Lie
Down
with
Dogs

Lie Down with Dogs

JAN GLEITER

ST. MARTIN'S PRESS
NEW YORK

A THOMAS DUNNE BOOK
An imprint of St. Martin's Press

Design by Ellen R. Sasahara

Library of Congress Cataloging-in-Publication Data

Gleiter, Jan, date
    Lie down with dogs / Jan Gleiter.   —1st ed.
      p.   cm.
    "A Thomas Dunne book."
    ISBN 0–312–14003–7
PS3557.L4415L54   1996
813'.54—dc20   95–38983

First edition: April 1996

10 9 8 7 6 5 4 3 2 1

For Paul

I would like to thank my sister Karin for her good judgment and intelligence and for never hanging up when I said, "So can I read you this part?" Sincere thanks, also, to Kathleen Thompson for her insightful advice and to Roger Allen and Dave Osberg for sharing their knowledge.

Qui cum canibus concumbunt cum pulicibus surgent.
(Lie down with dogs, get up with fleas.)

—SENECA

Lie
Down
with
Dogs

Chapter 1

T HE COUNTRY ROAD down which Robert Cooper was driving was a pretty one, but Cooper wasn't noticing the graceful arch of the trees that grew so close to the edge or the occasional play of moonlight on its dark surface. He noticed only that the road was lonely and that he seemed to be running out of gas.

"Just turn left when you get to where the Olsons' store used to be," his cousin Harriet had said, and his own eagerness to be away, to have his dutiful appearance at the family reunion over with, had kept him from pressing for more useful specifics. I'll find it, he'd thought. After all, I came down that blasted road to get here. Live and learn.

The fuel gauge had held steady at Empty for miles, but the emergency light hadn't come on. It still hadn't come on when the engine began to sputter. There was no shoulder to speak of on this deserted byway, just a foot or so of gravel and grass and a shallow ditch between the pavement and the woods, so when Cooper saw a rutted turnoff, he pulled the car onto it and as much as possible to one side, and rolled to a stop some thirty yards in.

Without much hope of success, he tried to restart the

engine, but it rapidly became clear that all he was doing was running down the battery. He was extremely annoyed. What good was an emergency fuel reserve if you didn't know you were using it? His irritation was intensified by the fact that there was no one available to whom he could assign the task of correcting the situation. The problems of day-to-day life were ones with which he had, for many years now, little experience.

It was cold outside, not cold enough to freeze a man, but cold, and—with the heater off—it was not long before he began to feel the chill. Had it been colder, he might have stayed inside the car for the margin of safety from the weather it provided. But it was not, and he did not. All roads led, he thought, if not to Rome, at least to somewhere.

There was another reason why Cooper left his car, locked the door, and strode off into the night. He thought he would feel less anxious if his helplessness was less apparent, if he looked like a man with a good reason for doing what he was doing. There might be a reason for trudging along a road, but no one had a reason for sitting in a motionless car in the middle of the night in the middle of nowhere—other than the obvious one of needing help. Cooper did not want to appear to need help. It was his belief that perceiving a need for assistance brought out the best in people or the worst, and the latter was as likely as the former.

At any rate, he turned up the collar of his soft suede jacket and began to walk, grateful for the warmth of wool trousers. He walked rapidly for a man who was not in particularly fine physical condition, for his nervousness made him desire a haven—and as quickly as possible. The moon had been sliding out from behind the clouds off and on all evening, but when it was not hanging noticeably in the sky, the darkness was almost impenetrably deep.

As he walked, the wind slapped his face and swayed the trees that extended far into the distance. He tried to whistle, feeling the same desire he had felt as a child to seem nonchalant in the face of potential danger while going on an errand into the dark basement, but the wind sucked away the notes. So he merely walked, refusing to hunch his shoulders against the cold. He walked in a way that would indicate to an observer that he was an important man with important things to do.

There were more turnoffs, here and there, along the road—narrow dirt tracks that led away through the woods. Some were marked with names—Jacobi, Larson, Miller. Others were anonymous. They probably led to hunters' cabins or houses, but Cooper had no idea how far away such structures might be or whether they would be inhabited at this time of year.

A sudden and unexpected noise caused his heart to lurch in his chest and his eyes to turn, wide and startled, toward the woods, all in the second it took for him to recognize the hoot of an owl. He stopped to take a deep breath and allow his heart to return to normal, and as he stood, he turned and gazed back down the road. There, behind him, bobbed a small white shape that grew steadily and silently nearer.

Cooper stood still, trying to make out the shape. He was not a superstitious man. He was afraid of realities, not fantasies, and it seemed hardly possible that this odd approaching shape could be anything dangerous to a grown man. So he watched with more curiosity than consternation until it was quite near. Now he could hear a faint, regular sound. Now he could see a form. When it was nearly upon him, he realized with surprise that it was a small boy, running purposefully and clothed only in a long white T-shirt. The child, whose eyes were fixed on the road, was unaware of the man ahead of him, dark and motionless; when Cooper called out softly and stepped in front of him, he leapt sideways in alarm.

"That's all right, now," said Cooper. The boy was very

young. Even to Cooper's inexperienced eyes, he was clearly not more than four. He was backing away, toward the side of the road.

"Hold on there," said Cooper, not knowing at all what to do but poignantly aware of the fear that was gripping that young heart. He spoke softly and did not approach the boy. "I'm afraid I'm completely lost and I wish you would tell me where to find some people."

The boy stopped. Cooper searched for words. He knew nothing about children. What did one say to them? He gave a small laugh. "Yes, I'm lost. Here I am, a great big grown-up, and I'm completely lost. Well, I know this road goes to Turner Falls, but that's quite a long way away and I don't think I can walk that far. My car ran out of gas, you see. It stopped running, and I left it back there along a lane." He gestured in the direction from which he had come. "Did you come past it?"

The boy shook his head. Cooper moved a few steps closer. He could make out the boy's face now, and it seemed that his eyes held more interest than fear.

"Ah," said Cooper. "You must have come from one of the other roads. Well, then, you wouldn't have seen my car. It's a big car. It goes very fast when it has gas in it. It doesn't go fast at all when it doesn't." He knew he was babbling, but the inane monologue seemed to intrigue the child. "Did your car ever run out of gas?"

"Don't got a car," the boy said in a small voice. He was silent a moment, then went on, his voice stronger. "Lisa got a car. We go riding to the store."

"Ah," said Cooper again, trying to sound knowledgeable. "Yes. Lisa would have a car, wouldn't she." He moved another step closer. The moon cast enough dim glow for Cooper to see the boy's rounded cheeks, his soft curls, and the unusually straightforward look in his dark eyes.

"But where is Lisa now?" he asked, attempting to indicate only the most casual interest. "Shouldn't you be with her?"

The boy shook his head. "Lisa said, 'Run away fast.'" Having been reminded of the order, he was reminded also of the fact that he was no longer obeying it. He looked up the road and then back at Cooper.

"Yes, well, I see," said Cooper cheerfully. "Why do you suppose Lisa told you to do that? Was she mad at you?"

The boy looked surprised. "Lisa never be mad at me. Mostly never. A crash waked me up and Lisa said the men are coming and she put me out the window and said, 'Run away fast.'"

They both, at the same instant, became aware of the sound of hurrying footsteps. Cooper felt a wave of relief until he saw the panic in the boy's eyes. The child turned and jumped over the ditch, heading for the trees. Cooper, moving faster than he knew possible, took three running steps and leapt after him. They crouched there, sheltered by the forest. Cooper's heart was racing. This is silly, he scolded himself. That's probably help, or maybe even Lisa, whoever she is. But it didn't hurt to stay where he was and see who was coming, embarrassing as it might be to appear out of hiding.

He put his hand on the boy's shoulder and whispered, "We'll just stay very quiet and see who that is." He could feel the boy trembling, could hear his quick, short intakes of breath. The footsteps were louder and the sound was mixed now with panting gasps.

Two shapes came into view and gradually defined themselves as men. They slowed to a walk.

"I can't see fifty damn feet! That kid could be anywhere!"

The first voice was answered. "You keep on. He could of got further than this. I'm going back to see what he wants us to do. He's probably called the boss by now. Maybe there's a neighbor the kid headed for. He's not gonna run the whole eight miles to town, at least not without you catching up to him."

Cooper and the boy remained frozen in place. Cooper found himself looking at the ground, afraid of pulling the newcomers' gaze toward the forest by looking at them. Eight miles to town!

The first man cursed loudly and broke into a jog, continuing up the road. The second turned and gradually disappeared in the direction from which they had come. Cooper found his breath coming a little easier. He sat back on the ground, stretching his aching legs out in front of him. Still, he whispered rather than risk the sound of a normal speaking voice.

"Were those the men?" he asked the boy.

The boy raised his shoulders in a shrug. "Maybe. Prob'ly."

"Well, you're a good, brave boy to do what Lisa said," answered Cooper. "Where did she tell you to go? Did she tell you to go to somebody's house?"

The experience of hiding together in the woods had intensified the boy's hesitant trust. He nodded. "Mickey's house. I s'posed to go to Mickey's."

"Well, we better get you there," said Cooper firmly. "And we better hurry. Now, what's your name?"

"Luke," said the child. "Luke Mc—" He broke off. "Luke."

"Okay, Luke. My name's Robert Cooper. You just call me Bob. That one man is on his way toward town. So if we listen carefully to make sure he isn't coming back this way, we can probably go on up the road without running into him. You put on my jacket and we'll get you up on my back, because that'll be a lot faster way to go, and we'll walk real quietly, and you show me the way to Mickey's house."

He didn't wait for the child's approval of this plan, but pulled off his jacket, fitted it on Luke as best he could, then hoisted him up, twisting to get him in position. He grabbed the small feet, which were cold as ice, even to Cooper's far from warm hands, to maneuver him around onto his back. He crossed his arms behind him to support the child's weight. "You just hang on around my neck, not too tight, and we'll get going. Does Mickey live all the way in town?"

"Up the Dog Road," said the boy mysteriously, but added, to Cooper's immense relief, "not near so far as town." His voice, so close to Cooper's ear, now seemed a little amused as he murmured, "At Mickey's house you not be lost anymore."

Cooper crossed the ditch and started up the road, hugging the side and walking as quickly as he could. After a few minutes of this unaccustomed effort, he stopped shivering despite the cold wind that pushed against them. He listened carefully. His own movement along the road was almost inaudible, though surely, he told himself, he would hear hurrying footsteps. He heard nothing, nothing but the wind. But the wind itself might well cover the sound of someone's approach. He peered ahead into the darkness, ready to disappear with the boy into the woods at the first suspicious shape.

He wasn't sure why he had become so quickly convinced that the men in the road were dangerous. But he had, and without powerful evidence to the contrary, it would remain his belief. That he knew.

Turning his head slightly, and trying to sound matter-of-fact, he began to question the boy.

"So, Luke," he said as heartily as possible in the low tone that seemed practical. "Tell me about Lisa. Does she take care of you?"

"Now she does," replied the boy. "She's my daddy's friend and she's my friend and she's got . . ." He stopped. "This is a secret . . ." He stopped again.

"Oh, that's okay. I never tell anybody's secret," said

Cooper. "You don't have to tell me if you don't want to, but if you do tell me, I won't tell anybody."

The boy hesitated for just a second. "Lisa's got a *gun*. Not a toy gun, a real gun, and it shoots real bullets and I saw some. But Lisa said don't touch it and it stays way up high so I *can't* touch it, but one time I tried to and then Lisa got mad at me and I had to sit in the chair for a long time, but she hardly never gets mad."

This was such a long speech the child had to stop for breath. Still, Lisa's gun was a fascinating subject that he could hardly bear to abandon. Wisely, Cooper did not say anything, and in a moment the boy continued.

"My daddy gived her that gun and he made her shoot about a million cans afore he went away. He wouldn't let me shoot it even one time." The child sighed and was silent.

"Well," said Cooper, aligning himself with the adult world and hoping that was not a mistake, "daddies don't want their children to get hurt, and guns are awfully dangerous."

"Not if you be really really careful. But he said no." The boy loosened one arm and pointed to the right. "Look. There's the Dog Road."

Striding across in the direction Luke was pointing, Cooper found a mailbox mounted on a post at the beginning of a dirt track. On the top of the box, a wrought-iron dog, tail stiff and knee bent, pointed up the turnoff. The box said simply "Luescher." Cooper, with his small burden, started up the track.

LISA JACOBI LAY curled on the closet floor, listening to nothing. She was not using her energy at the moment to struggle against the rope around her wrists. She was thinking. Thinking about what had just happened and what she could do about it.

Luke had been asleep in bed. She had been listening to

The Pirates of Penzance on the radio in the cabin's tiny living room, doing mindless background stitching on a piece of needlepoint and periodically looking out the window. The cabin was getting cold; she felt it through her bulky, dark green sweater. Luke would be warm under the blankets on his bed, but maybe, in a few minutes, she'd turn up the heat.

The wind made her jumpy. That and the fact that Sirius was at the vet's. "It's a nasty cut," the doctor had said, bending over the dog's injured paw. "I'll have to sedate him to deal with it, so he should stay overnight. But he'll be fine." Lisa was used to the constant vigilance the dog provided. She felt exposed and vulnerable now, with no shaggy bulk on the small hooked rug in front of the fireplace.

She had glanced at the framed photograph on the mantel, the picture she had taken for Luke's father and liked so much she'd made a copy for herself. Sirius stood laughing up at the boy whose hand rested on the big dog's back. Luke looked steadily at the camera—that peculiarly level gaze of his—but his fingers twined possessively in the dog's thick hair, as if he gained some substantial security in the animal's proximity. That, Lisa knew, was true for her. But, she had reminded herself, Sirius would be sublimely unconcerned about the wind. There was nothing unusual out there. Nothing at all.

She had almost stopped looking up, startled, at every new clatter of branches against the roof when she caught the flicker of light between the trees in the distance, a sweeping arc, as of headlights making the turn off the paved road onto the lane that led to the cabin.

Reaching to turn off the table lamp, Lisa had stared down through the trees. Nothing. If there really had been a light, it was gone. But her nerves continued to vibrate, and then the warning system she had devised worked—a small pewter pitcher was yanked from its shelf by the fishing line tied through its handle, and crashed into the wall. Someone was indeed coming up the lane from the road, someone whose passage had pulled and then snapped the clear twenty-pound test weight line that crossed the lane about two feet off the ground, someone who was moving without benefit of light up the winding track through the trees. Once before, the warning had sounded when a deer took a late-night stroll. But deer didn't need headlights to find the turnoff.

Lisa had bolted into Luke's room, pushed open the window, and snatched the child from his bed. Startled by the crash that had wakened him, he stared at her, eyes crumpling toward tears. She remembered her words. "No time to cry, darling. The men are coming. Run quick to Mickey's house. Go on the path through the woods to the road. And don't let anybody see you. Don't make any noise and hurry! I'll come find you there."

Luke had seemed to understand, bobbed his head in that odd way he had of indicating agreement or obedience. Oh, why hadn't they practiced! Why hadn't she taken Carl more seriously! She lowered the boy through the open window, not even taking the time to press her cheek to his, dropped him onto the soft dirt outside, saw him stumble once on his flight toward the woods, and yanked the window down.

Her heart slammed in her chest, making it almost impossible to close the window when all she wanted to do was slip out through it and follow Luke into the shelter of the trees. But there was so much clear ground to cover before the woods and there was so little time. She had to give him whatever extra minutes, seconds even, she could. She raced back into the living room.

Then the gun, that hated hunk of metal. She reached up to the shelf, snared it, and snapped off the safety as she crouched beside the window that looked out toward the lane. Shoving the window open a few inches and staring into the dark, she saw a shadowy form detach itself from the trees and start for the back of the cabin. Behind that form, another. They must have left the car down the lane. They mustn't be allowed to reach the back of the cabin, not yet, not until she was sure that Luke was hidden by the woods.

Lisa had aimed carefully and fired. Fired again. The garbage can sitting next to the garage some fifty feet from the house sang and rocked from the impacts. The creeping forms leapt back to the trees.

For minutes there was no sound at all except Gilbert and Sullivan on the radio. *Ah, leave me not to pine alone and desolate . . .* And then, drowning the ballad, shouts and breaking wood and a voice from nearby, from the direction of the kitchen. "There's four of us and one of you." She dropped the gun.

She remembered men flinging furniture, turning over beds, finally opening the bedroom window, and the sound of a triumphant voice. "He's outside somewhere! There's footprints in the dirt under here. She put him out the window! Get going! He can't have got far." She struggled against the rope that tied her wrists behind her back, but two of the men dragged her to the bedroom closet. She yelped and kicked out, then threw herself backward, but it was not difficult for the men to shove her in and slam the door. A minute later, there was the noise of hammering. Then silence.

She listened now, listened to the sound of her heart and the small noises of the night and to nothing else. There was nothing else. She smiled. The bedroom closet, against the confines of which she had put up a convincing struggle, contained her parka. And her parka contained a substantial pocketknife. Very slowly and very quietly she got to her feet. With her chin, she found the furry edge of the parka collar. Turning backward, she fumbled clumsily for the pockets, finally locating the zippered, inner one that held the knife. Opening the knife and cutting through whatever was binding her wrists was maddeningly slow and difficult and she fought against the enervating forces of panic and frustration.

Finally her hands were free. She turned the doorknob cautiously and pushed. The knob turned but the door didn't budge. It couldn't be locked—there wasn't a lock—but the door gave not the slightest bit under the full pressure of her 130 pounds. Well, that explained the hammering. The door was nailed shut.

How cooperative she had been to leave the toolbox out in plain view. But a moment's reflection changed her bitterness to gratitude. A nailed-shut door explained the hammering, all right, but it also explained why only her hands were tied. The men were convinced she was trapped. There was a chance no one was waiting outside the closet door, that the men who were not searching for Luke were in another part of the house. If so, small noises were safe.

Closing her eyes, she pictured the layout of the cabin. The back wall of the closet formed the east wall of the kitchen. What was on the other side of that wall? Not the refrigerator, thank God. The table. That was it, the table. She snapped open the longest blade of the knife, grateful for drywall and for the idiocy of those who thought that a modern internal wall restricted the free movement of anyone with a grain of sense. Apparently thugs rarely built houses.

A minute's exploration with the knife blade located a stud in the wall. Lisa inserted the blade at the edge of the stud and sawed up a foot and a half. In five minutes she had cut out a section of drywall large enough to fit through. She pulled out that section and started on the piece on the far side of the studs—the piece that formed the kitchen wall. In almost no time she was emerging onto the floor under the table. She reached back through the gap, fumbling for a pair of small sneakers, tucked them into the pocket of her parka, and crept to the kitchen door. It was ajar, the jamb splintered. She slid through, flattened herself against the back wall of the cabin while she peered into the darkness, and then darted across the yard toward the woods.

Chapter 2

TWO MONTHS, ALMOST to the day, before Robert Cooper's gas tank ran dry on a back road in the Wisconsin woods, Carl McCain had spent the evening working fitfully and without much success on a somewhat pretentious play. Raising his computer's monitor with three volumes of the encyclopedia had relieved the crick in his neck but did nothing to improve the stilted dialogue between his characters. Dialogue was not Carl's strong point— a problem in writing a play.

He was beginning to tire of being an actor. It was nearly impossible to make a living on the stage and he hadn't the patience for film or television work. It annoyed him to improvise a monologue and spend half an hour with a casting director discussing his character's background and motivations when he was auditioning for the part of a junkie who would be arrested in the background of a scene featuring the principal actor.

He'd had some small successes with just such parts. If those who knew him well went to a lot of movies and watched very carefully, they might catch a glimpse of him hailing a cab or selling hot dogs in a stadium. He was quite a good actor, but an increasingly unhappy one. For a while he'd been offered a significant number of auditions for commercials, but his agent no longer tried to get those for him since he refused to pursue them unless he approved of the products.

"You're an artist, not a consumer advocate," his agent had said, disgusted. "It's not really any of your business whether the damn muffler shop actually serves its customers better than its competition. Nobody expects you to believe what you say about it. You just have to seem to. It's called acting."

"Yes, it is," he had said. "And I respect it. So I won't use it that way."

Maybe she was right. Maybe he should be more willing to step back, to accept the way the world was. Maybe he should, but he couldn't. Reluctant to abandon his chosen field entirely, he had decided to try working in a different part of it.

But he hadn't immersed himself yet, hadn't been able to lose himself in his characters or their predicaments. He was too ready to abandon this first effort for whatever else entered his head. Still, he liked being able to say, "Oh, and I'm working on a play." He didn't add that he suspected it wasn't a very good one.

Next to the computer sat a spider, unhappily imprisoned in a glass jar. The spider represented Luke's latest effort to acquire a pet. The night before, Carl had discovered an egg, carefully wrapped in several towels that had gone missing from the bathroom, which attested to the boy's failed efforts to hatch a chick. The discovery had occasioned the first of what promised to be many discussions about the facts of life.

"Them eggs got no daddies?" Luke had asked, perplexed and incredulous, when Carl explained why a carton of eggs from the grocery store could be eaten or decorated for Easter but not, under even the best conditions, hatched. And the discussion had ended, as so many did, with Carl's promise to think about getting a cat.

The buzzer sounded and Carl, with a sigh of relief, pushed the button to unlock the lobby door. That would be Joanna. He was past ready for adult conversation after a day with Luke and an evening with his obdurate heroine. Maybe she should be more like Joanna, he thought, though Joanna might recognize the similarity and take it for more than it was.

It wasn't Joanna, though; it was Gerry, managing to look both dependable and dashing with his hat pushed back on his tousled black hair.

"You're not coming in here with those muddy shoes on," Carl said.

"Yeah, I know," rejoined Gerry, balancing to untie a black oxford and laughing at his friend. "You vacuumed at Christmastime and don't plan on doing it again before spring. Boy, am I beat! You got an orgy going or anything? I need a break after a long, hard shift upholding the law."

"Had to try to remember how to spell 'Illegal lane change,' did you?" said Carl. "No wonder you're worn out. There's beer in the icebox, but leave the Chenin Blanc alone. I'm expecting Joanna and I don't want to get stuck wooing her with Budweiser."

"Aw, jeez, Joanna? Joanna hates me," said Gerry, wandering into the kitchen and returning with a bottle of beer. "I think Joanna hates cops."

"Joanna does not hate cops," replied Carl. "She just hates you, like every girlfriend I've ever had. Probably because women tend to pick up on the subtleties in life—like who's a jerk and who isn't."

Gerry sat down on the couch and stretched out his legs. A toe stuck out from one sock.

"With two paychecks and no one to support but yourself,

why in heaven's name don't you own some decent socks?" asked Carl.

"Two jobs does not leave me time to shop for socks," said Gerry. "Besides which, I choose to spend my money in less plebeian ways."

Considerably less plebeian, thought Carl. Gerry had always had a taste for the luxurious and a talent for obtaining it.

"Besides," Gerry continued, "the few women in the world who do not find me thoroughly repulsive think the holes in my socks are endearing." He drank from the bottle he was holding and went on. "I stopped by to ask a favor."

"Forget it," said Carl. "When you want a favor, it usually has to do with getting a copy of the historical-studies exam and slipping it to you before finals."

"I asked you to do that once, only once, many long years ago, and you refused, indifferent to the misery of your loyal roommate."

"My lazy roommate. The one who would rather play poker all night than study, the one who finally ran through every introductory course and had to take one that didn't have '101' as part of its title, the one about whom it was often and truly said, 'You have to get up pretty early in the afternoon to put one over on *him*.'"

"We can quibble about the details," said Gerry cheerfully. "The fact is that you let me down. This time, the favor I want from you is minuscule. You will be in no danger of sullying your reputation as Mr. High-Minded. All I need is for you to hold on to a package for me for a few weeks." He walked across the room and reached into his jacket pocket for a small carton, wrapped in brown paper and taped.

"And what's in it? An emergency can of beer?" asked Carl.

"It's none of your beeswax what's in it," said Gerry,

sitting again and leaning back languorously. "I'm trusting you with it because you're so trust*worthy.* It's very important to me, and since I'm going on vacation for two weeks, I'd rather have it here with you than at my place. So is this too much to ask?"

Carl glanced at his friend. There was something akin to a plea in his voice. "Aw, what the hey. So I've got a box of plastic explosives in my apartment, the same apartment that houses an angelic three-year-old. So what. Sure." He took the box and placed it on the top shelf of the bookcase behind a row of tattered paperbacks. "Luke won't get at it there."

"Thanks, pal," said Gerry. "And now I'm taking off before the lovely Joanna arrives to hiss in my direction." He finished his beer and rose. "You going to the game tomorrow? Tell the guys I'm too busy getting the top off my suntan lotion to give them a thought."

"Depends on whether I can get somebody to watch Luke while I risk severe injury in that sport you call 'touch' football."

The next day Carl had somewhat grudgingly skipped football and spent the afternoon acquiring a calico kitten and the necessary accoutrements. Luke was overjoyed.

On her first afternoon in her new home, the kitten, escaping Luke's loving embrace, leapt to the top shelf of the bookcase and hid behind the books. Luke's efforts to dislodge her revealed a fascinatingly hidden package, most likely containing a delightful treasure that his absentminded father had forgotten he'd obtained for Luke's enjoyment. Carl wandered into the living room as his son, surrounded by ripped brown paper and tape, lifted a small statue of a strangely beautiful angel from its bed of cotton wool.

"No, Luke!" said Carl. "That doesn't belong to us!" He took the statue and carefully replaced it in its box. It was carved from stone, a dull, multicolored stone, and he stared at it, fascinated.

It was unfair to be cross with Luke, he realized. Three-year-olds couldn't be expected to understand what was their business to tear into and what wasn't. It was his own lack of imagination that had made him assume Luke would never be interested in the top shelf of the bookcase. He took the statue away and hid it under a stack of sweaters high in his closet.

A few days later, his mother called, sounding relaxed and happy. "I wish you had come with us," she said. "You would love it here, and Luke would have done just fine living the gypsy life. It's not like we're staying in Bavarian *dives.*"

She had never understood how Carl could turn down anything she offered him. That was all right. She wasn't one of those mothers who tried to control their sons; she just offered. And he, most often, politely turned her down.

"Have you been up to check the house?" she asked. "Frank was worrying about whether any of the plumbing might have frozen since we've been gone . . ."

"Sorry, Mom," he said. "I know I promised. I haven't been up there yet. I'll go. I'll go tomorrow."

He knew he'd been remiss. He should have gone weeks ago to check her house, the one he had been raised in, now standing empty. It was the house she had shared with Carl's stepfather in Lake Forest when they weren't in Europe or Jamaica or any of the other distant locales to which his stepfather's more than generous pension gave them access. When they returned from this particular trip through Germany, it would be put up for sale. Their possessions had already been moved to the kindlier environs of Phoenix. The house, however, needed some work that was awaiting spring. If pipes had burst in the recent cold, it would need significantly more work.

The following morning, after depositing Luke at the day-care center, Carl made his way through the tree-lined streets of Lake Forest to the house where he'd grown up. It was as imposing and unsullied as it had been left: the security system worked properly; no pipes had broken; no sodden leaves clogged the gutters. As he backed down the driveway, Mrs. Renfro waved from the yard next door.

"Carl! What do you hear from your mother?"

He rolled down the window and put the car into neutral. "They're having a great time," he said. "She called yesterday and asked me to check the house."

"Well, I've kept my eye on it too," said the neighbor. "With the rash of burglaries up here, you just never know."

This was surprising to Carl. Lake Forest's low crime rate was one of the things that drew people to it. "You haven't had any trouble, have you?" he asked.

"No, but we've been concerned. After what happened at the Minots, we've decided to put in a new alarm system."

Lillian Minot was his mother's closest friend, and Carl had known her all his life. "They got robbed?" he asked. "They're all right, aren't they?"

"Oh, yes. They're fine, just upset, you know. It happened while they were in Palm Springs, just recently. Lillian really hasn't seemed herself the last few days, but I guess that's to be expected. You might want to mention the situation to your mother. She'd want to know."

"I'll do that," he said.

He backed out onto Whittier and turned toward the Minot residence instead of taking the direct route to the expressway. He was worried about Mrs. Minot. She had always been interested in him, had come to see the plays he was in, had never forgotten to send a card on his birthday. Maybe talking about what had happened would make her feel better. Even if it didn't, he couldn't just drive home without stopping to sympathize.

Mrs. Minot opened the door, her beloved Pomeranian at her heels. Her white hair was stylishly short, her skin was lightly and beautifully tanned, but her eyes were dull and she looked older and wearier than he remembered. She brightened immediately on recognizing Carl, of whom she was genuinely fond.

"Doll baby!" she said. "Come in, you handsome boy." She put one slim hand on either side of his face and smiled delightedly. "How are your mother and Frank doing, have you heard?"

"They're doing fine," he said. "They're having a wonderful time. But what's this I hear about a break-in?" He lowered himself carefully onto a priceless love seat. "I'm so sorry."

"Oh, most of it was just *stuff*," she replied, sitting down across from him and patting her lap. The Pomeranian jumped up and settled itself. "We used Joe, like you recommended, to update everything a few years back," she said, rubbing the fur between the little dog's ears. "He found us some very good coverage and it was all quite thorough, so the situation could surely be worse. Bitsy wasn't here, thank goodness. She was safe from them."

"But how'd they get in? You have the same kind of security system Mom has, don't you?"

"They disarmed it, I haven't any idea how. There wasn't a trace of any kind except one set of footprints in the mud outside the dining room window. The police were actually impressed. It makes me nervous, of course. I don't want to be here at all without Hal, but at least they didn't wreck everything."

"Mrs. Renfro said there's been a lot of this kind of thing up here," he said.

"I don't know that 'a lot' is quite accurate," she said. "It's just that, up here, three or four seems like so many." She frowned. "When you think that what happened to us is so much like what happened to the Seiferts just a month ago while they were in the Bahamas . . . and we're not the only ones."

"It does seem odd," said Carl.

"It is! They seem to know where everything is, what's worth taking and what isn't. Hal was offended that they left his mother's hand-painted china, but you know as well as I do that it's hideous and not worth a dime."

She twisted the heavy silver ring on one hand. "It's funny, but the only thing I've really missed having around is the Tressori."

She smiled suddenly. "You know," she said, "I just thought of something. Your friend Joe is going to wonder about us. We were so happy with the coverage he found us that we told the Seiferts, so they used him too."

"You mean you're both covered by the same company?"

"Oh, I don't know about that. Joe gave us three or four estimates from different places. I don't know who the Seiferts ended up with. Do you suppose I should mention that connection to the police?"

"That you used the same broker? I can't imagine it means anything; there have been so many of these break-ins everywhere lately. But let the police decide it's irrelevant. Do you have other things in common? Do you use the same security system? Did you lose the same things?"

"Not the same system. I know because Marge and I talked about it. Their system isn't nearly as good as ours, but with a Rottweiler, they never thought they needed a terribly fancy system. They lost the same *types* of things we lost, naturally. Silver, jewelry, art. Of course, they didn't lose a Tressori, because they didn't have one."

"Please forgive my ignorance," Carl said. "Is the Tressori a painting?"

"A painting? Silly thing, of course it's not a painting. It's the dearest little stone sculpture you ever saw. Why, it's Gabriel! And to think I may never see it again." Her eyes misted over.

Carl wondered if she could hear the hollow thudding in his ears. Gabriel. The angel Gabriel.

FOR ONE FULL DAY, Carl tried to convince himself that whatever was going on, whatever Gerry had involved himself in, was none of his business. If Gerry was, in fact, doing something illegal, that was Gerry's problem; it was perhaps many other people's problem; it was not, however, his problem. He was unsuccessful in these efforts. What could it hurt to just look into the situation, try to find out what was going on? If he knew something, if it did involve Gerry, he could talk to him, help him fix it.

For the next three days, he worked feverishly. He searched the newspapers for the past six months, attempted to visit every victim of every crime that bore any resemblance to the Minot robbery. His training served him well. For one whose parts had ranged from Guildenstern to a young man dying of AIDS, playing a curious journalist was scarcely a challenge.

In the cases where he succeeded at interviewing a homeowner, none had been insured by the Minots' insurance carrier and, save for the Seiferts, they had worked through different brokers spread around the Loop. Each victim had been out of town on a scheduled vacation. Each had a security system, and each system had been disarmed. The thieves always found the items of most value, although hidden cash had been, it seemed, randomly discovered, if at all.

He had finished work the fourth day by breaking into his friend's apartment. No, he'd told himself, he wasn't breaking in. He was letting himself in, using the key Gerry left with him. It wasn't even against the law.

On the fifth day, Gerry called. "Hey! Glad you're home!" he said. "You know that package I left with you? A guy's going to stop by and pick it up for me tomorrow. Here's what I need you to do. Open the package. There's a statue, just an old stone thing, inside. Unwrap it and give it to him. Just give him the statue. Can you be home about six?"

Carl steeled himself. "No, Gerry, I can't. I'll give it to you when you get back to town."

"Don't give me a hard time, pal. Just be home tomorrow."

"Why? Why do you want me to give it to somebody else? I thought it was so important to you that you didn't trust just anybody with it. What's going on, Ger?"

"Look, Carl, something's come up. I absolutely have to hand the thing over." Under his bluff heartiness, there seemed to be an element of terror.

"We'll talk about it when you get back. I have to go now." Carl didn't wait for a response. He hung up the phone and sat staring at it, scared and sick at heart. He no longer believed that talking to Gerry would fix anything. The balance in the savings account passbook in his friend's desk was astronomical. Six jobs wouldn't account for it, let alone two. And a scribbled address next to the telephone on the same desk had tightened his stomach muscles to a knot. It was an address in Lake Forest, the address of a kindhearted lady with too much money, too little to do, and a missing sculpture of the angel Gabriel.

Two days later, Gerry showed up, flashing a grin. "I just stopped by for the package," he said. "I gotta get home to bed."

"Gee, Ger, I wish you'd called," said Carl, not opening the door wider than he had to. "It isn't here."

"Let me in, Carl," said Gerry. He put one hand against the door and pushed. Carl stepped back into the living room. "What's the problem?"

"That's what I want to know," said Carl. "I'm starting to get an idea, and I don't like it. What are you into, Ger?

Whatever it is, it looks like you're in pretty deep. But there's got to be a way out."

"You don't know what you're talking about, and you don't want to know," said Gerry. His eyes were soft and sad. "I'm sorry I got you involved at all, but I didn't know you'd *get* involved. It was a mistake, Carl, a big one. Why *did* you?"

"It was an accident," said Carl. "But I'm telling you the truth. The statue isn't here, and when it leaves where it is, the only place it's going is to the police."

"I *am* the police," said Gerry quietly. "And I'm not the only one who's involved in this thing. Don't be stupid, Carl. You go to the cops and there's a good chance you'll be talking to somebody who's interested." He sighed heavily and sank onto the couch. "Just pick out a guardian for Luke before you go."

"Okay," said Carl, his voice rising. "Then I won't go to the police. I'll just keep digging and eventually I'll figure it out. I'll figure out who you're working with and how you find out who's going to be out of town and how you disarm the security systems and whatever else I need to figure out. And then I'll find out who you're *not* working with and have a nice, long conversation with him. A really interesting conversation. What are you going to do about it?"

"It's not me," said Gerry. "You can make those big speeches about what you plan to do, but these people, they're not going to let you do any of it. You feel real safe because you know I wouldn't hurt you. Shit, man, you're right. But it's not me you got to worry about. They don't know who you are. They don't know where the statue is. But they know that they don't have it and that I know where it is. Eventually they're going to know who you are."

He put his head in his hands. "You know me, Carl. How long am I going to hold out? I panicked one week after I got the bright idea to keep something back, something for my-self. It was my first time inside; I'd always been on watch before. Hell, I deserved more than I was getting! But they already knew about it. Somebody must have seen me take it out of the haul, I don't know. I'm not letting them blow my brains out, Carl, even to save you. I intend to go on living. So how long can I protect you?"

He looked up, his eyes flat. Both his confidence and his charm were gone, and in their absence his features were stark and almost grotesque. "Even I don't know exactly who we're talking about here. I know some of the people involved, but none of us know who's at the top of it all. You can't stop this; it's like trying to catch smoke. Just give me the damn thing and get on with your life while you've got one to get on with. You're vulnerable, Carl. You're a daddy."

"Don't threaten me," said Carl, his voice hard.

A slight sound in the hall made Gerry wrench around. Luke stood wide-eyed, a calico kitten draped uncomplain-ingly over one arm. "We waked up," he said.

"Run on back to bed, Luke," said Carl. "Gerry has to go, and I'll come in your room in just a minute."

When he had disappeared, Carl turned again to his friend. "All right, Gerry," he said. "I've got to take Luke to day-care in the morning. Then I'll go to the safe-deposit box and get your package. I'll meet you here at noon."

When Gerry left, Carl sat beside his son's bed, looking at the small shape beneath the blankets, the smooth skin, the dark curls. Evelyn's curls. It was too late. He'd walked into hell and he'd dragged a three-year-old in with him.

Turning over the statue wouldn't make him safe. That was the one thing he knew for sure. If he'd given up the statue the first time Gerry asked for it, he would have been all right. Now it was too late. Now Gerry knew what he knew, and he had been willing to involve Carl's son. That willingness made Carl realize just how frightened Gerry was—frightened enough to do anything. Holding on to the statue might well be the only thing that kept Carl alive. Give it up, and he was a dead man. Luke would go on living, and there was no small value in that. But he'd be living without the person he loved the most, trusted the most, in the world.

Luke had been just a baby when Evelyn died, too young to mourn in an identifiable way. Still, he'd cried, night after night, and Carl had been unable to comfort him. Even a baby can know that things are different—horribly, painfully different. What would his life be like if he lost his father too?

The police. Gerry had clearly implied the police were involved, but it didn't make sense. That kind of corruption might exist in a police force as large as Chicago's, but it couldn't have permeated the entire department. As long as Carl went to a different precinct from the one where Gerry worked or, better yet, went as high up as he could go . . .

And then the realization of what he would be doing hit him, rocking him physically. He had one piece of solid evidence, and the police were hardly going to take him seriously without it. Once they saw it, there was no chance, no chance at all, they would let him hold on to it. And once it was out of his hands, the chances were good that he could count the minutes until he was just another mysterious fatality. The statue, and Gerry's pals' insecurities about where it was and what might become of it, was the only safety net he had.

He sat rigidly on the edge of the bed, rocking slightly back and forth, trying to calm his breathing and to think. There was a way out. One. Get Luke to a safe place. Keep the statue, the only proof of anything, out of the hands of Gerry, his associates, and the police. And then figure out exactly what was going on—and make it very, very public.

By noon the next day, Carl and his son were twenty miles south of Turner Falls, Wisconsin.

27

* * *

GERRY MARTELLI WAS almost as angry as he was scared. Damn Carl! Come by at noon! Gerry had been convinced he meant it. The look on his face when Gerry mentioned Luke had been one of such capitulation that Gerry had known he'd pulled it off. Now Carl was home again, ten hours after noon. His piece-of-junk car was in front of the apartment building; the light had gone on inside.

Gerry had jimmied the car lock and checked the odometer. The night before, it had read 94,624. It was 95,313 now. The same paranoia that had made him check the reading when he left Carl's apartment had prompted him to show up this morning four and a half hours before their noon meeting time. That's when he'd realized paranoia had nothing to do with the situation.

Carl had traveled almost 700 miles since last night. The glove compartment contained a battered map of Indiana and a new one of Wisconsin, so chances were he'd headed north. Somewhere within 350 miles of Chicago, Carl had left his son, his vulnerability.

Luke was Gerry's access to Carl, his only access. Gerry had realized long ago that Carl lacked the normal human drives—for wealth, for success, for power. After his first few fruitless efforts to help his friend by involving him in a variety of plans, which Carl had dismissed as schemes, Gerry had given up. He knew Carl well enough by now to realize that there was one way to get to him—through someone he loved. And he loved Luke more than life itself. He would not tolerate the smallest risk to his son. Once Gerry had found the boy, Carl would be as malleable as putty.

If Carl was really sharp, he'd have dumped the kid 35 miles out of town and spent the rest of the day driving. Gerry doubted Carl was that sharp. Luke was probably between 300 and 350 miles from Chicago. In Wisconsin. How much area did that cover? Not too much for Gerry. Wherever Carl had taken him, Gerry could find him. He may have flunked historical studies, but he knew more about finding people than Carl would ever know about hiding them. It would take a while. It might take days or even weeks. But it could be done.

He'd tried to protect Carl, and Carl hadn't appreciated it. Well, he wasn't going to keep it up, not if it meant throwing everything away. He'd level with his superiors, bite the bullet, and come out with it all. He had a good record with them. He'd just made a mistake. They'd see that; they'd have to. If they could be made to think that Carl knew more than he knew, that the whole operation was in danger instead of just Gerry . . . Well, that would keep Carl alive. More important, it would keep *him* alive. And give him time to find Luke—find Luke and get the damn statue back.

Yeah. He had to stay calm. Everybody just had to stay calm.

Chapter 3

T HE DOG ROAD, as Cooper himself was beginning to think of it, wound casually uphill. Small skitterings distracted him, but the only other indications of life were botanical. Luke's head had settled into the curve where Cooper's neck joined his right shoulder, and the child's clasped hands loosened as excitement gave way to drowsiness.

Cooper gently bounced his own hands, joined at the wrist, and coughed softly. As Luke's hands tightened their grasp, Cooper murmured the question occupying the front of his mind. "How far up this road does Mickey live?"

Luke propped his chin against Cooper's shoulder and yawned. "Not so far," he said. "Are I too heavy?"

"Oh, no, not a bit!" lied Cooper. The child seemed to have put on a staggering amount of weight over the last twenty minutes. "I just wondered if we were almost there."

"Sure indeed," replied Luke. "Look."

Straining to see in the moonlight, Cooper detected a clearing ahead. There was no light of any kind, but as he trudged on, he began to make out the shapes of two buildings. Now he could see them more clearly. The closer one seemed to be a cabin. To the left of it was some sort of shed.

He walked up three steps, which creaked under his weight, to the door of the house. The place showed no sign of current habitation, though it appeared to be well cared for.

"Mickey's not home," said Luke matter-of-factly. "Nobody here."

"How do you know that for sure?" asked Cooper, trying to hold on to his desperate hope that a rescuer slept within.

"Justice would be barking at you," replied the boy. "Justice wouldn't bark at *me.*" He said this with evident pride. "But you're a stranger." He thought for a minute. "He's at his girlfriend's house, I bet. Mickey's got a new girlfriend. He goes to her house a *lot,* and Justice too."

Cooper had envisioned Mickey as a playmate of Luke's. He would have parents, or so Cooper had told himself. And the parents would have a telephone, a coffeepot, a car. The discovery that Mickey was, instead, a carouser was a stunning blow.

Cooper's arms were aching; his back was stiff; his feet hurt. He slid Luke around to the side and lowered him onto the porch. "Let's look around and see if there's a bicycle or a wagon or anything we can use to go to town."

Luke shook his head solemnly. "Lisa said stay here. We gotta stay here." He sighed and gave up the effort to pass that off as truth. "*I* gotta stay here." He looked up at Cooper, his eyes very big and very dark in the dimness. "You going to town?"

Cooper's heart gave an unaccustomed lurch. Leave this child to the emptiness of the night? He was suddenly aware that he was not even resentful, as he had always been when a stray of any sort entered his life. Resentful of the obligations such helplessness imposed. Not responsible was a fine, even a glorious, way of life. Irresponsible was anathema.

"No," he said firmly. "We'll stay together until everything's okay." He stood for a moment, looking across the clearing to the shed. "But let's at least see what's around."

He stepped from the porch to the ground and reached up to lift Luke down. As he did so, the boy's eyes widened and he jumped away, startled. At the same instant, Cooper felt himself knocked off his feet and propelled to one side. A yell left his throat at the same moment his hip and shoulder hit the ground. "Run, Luke!"

He twisted on the sparse grass, trying to get up on his knees, to get to his feet, tearing at whatever was holding him down. Through the sound of his own gasps he could hear Luke's voice, desperate and afraid. *(Run, Luke, for God's sake, run!)* He got onto one knee, got his other foot under him, and pushed upward, muscles straining to free himself from the weight on his back. He twisted hard, flinging it off, and sprang away, turning to take on the enemy.

Lisa Jacobi scrambled to her feet, panting. She was holding a pocketknife, her fingers tearing at it to open the blade, and Luke was at her side, pulling on her arm. "No, Lisa!" he was sobbing. "Don't hurt that man!"

Cooper sank onto the ground, his knees no longer able to hold him up. "Lisa," he muttered. "Where the hell have you been?"

Lisa's terror left her as suddenly as Cooper's had left him. She had been confused by his yell, which took some of the force out of her attack. Now his remark dissipated the blind rage she had felt at the sight of a man reaching for the boy. Her struggle with him on the ground had revealed several things. Despite being strong and a game fighter, he didn't know much about brawling and hadn't done any in a while. More important, he wasn't carrying a gun.

Lisa also sank to the ground, scooping Luke into her lap, holding him and rocking back and forth, her cropped, fair hair falling over her face. She sighed softly, gripping the child whose arms twined tightly around her neck.

Cooper got weakly to his feet. He stood looking down,

relieved and exhausted. The woman on the ground looked up. "Who *are* you?" she said. "What are you doing here?"

Cooper spoke slowly. "My car ran out of gas," he said. "I was walking toward town, must have come past the turnoff to your place. Luke and I met each other on the road. There were some men that seemed to be chasing him." He nodded toward the boy. He knew how outrageous this sounded but also knew he had come to believe in the truth of what he was saying. "We hid in the woods and then came here."

Lisa's eyes narrowed momentarily as she weighed his words, judged the man who spoke them. She saw a man who was used to giving orders, not taking them, a man for whom the need to explain himself was both unfamiliar and distasteful. She didn't warm to him. But Luke liked him. Luke, who seemed to have an instinctual distrust of strangers, had trusted him. She made up her mind.

"They were chasing him, all right," she said. "Thank you for helping." She crossed her legs under her and got to her feet, smoothly and without relaxing her hold on the boy.

"We need more help from you," she said. "Mickey's not home, apparently. But we should be able to find some gasoline around. Enough to get out of here in your car. We need to get out of here." Lisa's gaze, like her words, was direct, though Cooper knew, with a stab of empathy, that her need was none the less for the absence of supplication. Her fear filled the space between them. "We need to get out of here," she said again, this time very softly.

"Yes," said Cooper, answering the unasked. "Can you find something to keep him warm? I'll look for gasoline."

"We have to hurry," said Lisa. "Look for a can in the shed. It's not locked. Mickey usually keeps some there for the chain saw." She turned and climbed the steps, dug into the dirt of one of several identical flowerpots, and pulled out a plastic-wrapped key. As she disappeared through the doorway, Cooper headed for the shed.

―――――

She was right. The shed door opened reluctantly when he shoved it. The interior was pitch-black. Cooper pulled his keys from his pocket and pressed the end of the penlight that dangled from the ring. It emitted the weakest possible glow, but sweeping the small structure, one section at a time, the faint light finally revealed a gas can. It sloshed reassuringly.

Crossing the clearing to the cabin, he met Lisa and the boy on their way out. Luke was wearing a pair of men's socks that bulged out above the heels of the sneakers he now wore and disappeared under a thick, hooded sweatshirt, much too big for him. Lisa held out Cooper's jacket, which he pulled on. She crouched with Luke behind her, and wordlessly he maneuvered himself onto her back.

"We're going to have to go mainly through the woods, at least past my place," said Lisa, rising again in that effortless way. "I don't know where they are, but I know they're around. They could be getting here anytime now." She wheeled and started for the woods, cutting across the clearing, perpendicular to the lane that angled up from the road. "Come on."

Cooper fell in behind her, irritated by the command but unwilling to argue the question of who should be deciding their actions. There were larger issues taking precedence, the most immediate being that he was experiencing an ugly, primal sort of fear—one that was intensified and complicated by his confusion about the situation in which he found himself.

There was a narrow path through the trees. Lisa knew it well and strode along at what seemed to Cooper a reckless pace. She was trying to think. Think! It was hard to think in any constructive way while her whole body ached with apprehension. Her chest was tight with it. She found it hard to breathe. She wanted to dig a hole in the woods and curl into it with Luke. Hide! But daylight would come. More men would come. Perhaps dogs would come. She couldn't dig a hole deep enough. They had to get out, get away, and the stranger stumbling behind her (but, she had to admit, without complaint) was her best hope of that.

The path curved around the largest trees but seemed to follow a set course. They walked steadily, crossing several lanes like the one that had led to Mickey's. Before each crossing, Lisa hesitated, listening intently before leaving the protection of the woods. After about fifteen minutes, she stopped so abruptly that Cooper nearly bumped into her. She slid Luke to the ground and squatted, tugging Cooper into a crouch beside her.

"My place is just ahead," she said quietly. "Your car must be on one of the lanes soon after the one that comes up to my cabin."

Cooper nodded and she went on. "Okay. Look, it's tricky getting around my place. The path goes into the clearing and out again on the other side, but we can't cut across the clearing. There's probably someone there. We're pretty close to the road here. If you can stay with Luke, I'll go on ahead with the gas and get the car. If anybody's waiting by it, they might get me, but they won't get him. Okay?"

There was something Cooper disliked about this plan. Not that he wanted to be the one to go on alone, to face whatever unknowns lay ahead. But he had never been able to tolerate helpless waiting. Was that it? Or was his problem with Lisa's proposal simply that it revealed that she didn't consider him to be in charge? He shook himself slightly, trying to free himself from habitual responses. Nothing about his position was familiar. He didn't know enough to debate her plan.

"Fine," he said tersely.

Lisa shot him a sideways glance. "Too many chiefs," she said softly, and was rewarded by a strained smile.

She led the way off the path, down through the trees to their right. They stepped carefully, testing their weight, wary of dry branches. The leaves had no crackle left, they were spongy underfoot, but branches could snap loudly at any time of year. During the worst blasts of wind, they moved more quickly, their small noises buried in the larger sound.

Lisa stopped and crouched again, Cooper following suit. "That's the road, right through there." Her voice was the faintest whisper. She shifted Luke off her back. Cooper took his keys from his pocket, handed them to Lisa, moved into a sitting position, and took Luke on his lap, cradling him so that the dark head rested right under his chin. The boy was almost asleep. He cuddled into the new position without complaint.

Cooper had put down the gas can, and Lisa now took it up. "I won't turn on the headlights," she said. "It will take me at least ten minutes, maybe fifteen, to get back here. If someone's right on my tail, I'll be going about sixty, and I won't stop. So stay back in the trees in that event. And if I don't come at all . . ." She faltered. She couldn't think of what to tell him to do if he was actually left alone in the woods with Luke. "Gosh," she said faintly. At that moment she sounded very young. "I don't know your name. Mine's Lisa Jacobi."

"You'll come," he said. "If you don't, or if you don't stop, I'll get him out of here. My name is Robert Cooper. PTS, Incorporated. Chicago. You can find me. Go."

Lisa put her hand briefly against Luke's cheek, rose, and disappeared into the trees. Cooper gazed into the darkness and began to count.

As she worked her way through the woods around the clearing where her cabin stood, Lisa calculated the risk of reentering the house. If she could just grab her backpack, she'd have money, a checkbook, a cash card. But that was insanity. Past the clearing, she glanced back. A light went on in the house.

She regained the path, moving quickly now, jogging. In another minute, she came out on a lane. Staying to one side, she moved down it, praying it was the right one. Ahead of her on the left, the darkness seemed thicker, deeper, and then there was a moonlight glint off chrome. She felt queasy with relief.

It took only a minute to get the gas cap off and empty the can into the tank. It took several more to do the other things she needed to do. Then she eased into the driver's seat—cursing the interior light that glowed as soon as she opened the door—released the emergency brake, and turned the key. The engine sputtered, coughed, caught. She yanked the shift into reverse and eased down the dirt track. When the tires crunched on gravel, she swung the wheel hard to the right. The moon provided enough light here in the road, out from under the canopy of trees, for her to faintly make out the macadam, and she started along the road, straining to see through the darkness.

Much as she preferred more rugged means of transportation, Lisa was grateful for this behemoth of a car. It purred. The headlights, had they been on, would have given away its presence, but she doubted if the engine could be heard more than five yards away, maybe less, given the noise of the wind. She stepped harder on the gas, relying on the feel of the road, on her familiarity with it, as much as on what she could see. A curve was coming up, and just past it, Cooper should be waiting. She came out of the curve and slowed. There, a dim figure separated itself from the woods.

Cooper jumped across the narrow ditch, carrying Luke in his arms like a baby. He came around to the left of the car. His driving was not part of Lisa's plan, but her heart was hammering with the need to get moving, fast. She pulled the shift into park, opened the door, and slid across to the passenger seat, taking the boy in her arms as Cooper handed him in. She felt hideously exposed in the interior light, which took long, breath-catching moments to fade.

"Oh, God, let's *go*," she muttered. "Lights, whatever, just *go*. I hope you know how to drive fast."

Cooper knew he couldn't have found his way through the woods, that was true, but he could drive a car. "Get in the back," he said. "And get down. Both of you. I'm just a lonely traveler on a dark road."

Lisa got herself and Luke between the front seats and into the back. She lay Luke down on the seat, where he promptly turned over onto his side and flung one arm across his face. Lisa crouched on the floor.

"I wouldn't plan on talking anyone into believing that," she said, speaking at a normal volume for the first time in what seemed like hours. "Anyone who stops you to chat about it can see back here. And we get almost no traffic this time of night, only the few of us who live here all year. If there's anyone on this road, he's going to try and stop you."

"Like the guy ahead of us," said Cooper, the headlights picking up a car that blocked the road as if wrenched sideways by a blown tire. Beside the car, effectively closing off what remained of the road, stood a man, waving frantically.

Lisa raised herself on one knee to see out. "Don't stop."

Cooper slowed to a crawl fifty yards from the man. "I can't get around."

"You can get around, on the left where he's standing. You'll go into the ditch, but you can make it," replied Lisa, wondering whether another car would box them in from behind. "He'll get out of the way. You're not going to kill anybody if you go, but you sure as hell will if you don't!" Her voice was low and savage. "Decide, damn it!"

Cooper had already taken sides in this war—when he first crouched among the trees with the sound of angry voices drowning out a small boy's shaky breathing. Ignorant as he was of causes and costs, this was clearer to him than any battle, for any prize, he'd ever engaged in. He stepped on the accelerator.

The car bore down on the man in the road. He gestured more violently and then, as Cooper swerved to the left, leapt to safety. The car jounced into and out of the ditch, spitting gravel as the tires spun and grabbed on the shoulder. Then they were back on the road, swaying into position as the big car found its balance, and away.

Cooper was shaking. "What if he'd had a gun? What if he'd shot at us?"

"What if you really were just a lonely traveler? Those people are very bad and very dangerous, but they're not stupid," said Lisa. "They don't know this car; they don't know you. They're not going to risk killing you."

"They don't know me *yet*," said Cooper. "But now they've seen my license plates. I imagine they can find me."

"They could if the license plates were on the car," said Lisa. She reached into her parka and tossed the plates onto the front seat. "Lucky for us, whoever put them on had a light touch. I wasn't sure if the screwdriver on my pocket-knife was up to the job, but the screws weren't rusted in place." She paused, then went on. "They may very well be coming after us. Don't slow down."

"I was planning to pull over and dig up a few wildflowers," said Cooper, no longer able to tolerate taking orders. "There isn't much blooming yet, but I like to get things in early. Get a jump on the growing season. Maybe I could borrow that handy little pocketknife of yours."

There was a moment's silence. "The one with a trowel was way too expensive," said Lisa.

The road was too dark, too narrow, and had too many curves for anyone to drive safely at sixty miles an hour, but that was the speed at which Cooper was traveling. When they came out of the woods and hit farmland, where the road was straighter and considerably easier to see, he hit eighty. After a couple of minutes, the scattered lights of Turner Falls came into view.

"I assume you want the police station?" he asked, slowing and taking a corner at a crawling forty-five. "I assume there *is* a police station?"

"No, I don't want the police station. Yes, there is one," said Lisa. "Look, I can't explain it right now. I can't go to the police and we can't stay anyplace near here. You weren't stopping in Turner Falls, were you?"

Cooper had slowed again, in the presence of houses and occasional streetlights, to something approaching the speed limit. If this woman didn't want to go to the police, he would just as soon not have the police come to them.

"No, I was just going to get as close to Chicago as I could tonight and go the rest of the way tomorrow. Turner Falls holds no attractions at all except perhaps a gas station."

"I put in about two gallons. There isn't a station here open this late, but we can make it to one on the highway. I know it's a lot to ask, but can you take us with you?"

"A lot to ask?" repeated Cooper. "You tell me to run a man down in the road, a man I don't know from Albert Schweitzer, and that's not a lot to ask. All of a sudden something's a lot to ask?"

Lisa curled her toes inside her shoes, hanging on to her temper. She knew her anger was unfair, that it came more from having to ask for help than from anything unreasonable in Cooper's sarcasm. The only people Lisa comfortably asked for help were people who were paid to provide it, like store clerks.

"That man had not the slightest similarity to Albert Schweitzer," she said calmly. "And I didn't ask you to run him down. I merely asked you to keep driving and pointed out that he would move. He did. Nonetheless, I can see that it may have seemed a strange request and I appreciate, we appreciate, your honoring it."

Cooper, appeased by her curiously formal speech, glanced into the rearview mirror and met her eyes. She went on.

"Mr. Cooper, would you please give us a ride to Chicago? We would be very much in your debt. We already are, of course, but we would be more so. I would ask Mickey for help if I knew where he was, but this new girlfriend is a recent one, and all I know about her is that her name's Maureen and she's 'a babe.' I doubt that's enough information for Directory Assistance. If you'd let us ride with you to Chicago, I could get help from Luke's father. We can't stay here or anywhere near here; we just can't."

Lisa paused, then added, "I should tell you, if you will take us with you, that there's a stop I need to make. Right up there at the vet's."

Cooper sighed. It was a long and a heartfelt sigh. By the time it was over, he was pulling into the driveway of the Turner Falls Animal Hospital.

Chapter
4

C OOPER PARKED BEHIND the animal hospital so that the car would not be immediately visible to unfriendly eyes. While Lisa was inside and Luke slept on the backseat, he reattached the license plates. Not having plates would attract attention from the highway patrol as well as from whomever it was he had nearly dispatched in the woods.

He worked quickly, anxious to leave Turner Falls behind, to get back to some semblance of what he thought of as safety. He had always wondered at people's attitude about the dangers of urban life. The illogic of it had struck him when he considered buying a lakeside summer home and asked a local handyman what kind of lock would offer the most protection.

"You gonna have any glass in the door? Any windows anywhere in the place?" the man asked. "If so, don't matter much what kind of a lock you put on there. Anybody really wants to get in, he's gonna get in. You can make it more troublesome, keep out the casual ones. The serious ones don't hardly need to break the lock; they can just break the door or any glass you got."

It was true, and it had filled him with a sense of vulnerability. Let the cabin dwellers of the world have their crickets and their peaceful summer nights. That life had lost its appeal. Unexpected attacks from marauding strangers might be more unusual out here in God's country, but if one occurred, there wasn't much protection against it.

Maybe that accounted for the plethora of dogs. Mickey, it seemed, had one, ready to charge wildly at strangers approaching his master's girlfriend's house. And now it appeared that Lisa had one and felt strongly enough about it to delay their flight. This was exactly what he needed. A fugitive dog, to sort of fill things out.

He finished twisting the last screw in place and stood, leaning against the car, waiting. The glass door to the animal hospital opened and Lisa came out. He saw her clearly, in the lit entrance, for the first time. Moonlight and streetlights through the car windows had not revealed the interesting shape of her eyes—green, were they green? He had seen immediately that she was fair but hadn't noticed how thick her short hair was. Tall, healthy, she looked, he thought, like the girl they'd pick to be Miss Dairyland.

She was accompanied by a staggering, shaggy brute who even at this distance seemed less than impressive. He was big and mostly black, with white on his face, chest, and legs. Cooper could make out rust markings, and a bandage on one paw and most of the leg above it. The animal stumbled disjointedly toward the car, carrying his injured and bandaged foot off the ground. Head slightly cocked, he surveyed Cooper in an uninterested manner. Cooper had the impression that the dog's main activity in life was drooling.

"No problem with the jailbreak?" he asked.

"I know the night attendant," Lisa replied. "He wasn't happy about releasing him without the doctor's okay, but I prevailed. I've been 'called out of town on a family emergency and won't be back for weeks,' you see. He pretty much had to let me get Sirius out of there."

"His name is Serious?" said Cooper, looking at the dog with distaste. "Is he a particularly earnest and sober fellow?" Lisa opened the back door, and the dog made an unsuccessful attempt to negotiate the distance from the ground to the floor of the car, landing on his chest and lurching to his feet again. "Earnest, maybe; sober, no."

"Not Serious," replied Lisa haughtily. "Sirius. Orion's faithful companion. The Dog Star. Sirius. And he's not drunk; he's been sedated." She leaned over and helped the dog get his hindquarters into the car. He settled on the floor with a slight groan of contentment.

"If you're sure he's completely comfortable, I'd just as soon get going," said Cooper, tension tightening his voice. "Or is there a canary, perhaps, in need of rescue?"

"I'm *sorry*," said Lisa. "Believe me, I don't want to stick around either!"

Cooper headed out of town. "Give me some directions here," he said. "Is there an indirect route to the highway? If those people on the road were who you thought they were, they're looking for us."

"Gee," she said. "I wouldn't have thought of that." Did the man think she was an idiot? "Go left up there at the bait shop."

Necessary as it seemed to be to take the circuitous rural routes Lisa directed him down, the narrow, empty roads increased Cooper's anxiety. Lisa sat sideways, looking for headlights behind them until they'd found the interstate. Even then, she glanced back regularly for the first fifteen miles.

When Cooper's heart had stopped sounding in his ears, he scrunched his shoulders into comfortable contact with the seat back and addressed his companion.

"Much as I hate even the suggestion that I condone pry-ing, meddling, or snooping, I have a question I must ask. Just what the hell is going on?"

She took in a deep and rather shuddering breath. "I don't know."

There was silence while Cooper suppressed a desire to pull the car to the shoulder and dump Lisa onto it. Not insensitive to what the man next to her must be feeling, she bent one leg and put her foot on the dashboard, hooked an arm around her knee, and went on.

"I really don't know, at least I don't know much." She told him about the men who had come to her cabin, about the closet, about getting out and making her way through the woods.

"Luke's father is a friend of mine from way back," she continued. "We went to college together and then we were, uh, involved for a year or so before he got married. I'd heard that his wife died and that he had a baby, but I'd never met Luke until Carl—that's his father—showed up one day. He said he was in trouble, that people were after Luke and would use him to shut Carl up, and he couldn't go to the police because that would make things worse. Anyway, he asked me to keep Luke for a few days. Carl's mother couldn't take him because she's off somewhere, in Europe I think, for months and months. Just keep Luke for a few days, he said. He'd get things straightened out and come back for him."

"And this was?"

"Six weeks ago. He called me after a week and said things were taking longer than he'd expected. He's called once a week or so ever since, but it's always to say it's not safe yet and can I hang in a while longer. The last time, I said no, I couldn't, at least not without knowing what was going on, but he said if I knew, then I'd be in danger too, and he wouldn't tell me."

Cooper rubbed the back of his neck. What kind of

scatterbrain took on the responsibility of somebody else's child without knowing why it was necessary? Was she lying? Or was she just a fool?

"Well, what *could* it be? What does Carl do? Let me get to the point. If you wrote a book called *Memoirs of a Moll,* would it be fiction or nonfiction?"

Lisa threw him a sideways glance. Was he serious? "He's an actor. A pretty good one from what I can tell. He doesn't make much money, I'm sure. Back when we were together, he didn't, as my grandmother used to say, have a pot to pee in. I don't know how he's managing to support himself and Luke. Maybe his wife had insurance. However he manages, he certainly isn't doing anything illegal."

Like you'd know, thought Cooper. "Of course, people who make their livings illegally usually want to be sure all their friends are aware of it," he said.

"Look, I know the man. I don't know the details of his sources of income, but I know the *man.* He didn't create this situation, whatever it is."

"So you know where he is, and we can just drive up, ring his bell, and find all the answers."

"No, I don't know where he is, but I can find him. The last time he called, he told me he was moving, but he gave me a number where I could leave a message. I'll call him and he can get some money to me and we'll be out of your hair."

Cooper greeted this news with mixed feelings. He was interested, interested in the personal details of someone else's life, and this was not a familiar feeling. The boy had unsettled him, had wrenched something out of its normal position. Exhausted as he was, he was feeling curiously invigorated. He'd never rescued anyone before. Still, these people's problems were too big for him; all of it was too strange; and it would be a relief to return to the predictability of his normal life.

"Well, we aren't going to get to Chicago until tomorrow," he said. "I've passed the age when I could drive all night. We'll get a couple of rooms."

"I can drive," she said, wanting to offer something.

Did she have to argue everything? "No," he said. "We'll stop at the next place we see"—he held up one hand to forestall comment—"which I will pay for since I doubt that your jacket pockets are conveniently stuffed with cash."

They turned off at the next exit and found a motel. While Lisa walked the dog, Cooper sat in her room watching Luke sleep. The boy lay curled on his side, his mouth slightly open, his eyelids flickering from time to time. Whatever dreams he was having did not seem to upset him. He smiled once, a sweet, happy smile.

Cooper put out a hand and pushed the curls away from the boy's forehead. It felt warm. Not feverish, but warm. He eased the heavy sweatshirt off, carefully removed the small shoes and the socks that covered the boy's legs, settled him between the sheets.

"Sleep tight," he whispered, feeling a dull ache of protectiveness.

He stood up as the door opened, nodded good night to Lisa, got his suitcase from the car, and went to his room next door. He had little hope of falling asleep much before dawn. It always took him at least an hour to let go enough to sleep. He washed his hands and face, staring at himself in the bathroom mirror.

I don't look like the kind of guy this would happen to, he thought. It was true. The face was not the face of an adventurer. The features were strong and regular but, he judged, bland. The blue eyes were steady but held no curiosity. The mouth was tight.

There had been a time, he thought, when every unknown offered the prospect of adventure, when he would have turned down that country road just because he didn't know what he'd find. But that was a long time ago.

Gazing into the mirror, he wondered what had happened to the boy who had spent so many hours in the old barn behind his grandparents' house. One summer he had rigged a rope from the window in the loft to a ceiling beam in the woodshed and split a section of inner tube to fit over the rope. Crouching in the loft, with Harriet aghast in the barnyard, he had stared out and down at the immense sweep of the ride he was about to have and felt nothing but joy.

"You'll crash into the shed!" Harriet had warned, frightened and fascinated.

"No, you goose!" he had yelled, triumphant in his wisdom. "I'll go right through the doorway!" And he had. Time after time.

That same glad anticipation had gripped him, years later, at the beginning of every track meet and, more intensely, each time he stepped into the batter's box, swinging the bat easily, waiting to see what would be offered up. He had never had the slumps that plagued some players and eroded their confidence. He had always been eager for the test. People talked about golf as a metaphor for life. They were wrong. It was baseball, where the whole world lay in front of you and the fences were merely borders to be challenged.

He decided to lie down for a minute before he took off his shoes, with the result that, when the sun streaming through the parted curtains woke him, he didn't have to put them on.

They had breakfast at the motel coffee shop. Lisa borrowed a pencil from the waitress and wrote down the price of everything she ordered for herself and Luke.

"It would hardly endanger my financial security to buy your breakfast," Cooper said. "Or you can tell me what you think of personnel testing, and I'll just put the bill on my expense account."

"I'll tell you what I think, but I'm paying you back," said Lisa.

"With what?" he asked, surveying the coffee, orange

juice, pancakes, eggs, sausage, toast, fried potatoes, and half a cantaloupe arrayed in front of her. "The proceeds from a Brinks robbery?"

"Breakfast," she said, "is the most important meal of the day."

Luke looked up from his waffle. " 'Cept lunch and dinner."

"Exactly," said Lisa. "Except for lunch and dinner."

"Need a good start on the day," remarked Luke. He had learned about nutrition, Cooper concluded, from a master.

"Besides," Lisa went on, "one of the orders of sausage is for the dog. To Sirius, the pursuit of sausage is a religion. Are you going to eat that biscuit or just let it get cold?"

Cooper put a protective arm around his plate. "Leave my food alone. I refuse to bolt my breakfast in order to retain ownership rights."

"Touchy, touchy," replied Lisa. "I was merely making conversation. So is personnel testing what you do?" she asked, carving out a pale orange spoonful of cantaloupe. "Those awful tests that ask people disgusting questions about their personal habits in order to find out if the prospective stockroom clerk is a psychopath?"

"No," said Cooper, "those are psychological tests which, for all your scorn, are actually pretty valid. But my company doesn't produce those. We develop tests that determine whether employees know how to do their jobs, not whether they should get hired in the first place."

"Because nobody can, like, *tell* that by watching them, or looking at what they produce . . ."

I need this? thought Cooper. "Not always; no."

"So if Joe Schmoe's worked for the Tasty Pies Company for thirty-two years and he turns out the best doggone apple tart anyone ever bit into but he takes one of your tests and blows it, he's out on the street?"

"Maybe. Maybe not. We don't make those decisions. We just make the tests."

"Oh. Then how they're used, well, that's none of your business. I see."

Cooper's jaw tensed. He did good work, valuable work. What gave her the right to question him—worse, to judge him? "I don't expect you to understand it. Most people don't."

"Excuse me?" There was a challenge in her eyes, which were, in the brightly lit restaurant, quite definitely green.

He swallowed coffee and regarded her. She met his gaze. Annoyance with her had animated his face. For a moment she glimpsed a hint of what had made the waitress border on the flirtatious with him.

"Let me make it simple," he said.

She sighed and sat back. Either the waitress was crazy or she was.

"The XYZ Corporation has four hundred and twelve employees," he began, giving Lisa the impression that she should be taking notes. "The company wants to promote six of them to work on some new machine. They want the most capable people, the ones who can learn the process the fastest, the ones who've best learned their previous jobs. That's not always apparent from productivity records or personal anecdotes about what a sullen fellow Basil Blithering is. You may never have worked for a supervisor who belittled your efforts and kept you from advancing, but good old Basil may have. And he deserves a more objective method of determining how valuable an employee he is."

"So he sharpens two number 2 pencils and shows his stuff on the Tasty Pies Test of Basic Skills. Unless, of course, he makes great tarts despite his inability to read—in which case, he's collecting unemployment."

"Yeah. It's all completely invalid, but it's a living." He scowled at her, giving into his impatience. "We don't develop tests that require skills unrelated to the person's job. Why would we?" He applied himself to his food.

Lisa, choosing the better part of valor, decided to regard this as a rhetorical question. The rest of breakfast passed in silence.

In the car, Sirius greeted his sausage with polite delight. Luke sat in the backseat doling it out, tossing a piece now and then for the dog to snap out of the air.

"Isn't that dangerous?" asked Cooper. "Mightn't he lose a finger?"

"Luke?" Lisa was aghast. "Luke could take the sausage *out* of Sirius's mouth without facing anything more than a reproachful look."

"What is he—some breed?"

"He's a Bernese. Bernese mountain dog. There aren't a lot of them in the States; they're Swiss."

"And big."

"Well, yeah. He weighs about ninety pounds. Of course, there are dogs a lot bigger. Like a Great Pyrenees, or a New-foundland, or, well, you know . . ."

"No, actually, I don't. I'm not a dog person. I don't much care for them; don't understand that slavering devotion; don't think they're worth all the hair they leave everyplace."

"To each his own." Lisa was calm. "I'm not a dog person" was, to her, ample indication of unfitness as a human being. What did he want her to do? She would give the remainder of her bank account and a few back teeth for some way to safety other than subjecting his car to dog hair. The man had helped them, helped them a lot. That didn't change the fact that he was irritating, had too much money, and was considerably too sure of himself. Lisa had dealt with the smug honcho type enough to know one when she saw one.

She glanced at him. A conceited, dull man. A man who thought *discuss* and *lecture* were synonyms. He wasn't actually bad-looking; there just wasn't anything engaging about him. He certainly didn't hold a candle to Carl the Beautiful. And he was old—must be in his forties. He was broad-shouldered, solid without the softness that so many executives conceal with tailored suits, but he had an indoor look, as if he'd pull every muscle in his body on a slide into second. He might even have been attractive once. Lisa shrugged mentally. She didn't have to figure out anything about him. She'd never see him again after today. That was all right with her; though, she had to admit, he might well be the reason Luke was singing Sirius a song about dear Liza and a hole in the bucket instead of . . . She shuddered.

"Cold? We can turn up the heat."

"No, I'm fine. Thanks."

Cooper pulled into a discount store lot and parked. He took twenty dollars out of his wallet.

"Luke's going to need something to wear. The tunic and leggings effect is real cute, but we can't haul him around looking like he was dressed out of a random dryer at the Laundromat. I'd go in and get him something, but I haven't any idea what his size is. Not that he seems concerned about precise fit."

It annoyed him that Lisa took the folded place mat from her pocket, found a pen in the glove compartment, and added, in large, bold numbers, the amount he was holding out. But he didn't argue with her. Within a few minutes she was back, and Luke, with a shout of glee, pulled a navy blue sweatsuit and a pair of socks from the plastic bag.

"For me? I put 'em on in here?"

"Sure," said Lisa, tugging Mickey's attire off the boy and helping him into the new clothing. "Hey, you look great!"

Cooper turned around and smiled at Luke. He looked older in regular clothes, and less pathetic. "How old are you, Luke?" he asked.

Luke held up one hand, fingers extended, then pushed

down his thumb with the other hand. "Four," he said with evident pride.

"As of a couple of weeks ago," remarked Lisa, whispering to avoid minimizing to Luke the impressive age he had attained.

Within a few more miles, he had slid down on the seat and dozed off. Lisa reached back and tucked Mickey's folded sweatshirt under his head. Sirius lay curled on the seat next to him. The radio played Mozart quietly. The farmland rolled by.

Cooper was the type to be involved with tests—boring, basically cold, somehow indefinable. The type who could come no closer to an apology than "I'm sorry you feel that way."

"Have you always been in the same line of work?" she asked.

"Pretty much always. I used to teach measurement courses. Decided I could do it better than it was often done. Ergo, PTS."

"Well," said Lisa, "I'm not much of a test person. I don't much care for them; don't understand all that summarizing a person by means of a score; don't appreciate all that damage by pigeonholing."

Cooper did not reply. He had heard it before and generally dismissed such observations as the product of ignorance and fear. Yes, tests could be used incorrectly. Yes, even good tests could be overinterpreted. There was, however, another side to this issue. He knew if he liked this young woman, he would have tried to explain. But he didn't like her. He didn't care what she thought.

The silence in the car began to drown out Mozart. Lisa resented it. "We could change the subject," she said. "I'm sure there's something in the world we don't have completely opposing views on. The post office? Imported beer?"

"Nah. I think we'd have completely opposing views on pretty much any subject. At least we would if I gave my views first."

"Meaning?"

"Meaning that saying something to you is like walking past a kitten while wearing an untied shoe. You pounce— back arched, claws out. Maybe practice makes perfect, but I keep wanting to say to you, 'For Pete's sake, it's just a shoelace.' "

"Gosh," said Lisa. "I didn't realize I was trying to have a conversation with Mr. Touchy."

"You're not trying to have a conversation at all. That's my point. You're trying to have an argument, and I guess you like them more than I do."

Lisa looked out at the green beginning to emerge in the fields they passed. "Do over," she said.

"Come again?"

"Do over. Like in sandlot baseball." She turned in her seat to watch his profile. "So, do you have to know a lot of math to do what you do?"

Cooper glanced at her. No, he decided, it wasn't a setup. "To do what I do, yeah. Not necessarily to write the tests, but to analyze the data."

Lisa started to sing quietly.

"I'm very well acquainted too with matters mathematical,
I understand equations, both the simple and quadratical,
About binomial theorem I'm teeming with a lot o' news—
With many cheerful facts about the square of the hypotenuse."

"They were playing that on the radio last night," said Cooper. "Just before I ran out of gas."

"Uh-huh," said Lisa. "Before my uninvited guests appeared."

"About those men, could you identify them?"

"No, I'm sure I couldn't. They were wearing ski masks. They had on ordinary clothes—the ones I saw anyway." She stopped, thinking. "One of the men that shoved me in the closet had a mark, like a stain, on his right arm just above his wrist. But there wasn't anything else odd about them that I saw." She stopped again. "Except . . ."

"What?"

"Well, it's nothing, I guess, but the guys that grabbed me both had on black shoes."

"Now, there's a distinguishing characteristic . . ."

Lisa was getting used to his sarcasm. "But, see, they weren't athletic shoes or hunting boots or anything you'd expect people tramping around in the woods to have on. They were . . . like oxfords. Very plain. Dress shoes."

"Perhaps they had a dinner engagement right afterward. A formal one."

"That would make as much sense as anything else does."

That was, Cooper thought, the issue here. Some fact or set of facts would bring this whole situation into focus. "Why are you living there, out in the middle of nowhere?" he asked.

"It lets me concentrate on my work," said Lisa, "which is replicating DNA. When the Nobel Prize money came in, I was able to go off on my own."

Cooper sighed, but glancing at him, Lisa detected the beginning of a smile.

"I'm between things," she said. "I've had different jobs, but nothing I wanted to stick with. I was in graduate school for a while. Lately I've just been hanging out, stretching some money my grandfather left me, trying to figure out what I want to do. Part of what I got from my grandfather was a little ramshackle cabin, and I've been living there, working on it."

Inside the city limits, Cooper turned off the highway and, at Lisa's request, stopped at a pay phone. He watched her make the call, one hand over her free ear. She hung up, stood for a moment with her hands pressing against the shelf below the phone, then turned and came back to the car. She opened the door and slid in.

"Carl's not there. The woman who answered the phone said that he just comes by to get messages, but he hasn't been there yesterday or today." She looked worriedly at the backseat, where Luke was sitting up, groggy and confused. "Look, is there any way I could borrow, like, fifty dollars? I just have to get in touch with Mickey and have him go to my place and get my wallet or even just a bank card and UPS it to me. But it can't get here until tomorrow or the next day. I'm sorry. I was so sure I'd reach Carl. He *said . . .*" Her voice trailed off.

"You think you're going to find a hotel that'll take ninety pounds of canine? For fifty dollars? Not in Chicago. Some of the big ones downtown will take a cougar if you walk in draped in sable, but you're a little short on sable."

He stopped and thought. There didn't seem to be any way around it. "Come on to my place for a day or so. I've got room."

Lisa shook her head.

"You don't have much choice," said Cooper with excessive patience, as if speaking to a child. "I've got to get to the office this afternoon, and I'll be there all day tomorrow while you get things straightened out." He was aware that this idea held no appeal for Lisa and resented it. "Or tell me where to drop you. Just decide."

Lisa turned and looked into the backseat again. He was right, she didn't have much choice. "All right, we'll come with you." She knew she sounded curt. "I mean, that's awfully nice of you."

Chapter
5

THEY DROVE FOR a while, winding through neighborhoods more pleasant than Lisa remembered from her days as a Chicagoan, and pulled up in front of a small white house. A deep porch extended across the front and around one side, and masses of spring foliage had begun to emerge on either side of the steps.

"This is where you live?" asked Lisa. "Amongst the narcissus?" She had expected a high-rise, a doorman, a stainless-steel kitchen with a wine rack and a jar of olives. "Look, Luke, Mr. Cooper's got a swing on his porch."

Luke slid out of the car and ran up the front steps, where he clambered into the swing. Sirius stepped out gingerly, favoring the bandaged paw, head up, eyes lively and watchful. The air of vague foolishness was gone. The black of his coat was brilliant in the sunlight.

Lisa and Cooper went into the house, Lisa insisting that Luke was perfectly safe on the porch with Sirius nearby.

"He won't run off? Or bite the neighbors?"

"He might try, but Sirius would stop him."

"The dog."

"He doesn't run off when he's got a job to do. They're

cattle dogs, protectors of the herd. Luke and I are his herd. So no, he's not completely harmless. He's suspicious of strangers, so if you think there's the likelihood of a neighbor racing into the yard swinging a club or trying to push Luke off the swing, you might want to advise him not to. Well, unless he's four years old himself. I'm not worried, but then I don't know your neighbors."

"The elderly gentleman to the west has a paranoid schnauzer," said Cooper. "That's about as dangerous as things get."

Lisa looked around at old, comfortable furniture, rugs, and potted plants. "It's more domestic than I would have imagined. Are you by yourself here?"

"My wife lived here before she found someone else she'd rather live with and, consequently, someplace else she'd rather live," replied Cooper.

She turned and gazed at him, a hint of sympathy in her eyes. Cooper felt his shoulders go rigid. "It was a long time ago."

He told her where to find the guest room upstairs and to feel free in the kitchen, and excused himself to change. He came back downstairs, somewhat daunting in a dark gray suit, a blazingly white shirt, and what Lisa assumed was this year's power tie.

She looked at him appraisingly. Some men were born to wear suits, and he was one of them. He looked restored, as if it were a relief to have shed his temporary disguise as a minion, to be adorned, once more, in the trappings of his position. Before leaving, he took two more twenties out of his wallet.

"Go ahead, write it down. But I'm leaving this so you can at least get toothbrushes. There's a drugstore down a block and over that way." He pointed. "And there's a park with a playground three blocks farther along the same street. I'll be home about six. The number's in the phone book. PTS, Inc."

He handed Lisa the money and a house key. Halfway down the front steps, he turned. "I'm going to drop the car at the shop and get the broken gauge taken care of, along with a few other things. So I won't be at the office for half an hour or so."

The kitchen didn't go with the rest of the house. It was large, high-ceilinged, but austere and unused. The cabinets were dark oak, custom-made. There was a commercial-grade range, huge and gleaming, and a large table. In a nearly empty refrigerator, Lisa located a waxed round of Gouda, an unopened carton of butter, and half a loaf of bread, none too fresh, that would be usable if grilled. She fixed some cheese sandwiches and settled Luke with his in front of the TV. Luke, who had spent six weeks without a television set, was delighted.

"It's the Rifleman!" he crowed. "He's got a big, big gun and a boy and," with a certain smugness, "my name."

The Rifleman, which Lisa remembered fondly, seemed a better choice than the other available options. She rationalized that TV containing basic moral lessons and at least some information about the world was unlikely to do the boy any real harm, despite Lucas McCain's predilection for spraying bullets around North Fork. She disappeared into the kitchen and picked up the phone.

Mickey had returned home. He answered after eight rings.

"Hey, Lisa!" he said. "Weren't you going to bring over your miter box? I've been cutting firewood—criminy, it's cold—but I've been watching for you."

"I'm not at home, Mickey," she replied. "Had some trouble last night and split. I need your help."

"Yeah? Sure. What?"

"Don't go by yourself, but get some guys and go over to my place. If my backpack's there, get my wallet out of it and send it to me overnight. If you're too late for the UPS pickup at Knight's, send it FedEx. If my backpack's not there, just send my spare bank card. It's in the back pocket of a pair of jeans on a hook in the bedroom closet. If there's anybody around, just act like you thought I'd be there and leave."

"Who would be there? And where *are* you? What's going on?"

"If there's anybody there, they're not nice and you don't want to deal with them. It doesn't matter who they are; I don't even know. I don't want to tell you where I am because . . . Look, it's just better not to. And I don't know what's going on except that somebody's after Luke. I'll tell you about it in a few days, when this is over. Okay?"

"Yeah. Okay. But can't I help?"

"You are helping, Mickey. Really. As a matter of fact, I already took your gas can, and you loaned Luke a sweatshirt and some socks last night. Your only clean ones."

"So that's where they went! I thought maybe I'd just imagined them."

"I'll get them back, clean again. Now, this is going to seem weird, but don't address the package to me. Use your sister's name. And send it to . . . wait a minute." Lisa found the phone book and PTS, Inc. "Send it to your sister at PTS, Incorporated." She gave the address. "I mean it about not going alone, Mick."

"Yeah. All right. Whooo, but this is creepy."

"Tell me. Thanks, Mickey. Say hey to Justice." She hung up and sat staring at the phone, then picked it up again and called PTS.

"Good afternoon. PTS." The voice was brisk, pleasant, very British.

"May I speak to Mr. Cooper, please?"

"Dr. Cooper is tied up at the moment." The correction was polite but firm. Lisa found it intensely irritating. "May I take a message?"

"Well, when the *doctor* is free, just tell him that Lisa called and—"

Great Britain cut her off. "Oh, yes, well, hold on, please."

Cooper's voice came on. "Lisa? What's wrong?"

She couldn't recall a single time since the age of eight when giving her name had made an unavailable person instantly available. It had happened once when she'd called her father at work, galvanized into the action of using the phone without permission by the terror of coming home to find no one there. Her father had answered the same way.

"Nothing's wrong. I didn't mean to interrupt you, especially if you're with a patient . . ."

"What?"

"Never mind. I can talk to you later."

"No, it's no problem. What's up?"

Lisa explained what she'd done. "So something may come tomorrow or the next day, addressed to Adrienne Luescher. Is that okay? Will somebody accept it?"

"If I tell them to," said Cooper.

Lisa hung up and carried her plate to the sink. She was gratified that he had told the receptionist to put through any calls from her, but couldn't shake the annoyance that his answer to her question wasn't "Sure" or "I'll take care of it" instead of a declaration of authority. He must be a real joy to work for.

As soon as the Rifleman had dispatched a gunslinger and explained to his son, in a few well-chosen words, the ways of the world, she gathered up Luke and went in search of the drugstore, the playground, and a grocery.

LISA LAY IN BED, staring at the ceiling. On this side of the house, streetlights cast no glow, but the moon was out and, shining faintly through old lace curtains, kept the room from total darkness. Luke's bed, six feet away, creaked softly as he turned. Sirius was aware that she was awake. She must breathe differently asleep; he had never wakened her in the night by pushing his nose against her hand as he was doing now. She stroked the top of his head absently.

Where was Carl? How long would she have to impose on the generous but overbearing stranger who, for some inexplicable reason, had offered refuge? When could she go home, get her own life back? The constraints of her situation weighed heavily. Obligation, which would normally dismay her, was not the root of the problem. She could find ways to return the favor of hospitality, but there was no way around the fact that she was only peripherally in control of her life.

Alone, a dog her only responsibility, she would have had options. Her bank account could handle a cheap motel for some time. Or an airplane ticket to her college roommate's home in Seattle. Or . . . But alone, she wouldn't be in this predicament. And the predicament was considerably more complicated than finding a place to stay for the foreseeable future. She moved fitfully on the bed—Cooper's bed, in Cooper's house.

He wasn't the worst she could have run into. Not the kind of man she'd choose to spend time with, but all right when he wasn't imperious. She had friends who, if they'd seen her with him, would have cocked an eyebrow, made an approving face. But she had never cared for men with carefully arranged sock drawers. Not that her investigation of his house had gone so far as opening his sock drawer.

She'd gone upstairs, wondering about the house, when she and Luke came back from their outing and before making dinner. The rooms had the potential for being pleasant, occupied as they were by the same kind of solid and unpretentious furniture that she had seen downstairs. They did not, however, seem to be part of anyone's home. The furnishings had been put in logical places but not arranged to meet anyone's needs. The rugs were hooked and muted—dusty-colored flowers on pale backgrounds. Someone had needle-pointed a seat cover in the same subdued colors for a walnut rocking chair. At Luke's bedtime, she sat in that chair with him on her lap as she told the obligatory story. But, nice as any individual piece of furniture was, the rooms seemed to reflect an absent personality, as if Cooper, as well as she, were a visitor in what had once been another's home. Well, she thought, the ex–Mrs. Cooper had charming taste.

Luke accepted their situation with his usual unquestioning adaptiveness. He felt safe and, at least for the moment, that was enough for him. He was delighted by the playground after six weeks with only a tire suspended by a thick rope from a tree in the clearing behind the cabin. Tired but cheerful, he sat cross-legged in the bottom of the cart as Lisa strolled through the grocery store.

By the time Sirius's ears pricked at Cooper's key turning in the lock, the table was set and dinner was ready.

"You cooked?" He was surprised, a little taken aback. "We could have gone out."

"It was fun. I like strange kitchens," she'd replied. "Though even the strangest usually have measuring spoons *some*where."

"I don't cook much," said Cooper unnecessarily. The quickest glance into the virtually empty pantry, the drawers holding little besides a corkscrew and a garlic press, had revealed that fact. He sniffed. "What is it?"

"Meat loaf," said Lisa. "Mashed potatoes. If your idea of dinner is to divide a kumquat into six parts and eat half of it tonight and the other half tomorrow along with one smoked oyster apiece, you'll need to find a different houseguest."

Luke dominated the conversation during dinner. "Does your mother and your dad live with you?" he asked Cooper. Learning that they had died long ago seemed to establish a new level of camaraderie.

"My mother, she died a long, long time ago too," he

announced matter-of-factly. "She got sick, sicker than I ever got, and then she died. When I was this big." He held his hands about eight inches apart. "Now I live just with my dad when I'm not visiting Lisa. And we got a cat."

He ate steadily for a few minutes and then looked up hopefully. "You got a cat anywhere?"

"I had a cat," said Cooper. "He was as big as this table and he ate nails. The neighbors were scared of him."

Luke put down his fork, drank some milk, replaced the glass, and shook his head. "You made that up."

"Why do you think so?"

Luke grinned. "There's no cats big as a table. Maybe a tiger, but people don't got tigers in their house. And nails would poke his mouth. You made it up."

"Well . . . *maybe*. But I don't have a cat anymore, anyway."

"Not in the basement?"

"Nope. Not anywhere."

"Well, *I* got one. You got any friends to play football with?"

Cooper shook his head. "The neighbors were scared of them too."

Luke looked doubtfully at him.

Cooper relented. "I don't have any friends to play football with, but I used to. Now I have friends to play bridge with. That's a card game."

"I *think*," said Luke, "football is more fun."

Lisa was glad to leave the conversation to them. It was nice, having another adult around, even if he wasn't a friend. And Cooper was less annoying when he was dealing with Luke than when he was dealing with her—less taut, almost blithe. In defense of intellectual pursuits, he slid open a box of bridge cards after dinner to widen Luke's horizons.

"We going to play bridge?" Luke asked.

"Nah. You might not be able to learn how before bedtime. Let's try war."

While they played at the kitchen table, Lisa did the dishes, listening to their discourse, to the slap of cards and Luke's pleased exclamations at each small triumph. Then she took him up to bed.

When she came down, she found Cooper in the study, papers spread out on his desk. He was wearing glasses, which made him look milder. He waved her toward a large leather-covered chair, took off the glasses, and leaned back.

"Luke settled?"

"Yup. He was pretty full of himself after beating you at that grueling game. He likes it here. Thanks for letting us stay."

Cooper made a dismissive gesture. "More room than I need." Then, casually, "You have a plan?"

"Not much of one. I'll leave a message at Carl's number, try to think of how to find him. I should get at least a cash card, tomorrow or the next day, depending on when Mickey was able to get it sent. I guess I should call him to make sure he found it."

"No," said Cooper. "The first call was probably safe. There was no good reason for anyone to think of Mickey as a possible contact. But once he went to your house . . . well, that identified him. If these guys are small-time, they won't be able to find you through him unless you go hide under his bed. But they didn't strike me as small-time. If they've bugged his phone, you don't want to call him."

He was right. Lisa chafed at the imposed isolation, but he was right. "Well, he probably got what I need. I'll find out when it does or doesn't show up. Assuming it comes, Luke and I can get a room someplace."

"You've got a room. You've got a whole house." Cooper's voice was annoyed. "I thought this was settled. If you don't want to stay here, don't stay here. But there's no reason to keep remaking the decision."

Lisa felt her back stiffen, pulling her forward in the chair. "I simply," she said with clipped dignity, "don't know how long this will go on. And I have no intention of being dependent, day after day, on a man I met yesterday." She stopped short of "and don't particularly like," but the unspoken ending hung in the air.

He gazed dispassionately at her. "Fine," he said quietly. "Leave when you get your ATM card. Do whatever you want. However, in making your eventual decision, consider this. I liked coming home today, being jumped on by a four-year-old, dinner in the oven. It's like getting a chance to have, for a few days, parts of a life that was always mere speculation. You and Luke get some measure of comfort, some bits and pieces of security for a few days, and I get that. It seems balanced to me."

His speech disconcerted her. She knew it had cost him. For whatever reason he had decided to abandon aloof autonomy, it behooved her to let him.

"All right," she said. "I'll get some more groceries so the smell of dinner that greets you isn't that of boiled Nikes."

He nodded. "I keep some cash in this drawer." He jabbed a thumb toward his desk. "Take what you need."

Lisa had borrowed a T-shirt, taken a shower, and gone to bed. And now, waiting for her restless brain to develop a plan, she sighed and willed herself to relax. The one-day-at-a-time approach involved increments too bulky for her purposes. She'd have to deal with things one hour at a time.

She turned on her side and prodded the feather pillow into a more comfortable shape. The sheets were soft and smooth against her bare legs. Under the heavy quilt, she felt snug. There was absolutely nothing she could do before morning. She slept.

Chapter
6

L UKE SAT, ALTERNATELY looking out the window and turning to chatter up at Lisa. He had stood, holding on to a pole and rocking delightedly with the swaying motion of the bus, until a lurch flung him into Lisa's shoulder and she decided he was better off sitting down. After breakfast and another visit to the playground, they had gone to visit three of the thrift shops Lisa remembered as offering particularly wide selections and were on their way back to Cooper's.

"That boy got a bike. I don't got a bike, but my dad says someday. You don't got one neither. Maybe my dad will get you a bike too. There's the stemetary where the people goes when they smashes their cars. Waaaay down there is the lake. Pretty soon we see where Rick Wilkins plays."

Rick Wilkins? Ah, thought Lisa, the boyish, sweet-faced catcher who used to play for the Cubs. Luke was right; they were approaching Wrigley Field. But how had he known that? Why was he so familiar with this neighborhood?

She reached up and yanked the cord. "Come on, Luke. We're getting off."

Half a block later, the bus shuddered to a stop. She

guided Luke down the steps and stood gazing around.

"Did you and your dad live near here, Luke? Did you ever walk over to see a Cubs game?"

The boy nodded vigorously. "Lotsa times. Me and my dad like the Cubs. But they only win some of the time."

"Do you know how to get to your house, the one you lived in with your dad?"

"That way," said Luke, pointing off to the left. "We going there?"

"Sure, let's go there," said Lisa. "You know your dad's not home, don't you? He moved to a new house, and you'll move there too, soon. But we can go by your old house. That will be fun."

Her heart was thumping with sudden hope. It was unlikely that there would be any way that she could use Carl's old address to find his new one, but the small chance was a bigger one than she'd had before. She had asked Luke where he lived, but all he had known was that it was in Chicago. Even she knew the need to teach children their addresses. Why hadn't Carl?

Luke seemed to have no trouble finding his way from Clark Street. He ran ahead, waiting politely at the corners for Lisa to catch up.

"Here's my house!" he announced at last, running up the walk of a neat courtyard building and pushing open the vestibule door of the second entrance on the left.

The mailboxes held no "McCain" nameplate. Lisa had been certain they wouldn't. Carl had told her that he was moving, claiming that he didn't know yet where he would go but that he would tell her as soon as he did. He had never told her.

"Do you know any of these people?" she asked, reading names off the boxes.

"Mrs. Peavy," said Luke. "She lives upstairs and she has cookies."

Lisa pushed the bell. After a few seconds, a woman's voice came over the intercom.

"Yes?"

"Hi, Mrs. Peavy? I'm a friend of Carl and Luke McCain's. Could I talk to you for a minute? Luke's with me."

"Why, gracious! Come right on up!"

The buzzer let out a piercing whine. Lisa pushed the door open and followed Luke up the stairs. Rounding the last turn, she saw him with his arms flung around the legs of an old lady in a flowered cotton dress.

"Luke, you little darling, let me see that handsome face!"

Luke let go and beamed up at Mrs. Peavy.

"But you're so big! Are you really Luke McCain or are you a twelve-year-old just pretending to be my little boy?"

"I'm me; I am!" said Luke, and then his eye fell on the calico cat that had wandered out into the hallway and was winding itself around the woman's legs. "Mayor Lin!" he exclaimed. "It's Mayor Lin! What you got Mayor Lin at your house for?"

"Marilyn got lost before your daddy moved, honey, and then she came back after he left. She's still your kitty. I've just been taking care of her for a while."

Mrs. Peavy turned to Lisa with a smile. "Why, come on in. We don't need to stand here in the hall."

She ushered her visitors into a dim apartment full of pleasant smells—a subtle mustiness like old sachets and a lingering heavy sweetness. Lisa sniffed and grinned. "Doughnuts?" she asked. "It smells wonderful in here, like my grandma's house used to smell."

"Doughnuts, you bet," said Mrs. Peavy. "You just sit down and let me get some. Would you like coffee, dear? It's all made. Or tea? Or herb tea? Carl always likes herb tea, so I keep some around. Why, the first time I offered him tea, he asked if I had any, and of course I didn't. But he drank the regular, old orange pekoe without so much as a grimace, being such a nice, polite boy. Anyway, the next time I went to the store, naturally I got some, and after that, well, he could have what he liked."

"And I'm sure he was grateful," said Lisa. "He's the herb-tea type. But I'd like coffee. No, I'd *love* coffee. Thank you." She dropped her bags and sank into an overstuffed, claw-footed chair. She leaned back, resting her head on the crocheted antimacassar. "Black, no sugar. You've saved my life."

Luke sat cross-legged on the floor, stroking the cat, who was stretched rapturously on her back, purring so loudly that Lisa was surprised the windows weren't rattling. Next to her, on a small mahogany table, was a photograph of a beautiful girl, her arm tucked possessively through that of a grinning soldier. They seemed oblivious to the camera that had captured them. Lisa, picking up the picture in its heavy, silver frame, was transported to a white frame house in a small Wisconsin town, a house with the same picture frames, the same fragrances, the same antimacassar-draped armchairs.

Mrs. Peavy returned with a tray that held a plate heaped with sugared doughnuts, two cups of coffee, and a glass of milk. She nodded at the photograph in Lisa's hands. "Fred was a looker, wasn't he? Was I proud to be out and around with him! Everyone just used to *stare*."

How odd, thought Lisa. Fred was just an ordinary, pleasant-looking young man. It was the young Mrs. Peavy who must have turned heads. She was still quite lovely, with the appeal of the intensely mild.

"Now, tell me who you are and what you're doing here with Luke," said Mrs. Peavy, holding the doughnuts out to Lisa. "Where's Carl?" But Lisa shook her head a fraction with a slight motion toward the boy. After introducing herself, she steered the conversation to Fred, about whom Mrs. Peavy was delighted to talk, until Luke had eaten his fill and wandered off to open the door of a telephone stand, where, it was clear he was aware, Mrs. Peavy kept a stash of small toys.

Lisa began in a carefully casual but lowered tone. "I don't know where Carl is, Mrs. Peavy. That's what I'm trying to find out. Gosh, these are good!" She picked up a third doughnut and went on. "I've been keeping Luke for a while—"

"Yes, I knew Carl had sent him somewhere, though he never said exactly where. He said he had a lot of work and wanted Luke to have more attention than he could give him for a while."

"Uh-huh. Well, now I need to find him. I was hoping you might know something about where I could start looking."

Mrs. Peavy contemplated her hands, folded in her lap, and considered the situation. She liked Carl, and he had chosen not to reveal his whereabouts, had gone so far as to hide his whereabouts, from what she could tell. What a nice, good-looking boy he was. Not as handsome as her Fred had been, not by a long shot. Too thin, really. But she could see why there were often pretty girls going in and coming out of his door. He had those eyes that crinkled at the corners when he smiled, and he smiled so often.

On the other hand, there was his child, his adored child. Carl had entrusted him to this nice girl. And she, Mrs. Peavy could tell, came from a very good family. Why, she had recognized the smell of doughnuts, right off, not like so many youngsters these days. A sensible girl too, that was obvious, and attractive, with her short, thick hair and that direct gaze. Mrs. Peavy could feel the gaze on her now.

Oh, it was too much, the constant need to judge. So what if she wasn't—what had Fred always said in his gentle, teasing way? A mental giant—that was it—heaven help her if she didn't have some sense! She made up her mind.

"I don't know where he is," she said, looking up. "But he called a few days after he left, to ask if Marilyn had come home. Of course, she hadn't yet, though it wasn't too long before she did, all bones and soot she was when she made it back. I guess she'd gotten locked in somewhere, poor little thing. And he gave me a phone number, in case Marilyn showed up, you know. But he said not to give it to anyone and to pretend I didn't know anything at all about where he was. So I didn't tell anyone. Not even his cousin."

"His cousin? Carl's cousin?"

"Yes. His cousin came by looking for him, but I told him that I didn't know where Carl had moved, just that he'd moved. I felt a little bad about it. Probably he didn't mean not to tell his own cousin. But how could I be sure? And not everyone gets along with their cousins. I had one cousin I just couldn't abide. A snoop and a tattletale, that's what he was. But cousins can be almost like brothers and sisters, and if you don't get along with them, well, it's too bad, really."

Lisa nodded. "Really," she said. "This cousin—what was he like?"

"Oh, a sweet boy. Friendly and polite, like Carl, and handsome in an unusual way. From Texas or someplace down there."

"He told you that?"

"No. He didn't have to. He talked like he was. Like my Fred, who came from near Dallas." She sat silently for a moment, her eyes fond, then brought her hands down firmly on the arms of her chair. "Let me get that number for you."

She got up carefully and went over to a small cherry desk, took out an address book, and copied something onto an index card. She returned and handed it to Lisa. "Try this, dear," she said. "I hope you have better luck finding him at home."

Lisa sat very still, holding the number. Carl didn't have a cousin. He had told her once, in deep, mock seriousness, that they could never marry because they were both only children. "My parents were only children," he had said. "I can't have Luke grow up deprived of cousins like I was. Surely you understand."

Lisa had understood precisely. She was so far from being a person that Carl would want to marry that he could joke with her about the reasons. It still stung.

She folded the card and hitched forward on the chair to put it in the back pocket of her jeans. "Did Carl's cousin tell you his name?"

"I don't think so. I'd remember if he had, wouldn't I? Well, maybe not! But I don't think he did. Matter of fact, I know he didn't because I remember now, I almost asked. So I could tell Carl about it if he called. But then I didn't, because it seemed a little nosy. I was going to tell Carl about it the next time he called. And then, when Marilyn came back, I tried calling him every day to tell him she's safe, but he's never answered the phone. So, of course, I couldn't tell him about his cousin either."

"Shall I? When I reach him?"

"You do that, dear," said Mrs. Peavy. "I don't mind if he knows where you got the number. He can't expect me not to use my common sense, for heaven's sake."

She walked them to the door and put one hand on each of Luke's shoulders. "You call me up, you hear? And come back to see me."

Luke nodded. "I gotta come back to get Mayor Lin. She wants to come home with me."

Mrs. Peavy smiled and watched them go down the stairs. As she carried the cups to the kitchen, a memory crinkled her brow with worry. That nice policeman who was friends with Carl had come to the door not more than a day or so after Carl's cousin. But he hadn't, after all, been looking for Carl. He'd just seen Marilyn in the window, where she sat of an afternoon looking out at the birds, and he'd wanted to make sure Luke was all right.

"I saw Luke's kitten," he'd said with casual affability,

accepting a chair and her offer of coffee. "Just wanted to make sure Luke wasn't sick or anything. I know how much he loves that cat."

She had just been trying, unsuccessfully again, to reach Carl, and his request for secrecy was fresh in her mind. She'd pretended ignorance. "Oh, I don't think so," and she'd smiled back over her shoulder as she went into the kitchen. "I haven't any idea where he is, but I'm sure he'll be back for her soon."

The policeman (Martin was the name on his uniform . . . or was it Martell?) hadn't pursued the subject. He had chatted in a friendly and offhand way about going to school with Carl, and then he'd left.

But now, thinking back, she wondered about the visit. Had the address book still been out on top of the desk when she'd gone into the kitchen? Was it later that evening that she'd seen it there, open to the Ms, and put it away?

"Oh, don't be silly! He's Carl's friend and a *policeman*!" she said, and, hearing her voice in the quiet apartment, was surprised that she'd spoken out loud.

FOLLOWING LUKE BACK to the bus stop, Lisa gritted her teeth against the memories. She had kept them tucked away, tucked deeply away, for a long time. She'd gone on. As long as the memories did not resonate in the present, she could count herself recovered. She had formed other attachments, had refused to measure them against what she had felt for Carl. Even after he had showed up at the cabin with Luke in tow, needing her help, she kept the past tucked away. Hearing his voice on the phone and then, a few hours later, opening the door to him, she had felt her heart thud painfully. But she had willed herself to stay in the *now*, to smile a welcome, to listen and nod. She couldn't have refused him, and that, she knew, was because of the past. But she didn't have to live in it. She didn't even have to visit it.

Now a casual comment about a cousin Carl didn't have had begun the recollections. Not having her guard up against that one memory had allowed the flood to begin, and they washed over her, steady and insistent. She could see Carl at twenty as clearly as she could see his son today. Carl in an army jacket, walking in his long-legged stride down the sidewalk in front of his dorm, shoulders hunched against the cold. The wind had pushed his dark hair off his forehead. *Cutting classes tomorrow, Lisa. Going to Chicago to see a man about a job.* Lisa, pulling a handful of change from her jacket pocket and holding it out. *I've got money; can I come too?* His laughter and response. *Sure. Meet you at the train station.* But she had meant it. Can I come too—while you look for a job, while you grow up—can I come too? Then, meeting him again, years later, and getting another chance. Another chance! She had never had a chance at all. *We can never marry.* His eyes laughing. She knew he hadn't the slightest idea. *Surely you understand.*

No, she hadn't. Hadn't for a moment understood how one person could be consumed, could cherish, adore, while the other went on, affectionate but unchanged. *Too bad, because the two of us could produce an entire NBA team.* They were lying, propped on pillows, on the bed in the tiny apartment they shared, and Carl had stretched out one denimed leg next to hers. Tall as he was, the sole of her foot came to his ankle. She laughed, shortly, lightly, returned to the crossword, erased a word, some word, any word, pretended concentration. It would be like that forever, or until he fell in love with someone, whichever came first. She had known it.

She moved out the next day, needing, she said, a place of her own, needing, really, to hide from him so she could stop hiding from him. When she moved to Wisconsin, she sent a note to let him know, hardly able to bear the knowledge that he would see her handwriting on the envelope among his mail and would not tear it open first, would not save it until last, would merely open it in whatever order it came to hand. And, because he liked her, maybe even liked her a lot, he would be glad to know where she was. Breezily, cheerfully glad to know. Period. How could it still be so painful?

Luke stopped to press against a fence, on the other side of which surged a boxer puppy, its entire hindquarters quivering with the movement of its stub of a tail. Luke could get his arm between the pickets, as far as his elbow, and the puppy was gnawing rapturously on his wrist. Luke's giggles pried Lisa out of the past.

"Come on. We've got to go get Sirius some food, or he'll be eating your arm too."

THEY ATE THAT NIGHT, again, in the kitchen. Lisa had roasted a chicken and made a shortcake with small, sweet strawberries she'd found at the grocery store. Cooper felt odd, being cooked for in his own home by a woman he barely knew. The fact that the atmosphere in the room was not tense just made the situation seem even stranger. He'd found himself whistling that morning while he spaded what would be the annuals bed, and then singing in the shower. The kitchen table, when he came downstairs, had been set for breakfast. Things were supposed to feel strained when they were so unfamiliar, so why did he feel at ease? Chasing tiny peas around his plate, Luke sat across the table and told about the afternoon.

"We ate lunch and we went shopping and Mrs. Peavy gave us *doughnuts* and we rode on the bus and Sirius was glad when we came back."

"Mrs. Peavy?"

Lisa explained, neglecting to mention either the telephone number she'd obtained or Mrs. Peavy's visitor. This man was their host and that was all he was. She was not interested in forming a partnership.

"When we got back, I did some wash. I hope that's

okay." The laundry area in the basement looked as though surgery could be performed there. It was a little unnerving.

"Of course. But what did you have to wash?"

"We bought some things at a couple of thrift shops. They seem perfectly clean, but I'm just happier if I wash them myself."

When Luke had been bathed and put to bed, Cooper emerged from his study and joined Lisa in the living room. She sat on the rug in front of the fireplace, folding the clothes she had bought.

"Wait a minute," said Cooper, spotting the designer's name on the tag in a heavy, cotton sweater of myriad subtle colors. "That cost about two hundred dollars."

"Once," said Lisa. "You think people who drop a fortune on clothes keep them forever? That's the whole point. Some lady bought this for two hundred dollars and wore it one winter, maybe three times. Then I bought it for ninety cents." She shrugged. "It's the only thing I like about rich people—their tendency to get bored. Great sweaters are hard to find, though. The easiest clothes to get hold of are the ones people give away the instant they've lost twelve pounds on some absurd diet. They refuse to believe their new, starved bodies are temporary."

Cooper looked at the stack of clothes—some children's pants and long-sleeved shirts, a pair of Lisa-size jeans, beautifully made Italian shoes, a challis skirt, a long-sleeved blouse. The skirt surprised him. It was hard to imagine Lisa in a skirt, in any kind of feminine clothing except maybe some calico, pioneer getup. Not that she wasn't obviously female, but in such a . . . rugged way. He preferred women who took his arm in the woods to keep from turning their ankles. Still, it was easy to watch her, easy to sit there with her, as if she were . . . just a person.

He wondered what she'd look like in the skirt. It had surprised him that she could cook at all, much less that she could cook something as good as what he'd eaten the last two nights. Her head was bent over the child's shirt she was folding, and the back of her neck was smooth and vulnerable.

"How much did that haul cost?"

Lisa looked up and smiled. She looked about fourteen when she grinned like that. "Twelve bucks. You might have noticed we didn't take time to pack the other night. I should get at least my bank card tomorrow, and I could have waited until then to get something to wear. But Luke and I needed something to do, and these jeans"—she looked down at her crossed legs—"were on their fifth day and had been worn for a scuffle in the woods."

Cooper remembered the force of her body hitting his and tried to suppress the embarrassment he felt in recalling the struggle. If he'd been expecting the assault, it wouldn't have been difficult to free himself. Even so . . . His mouth twisted. He needed to get back on the weight machines at the club.

"It was nice for Luke to find his cat," Lisa continued, twisting around to lean back against the couch across the room from Cooper, stretching her legs out in front of her. "She makes the most wonderful doughnuts. Not the cat, Mrs. Peavy. And she's the sweetest old lady. Still gaga over her late husband, and he's been gone for eight years. One of those lucky ones who find their true loves and keep them." She blushed suddenly and fiercely. "Oh, I'm sorry."

Cooper laughed shortly. "Forget it. Whatever a true love is, Allison wasn't mine. We were . . . comfortable for a number of years and then not." Why did that statement seem so evasive? It was true. It was just incomplete. So what? He barely knew this girl; why should he tell her anything about his life?

He's practiced that line, thought Lisa.

"That was too glib," said Cooper. He hesitated, then went on. "She was happy while I was teaching. Her parents were professors; she thought that's what smart people did, if they didn't go into medicine or maybe law. She . . . liked the accoutrements—the faculty parties, the awed, respectful students, the intellectual chatter. I hated it."

He paused, remembering how deadly his life had seemed. "The classes were okay, better than okay, but I did so little of that. And the committees and the meetings and, worst by far, those dinner parties she liked . . . It was all so boring. I had tenure. There wasn't any challenge anymore. Allison thought the research money counted as a challenge, but it was so easy to get, so easy to spend, and I never felt I'd earned it. I quit and started PTS and she never forgave me. I pretty much lived at the office for a few years. I guess it was a relief when she left. She found a nice fellow with suede patches on his elbows who'd just been made chairman of economics. She's happy again."

"And you?"

"I don't think of things that way. Happy. Unhappy. I like my life all right, I guess."

Lisa was quietly shocked. He doesn't think of things *that way*? No wonder his wife left him.

Cooper interrupted her thoughts. "No luck reaching Carl, I assume?"

"None." That was true. It was also true that she had called the Name and Address service and found out that the number Mrs. Peavy had given her corresponded to a listing for a Martin Lazarus at an address near Diversey.

"I thought I'd go out for a while tomorrow, check with some people Carl and I used to know, people he might still know. Maybe Mrs. Peavy can watch Luke. It seems better not to have him with me while I'm asking questions about his dad."

"But while you're looking for him, there are people looking for you."

"Uh-huh. So maybe I should, oh, wallpaper the upstairs bathroom instead? Look, Carl's out on the West Coast auditioning for some sitcom. Or he's on location for a commercial. He's out of town, just like he told Mrs. Peavy. And somebody knows where."

Carl would not have gone to the West Coast, or anywhere else related merely to his career, without bothering to tell her. She knew that. She also knew that telling Cooper of her plans to check out the home of Martin Lazarus would result in an argument she had no intention of having. It wasn't any of Cooper's business what she intended to do or how she intended to do it.

She's planning something, thought Cooper. This vague scheme is not the best she's come up with. She's decided something and she's not going to tell me what. He was furious. He kept his voice mild.

"Whatever you're contemplating, for the record I think you're nuts. From what you've told me and from what I heard in the woods, those people are not kidding around. Stay away from anyplace they might be or might arrive at."

"Don't tell me what to do." Lisa's tone was cold. "If they know where Carl is, if they've done something to him or are planning to, then why did they come looking for Luke? Come on, *Doctor* Cooper, make sense."

I wonder if she's always petty when she's annoyed, thought Cooper.

Lisa went on. "They came after Luke because they can't get to Carl. And if you think I'm going to just sit here and worry, wondering who they are, what they want, why they're looking for Luke, how the heck they ever found him, and whether they can do it again, well, you're just as wrong as you can possibly be."

Cooper opened his mouth and shut it. He had almost told her to be practical—not a wise comment, he realized, with an andiron within her reach. "Fine. But you don't need to go back to Mrs. Peavy's," he said. "There's a woman who works for me who doesn't live too far from here. Her neighbor watches her kids. Maybe she'd take another one."

Lisa's eyes lit up. "That would be great. The one thing, besides TV, that I haven't been able to give Luke is kids."

Cooper went off to the phone and came back a few minutes later. "She gave me the number and I called her neighbor and everything's set. Anytime tomorrow. But call first to make sure they're not out and around."

A sudden nervous dart of Lisa's eyes made him hold up his hand. "Yes, one pays her. You can put another entry on that list you're keeping."

Maybe his wife didn't leave him because he was a boor, thought Lisa. Maybe it was because he always knew what she was thinking.

Chapter

7

THEY HAD CLEAR objectives and strict rules. The services the public counted on them to supply were to be provided in a dedicated and competent fashion. Gerald Martelli had worked for them for some time before he was considered for inclusion in the inner circle, the elite and carefully selected employees who carried out the group's other activities. These were the ventures that provided the bulk of their quite considerable income. Martelli survived a probationary period of another four months without knowing he was undergoing it. A videotape of a series of his petty violations of the law was made, unbeknownst to him, during this time, to provide them with a measure of protection in the event their judgment of him was inaccurate. They had not needed the tape; their judgment had not been inaccurate, except for a lack of perception regarding how deep and how impatient was his greed.

He was informed of the rules. The trivial but adroit transgressions that had indicated his suitability and netted him an extra five thousand dollars or so a year were to stop. He was to become a model officer, steady, reliable, and above reproach. Only when he was working for them was he to give vent to his long-standing desire to augment his income with whatever opportunities presented themselves. And he was to pursue those opportunities with a minimum of risk and a complete absence of violence. Gerry knew his bosses created no messes, tolerated no excesses, and permitted no insubordination. He knew they avoided violence because it was impractical. What he failed to realize until too late was that they were quite capable of recognizing the point at which the impractical became necessary. And they were willing to do what was necessary.

The danger they avoided was that which was counterproductive. If it was practical to harm the boy, in order to recover what was theirs and to protect the operation, they would do so. Since Gerry had created the situation involving the boy and his father, it was reasonable that he bear the largest part of the burden of carrying the strategy out. This was explained to him, and he understood.

What he didn't understand was how they had found out about the statue. He'd been alone in the upstairs study when he'd seen it. It was standing in a niche in the wall, all alone, just the statue surrounded by dark green wall. A small light, recessed in the top of the alcove, would bathe it in a soft glow. He'd gone into the study to locate the stamp collection. The insurance file photo showed it spread out on a desk. It was likely that the collection was kept in the same room where it had been photographed. It was. He spotted the statue as he stood and turned, the albums gripped securely in his left hand. His right hand shot out, without conscious thought guiding it, closed around the statue, and dropped it in his pocket.

They had gone over the list carefully the night before, as always. They had gathered around the gleaming oak table in the small room they used for such purposes and made the assignments. They were all there, all except the boss. He was never there. It was worrisome to Gerry not to know who the boss was, but he no longer expected to find him at one of these meetings. They had gone over the details. The burglar alarm was the normal kind most respected by insurance agencies. It would call the closest police station at the first indication of a break-in. Thanks to Jefferson's skills, there would be no call. Jefferson was the highest paid member of the inner circle for one reason only. He had spent fifteen years in the burglar alarm business. He could install every common system in existence. He could deactivate anything he could install.

The best part, Gerry had thought, glancing around the table, was the sheer bulk of the information they had. They knew what methods had been used to keep them out of every house they wanted to enter. They knew the residents were away and where they were. They knew what was there, exactly how much each item was worth, and at least generally where it could be found.

There was no statue on the list. Each item on each schedule was described in detail, its appraised value noted. The statue, for whatever reason, was not on a schedule. That should have meant it had no particular value. Yet it had to be valuable. The niche in which it stood had been designed to hold it. Even he was stunned by its beauty, and he had little appreciation for the vast majority of the items he so zealously participated in seeking, stealing, and turning into cash. Clearly it was worth stealing, yet there was no plan to steal it. They couldn't know he had done so, but they did. He knew it the moment he ambled into the bar at the resort where he was staying and saw Menendez at a table facing the door.

"He wants it back, Martelli," the boss's messenger remarked shortly. "Now."

"Hey," Gerry said, spreading his hands and grinning, knowing with certainty that attempting ignorance would be disastrous. "My mistake. I knew the thing was worthless—

it wasn't ridered. I thought it was pretty. You mean you've never lifted an imported chocolate from the candy dish on your way toward the silver service?"

"I didn't get sent down here to talk about candy." Menendez did not smile back. He lifted a Scotch and soda, drawing Gerry's eyes to the port-wine stain on his wrist. "We want the statue and we want it now. It'll end up in Lake Michigan, but we're the ones going to put it there. It's not at your place; we already know that. So where is it?"

"I'll get it." Gerry gave up his attempt at joviality. "I swear. I know where it is; I know exactly where it is. I'll have somebody pick it up and bring it down to the office."

The man merely gazed at him. Gerry waited, terror beginning to spread, his fingers and toes losing sensation. "Look, I'm sorry. Like I said, it was a mistake. It won't happen again. What's the big deal?"

The man looked at him silently for a moment before he responded. When he spoke, he did so with exaggerated patience. "This is a team," he said. "But the team has a manager. Nobody—and I mean nobody—goes off on his own. You do this kind of thing, you can't be trusted. You can't be trusted, you're out. If all you are is out, you're lucky. My plane ticket down here cost one heck of a lot more than the stupid knickknack you filched. That's not the point. The point is"—he leaned back and waited for Gerry's eyes to meet his—"that it's *evidence.* The statue ties you to the event during which you obtained it. *You* can tie a number of other people to that same event, not least among those people, me. That's the big deal. And the big question is, can Gerry Martelli be trusted? We're concerned that the answer is no."

Gerry swallowed, tried to smile. He put his hands, which had started to tremble slightly, under the table. "Tomorrow. You'll have it tomorrow."

Menendez nodded. He'd known about Gerry's deceit almost immediately, as soon as the contact on the Lake Forest force had faxed the police report. It had listed a statue, valued at three hundred dollars, stolen from the room Martelli alone had been in. Menendez had reported to the boss. His reaction had been, Menendez thought, quite reasonable.

"You realize, Martelli," Menendez said now, tapping his fingers on the table, "that, so far, the boss finds this merely annoying. You run into any problems retrieving it, things are going to get a whole lot worse than annoying."

"Sure," said Gerry. "I understand. There aren't going to be any problems."

But what had seemed so easy turned out to be, like his misguided acquisition of the statue, more complicated than he'd thought. His "tomorrow" had stretched as far as he could stretch it. After his visit to Carl's apartment, once he knew he couldn't deliver, at least not right away, he'd had to explain. Menendez had not reacted well.

"You stupid shit! Somebody *knows* about you? About *us*?"

"Not precisely," Gerry had said. "He knows more than he should know. He knows I'm involved in something and he has a glimmer . . . but exactly how much he knows, I can't say. Yet. But, look, I know how to get to him."

"You're not paying anybody off," said Menendez. "You're not blackmailing anybody. You're not doing *shit*, you . . ." He stopped to regain control. His ability to control himself was a large part of the reason he had as much power in the group as he had. "Not one tiny little part of what is going to happen to your friend is up to you. Understand?"

Gerry nodded. He waited. When Menendez sat down and reached for the phone, Gerry held up one hand. "Nothing like that would work anyway. He's out of control. He's a crazy man, like a fanatic or something. But there's one way, and I know what it is. I know what it is, and I know how to pull it off."

Menendez listened, and when the idea had been laid out,

he nodded grimly. "Write it down," he said. "Name, address, everything you know about this McCain person. *Everything*. I want to know what he friggin' eats for breakfast." He let his hands fall, palms down, on the top of the desk he sat behind. "I'm telling the boss. You realize that, I assume. One thing you better understand—the kid isn't going back to Daddy. What happens to the kid depends on how much he knows, but he isn't going back to Daddy, no matter what. Once we get the statue, your friend is out of the picture, and maybe the kid too. You got a problem with that?"

Gerry's desperation over the past several days had made him angry. His anger had eaten away at his affection for Carl, at any protectiveness he had felt for him or his son, until those tenderer emotions ceased to exist. Now he hated Carl, the source of all that threatened him. "No," he said truthfully. "I got no problem with that."

Carl's moving was an irritation. He did it quickly one day while Gerry was at work, and it was a setback. Gerry's hatred deepened, but he didn't panic. When Menendez told him to find a reason to visit Mrs. Peavy, to find a way to search her place, he did so. It was with grim satisfaction that he had left her apartment. It was with an invigorating blend of fury and determination that he watched Carl's apartment, and waited, and climbed through the window. When he passed on the photograph to the team that took over the search in Wisconsin, he had already done the necessary research.

"Yeah," he said, smugness taking the edge off what had been, for too long now, a throbbing ache of fear tightening the muscles in his neck. "I thought it was just a mutt too, at first. But I know dogs, and this one didn't look accidental enough. For one thing, there aren't a lot of tricolor mutts. So I spent a little time at a few bookstores. This is no Heinz 57. Matter of fact, we couldn't have asked for a better situation. It's a Bernese mountain dog. They're noticeable, as you can see, but uncommon. Vets, pet shops, trainers, kennels . . .

Somebody's going to have seen this baby. Maybe we'll get lucky right away."

He hoped they would get lucky, that he'd never have to play his ace in the hole. As soon as he had to use that, his days in the inner circle were over. It would save his life but destroy his lifestyle. He didn't need to find Carl to play that card. The information that Carl had, that Carl didn't know he had, was by no means the only set of notes he had preserved. He only hoped he wouldn't have to use it. Yes, he hoped they'd get lucky.

But it wasn't luck that located the dog and therefore the boy. It was persistence. Persistence and, from what Gerry heard, some direct involvement from the boss himself. And it almost paid off.

They went to pick up Carl the night after they failed to get his son. Their confidence in the power they would wield, once they had the boy, had kept them from serious concern until Luke slipped through their fingers. They were leaving nothing else to chance. They'd find the boy again, and this time he wouldn't get away. In the meantime, they'd keep Carl safely isolated. Carl, however, was not at home. And he didn't come home during all the hours that his former college roommate sat in a darkened living room, waiting. Nor did he come home the next day, or the next night.

Gerry's shift was over before daybreak. He had time to confer with his reliever, go home, and grab a few hours' sleep before reporting at the precinct. He was bone-tired these days, always bone-tired.

He walked down the street and bent to talk through the open window of the car. "We know he's not at his girl-friend's. Chaco's been on her place. He's split. I say, let's get whatever we want out of there. He's not coming back to notice it's gone."

Menendez, in the car, stretched out an arm to look at his watch. He picked up the phone lying next to him. It appeared that Martelli had exhausted his ability to help locate Carl. Menendez had a feeling the time he'd been waiting for had come. He spoke into the phone.

"Menendez here," he said. "Nobody's home. The thought is nobody's comin' home. You want us to clean up?" He waited, nodding. "Roger."

He hung up. "Get in. Chaco or Phelps'll take care of this place later today," he said. "Right now, the boss wants us at a meeting at his place."

Gerry slid into the front seat. "In the middle of the night?"

Menendez shrugged. "You want me to call him back and tell him you'd rather go home to bed?"

Gerry grinned. "Yeah, right. I was just wondering why he wasn't nestled in the arms of Morpheus, knitting up the raveled sleeve of care."

The other man ignored him, but Gerry was used to that. Despite his sleepiness, he was curious and deeply flattered. His single-mindedness over the last six weeks had been noticed. The boss must have been told who had located Carl, kept such careful watch on him, and come up with the dog connection. The result was an informal kind of promotion. He was being included now among the few—how many, exactly, he didn't know—who met face-to-face with the boss.

"So this'll be interesting," Gerry said, enjoying his new status. "Why'd he decide . . . do you know? Was it that I figured out about the dog, found the vet for him to visit?"

"Nah," said Menendez. He loathed the handsome, shallow, stupid young man beside him. "It's probably that you've turned out to be an even bigger scumbag than he thought you were when he recruited you."

"You recruited me, Menendez," said Gerry. "After knowing me while you were on the force."

"Because he told me to. He knows you too. He's known you for a long time."

Gerry was intrigued, but a glance at the expressionless man beside him stilled the next, eager question. It would be answered soon enough.

The route they were taking indicated that the man they were going to see lived somewhere in the Ravenswood Manor neighborhood. Gerry looked out the window, sleepy but curious, wondering how the people in these solid, brick houses with the mission-tile roofs would respond to the knowledge of who resided with them in this quiet community. He was sure the boss was a perfect neighbor, pruning his rosebushes after the first bloom, keeping his lawn thick and trim, ordering Girl Scout cookies from the local adolescents.

The Pontiac turned in to a narrow street that curved back toward the river they'd crossed two blocks earlier and stopped at the dead end.

"We'll cut through here to the back door," said his partner. "He doesn't want us parking in front."

"Right," said Gerry. He'd expected precautions.

They got out of the car and entered the woods, proceeding along a narrow path. Gerry followed obediently, removing his hands from his trench coat pockets to push aside an occasional twig or bramble. The man ahead of him turned toward the river. It was sluggish and none too clean.

"Where are you going?" asked Gerry.

Menendez swung around, the narrow end of a silencer protruding from his gun barrel. And Gerry Martelli became abruptly but belatedly aware that his ace in the hole was useless. He'd played his hand considerably too close to the vest.

Chapter

8

L UKE WAS AN ADVENTURER, and the three children
tumbling over Carol Murphy's overstuffed couch
seemed to herald great times to come. His customary
distrust of strangers had abandoned him. He let go of Lisa's
hand and allowed himself, with a wide grin, to be led by a
solemn-eyed toddler into the fray.

"Gosh, this is wonderful," said Lisa. "I don't know how
long I'll be gone exactly, but not more than a few hours."

"Oh, leave him here for lunch. Lunch is fun," said Carol,
swaying rhythmically with an infant against her shoulder as
she talked. "After that is nap time. They all nap. Or there's a
seventy-five-dollar-an-hour surcharge. So if it's okay with
you, why don't you pick him up around twelve-thirty. I
mean, he's welcome to stay all day if you want . . . *if* he naps.
Or you're rich."

"After lunch would be great," said Lisa. "Assuming he
gets along, maybe he could come again another time?"

"Sure," replied Carol. "And he's going to get along. Look
at him."

Luke was somersaulting off the couch. He had a slightly
dazed, ecstatic look.

"It's not like this all the time. We color and I read to them and we go places. It's not constant mayhem."

"He needs some mayhem," said Lisa. "Bye, Luke. I'll be back after lunch."

Luke threw her a distracted wave.

At the two-flat on Oakdale, Lisa found Martin Lazarus's name. He had the first floor, the left of the two doors on the porch, but there was no answer to the doorbell or to her knocking, and the door itself was firmly locked. There seemed to be no one at home on the second floor; the morning newspaper was still propped against the right-side door.

She wasn't discouraged. Carl was that combination of scatterbrained and practical that planned for predicaments caused by absentmindedness. He always kept a house key outside the house. The only question was where, and even that wasn't difficult. The top of the door frame was too obvious; Carl wasn't stupid. It was probably around back. She let herself through an unlocked side gate and made her way to the back porch. A tall privacy fence surrounded the backyard on three sides, with another gate, this one locked, leading into the alley.

The back porch was cluttered with a bicycle held by a Kryptonite lock to the railing, empty flowerpots with dry soil encrusted around the rims, a basket of cheap outdoor toys. Lisa stood thinking, trying to get inside Carl's mind. A dull, shuddery sound startled her, and she crouched beside the bicycle, silent and still. Nothing. Then a rustle. Then, again, nothing. Lisa's heart hammered sickeningly. She stared at the corner of the house, tensed and waiting. Another sound, above her, wrenched her eyes skyward. A squirrel jumped from the porch roof to the branch of a nearby tree. The flood of relief made her feel weak and foolish. Squirrels.

She glanced around again and focused on the basket of toys. Perfect. The key was inside a plastic egg at the bottom, and it smoothly opened the back door. Once inside, she inserted the key on the indoor side of the lock and turned it.

She was in the kitchen. It was a distinct contrast to Cooper's—disorganized, cluttered, filled with the things that Carl loved. His Mexican bowls stood along a shelf above glass jars of pasta, beans, and grains. Just standing in the room made Lisa catch her breath. But no one was there. That she knew. The apartment contained no breathing except her own, no living thing.

She walked, forcing herself not to tiptoe, toward the living room. The floor creaked faintly under her feet. She passed a bedroom, the dresser top in disarray, the bed unmade. But there was nothing peculiar about that. Carl had often remarked that good housekeepers aired their sheets daily. There was another bedroom containing a single bed with a comforter of bright cars and trucks, a toy box, a dresser. She passed the bathroom, empty, the shower curtain closed, and went on to the dining room.

Here the modern art, which Carl loved and Lisa usually detested, was much in evidence, and a typical argument surged unbidden into her memory.

"That's supposed to be horizontal, Leese," Carl had said, a hint of exasperation in his voice.

The frame contained properly placed eyes for either orientation. The picture wire itself had come loose. Lisa, in refastening it, had evidently chosen the incorrect pair.

"The painter's name is in the lower right corner. Where painters' names always are. Wasn't that a clue?"

"Oh, hang it yourself," she'd replied, irritated, gazing at what she would describe as blotches of muddy color. "If a person's only clue is where the painter signed the blasted thing, what possible difference could it make which way it hangs? How could you bring yourself to pay money for this? *Disillusionment with Fruit.* Is there supposed to be fruit in here? Or had this guy bought too many mealy peaches and this represents produce-based annoyance? I don't get it, Carl, and neither do you."

It was an old disagreement, and Carl was tired of it. "What I don't get," he had said with maddening dispassion, "is why we're fighting about art."

They hadn't been, of course. What a lot of stupid quarrels people have, she thought now, when they're really upset about something else. So he loved modern art too much and her not nearly enough. These two flaws were not actually related. The muddy-blotches print had moved to this new apartment and was correctly hung, horizontally. Lisa glared at it as she went by.

The living room looked as if Carl had just left. An untidy pile of magazines littered the floor near the couch. An empty, tea-stained mug stood next to an easy chair. There was a desk holding only a computer and a jar of pens, a fireplace, its mantel crowded with photographs of Luke, a bookcase full of books, a rug in need of vacuuming.

Carl had taken some care with only one aspect of the decor—the pictures of Luke. Each was carefully framed and angled slightly, to allow them all to be seen from one position. Luke as a baby, on his stomach on a rug, head up and smiling. A close-up of him at about two, staring seriously at the camera. Luke rolling in the grass, going down a slide, hanging from a tree branch, holding a calico kitten. There was, however, no picture of Luke with his fingers twisted in the ruff of a Bernese mountain dog.

Odd, thought Lisa. He told me he put it on the mantel, that it was nice to have a new one, that he looked at it every day. Maybe he was just being polite and the photograph is really stuck in the bottom of a drawer somewhere.

Her eyes moved around the room again, stopping at the desk. The accustomed stack of journals and notepads was not there. And there was no disk holder with floppy disks spilling out of it.

Gazing at the computer, Lisa sighed. Hours of work faced her, and it would probably be completely fruitless. But with nothing else to go on, she'd have to skim everything on the computer's hard disk. She flipped the switch. Nothing happened. She glanced at the outlet above the baseboard. The cord from the surge protector was firmly plugged in, but the computer was not plugged into the surge protector. She leaned over and plugged it in.

Something to eat would make the next few hours more bearable. Whatever was in the refrigerator would be suspect, since she didn't know how long Carl had been gone. But there was a pantry. She walked back toward the kitchen, noticing again, as she passed the bathroom, the neatly closed curtain around the tub. Carl didn't close shower curtains. He rarely even closed drawers. The condition of the living room, save the tidy desk, had been in character. This wasn't.

Lisa stepped inside and glanced around. It was cooler than the rest of the apartment. The bottom half of the window above the bathtub was hidden behind the curtain. Perhaps it had been left open.

She stepped toward the tub, a spasm of fear shivering up her spine. One of the trivial indications of incompatibility between Carl and her had been his insistence on closing every window she opened between the months of October and May. She put her hand on the curtain, wrenched it aside. There was nothing there. Nothing except the reason for the coolness of the room. The window was open about an inch.

Lisa stepped into the tub to reach up and shut the window, yanked at the window frame. The wood was swollen and resisted, but finally the window thudded shut. Outside, the first green of spring was emerging on the branches of an apple tree. She pushed on the lock at the top of the frame to jam it closed, but it was frozen in the open position. Irritated, she stepped out of the tub. Why Carl preferred living with things that didn't work to fixing them was beyond her. She glanced down. She had left a faint muddy footprint on the bottom of the tub. On the rim, the indistinct outline of the toe of a shoe was visible.

She hadn't stepped on the rim.

Lisa stood very still, gazing at the bathtub. Even the footprint she could account for, the muddy one on the smooth porcelain bottom of the tub, was wrong. The ground outside was beginning to soften as the weather warmed, but it was crumbly and dry. It was the bottom of the tub that was wet. Drops of water were beaded on the drain.

The tree outside was very close to the house. The shuddering noise she'd heard earlier came back, echoing in her memory. A window closing. Sudden comprehension hit her, washed over her, left her breathing shallowly. Someone had rinsed out the tub, had noticed the footprints left by stepping down into it from the window and rinsed them away. Leaving, he had been unable to wipe away the toe mark left on the rim.

Was the person who had been inside when she arrived now watching the house?

Back in the living room, she edged up to a window, moved the curtain a fraction of an inch, and peered up the street. The parked cars were empty. A woman was walking a cocker spaniel. She moved across the bay for a better view of the other direction. Across the street someone sat in the driver's seat of a dark blue Pontiac. A dutiful son waiting for his elderly mother or a siding salesman early for an appointment. Or someone watching Carl's apartment. Suddenly the unplugged computer made sense. No one unplugged a computer from its surge protector unless he intended to move it.

If the man in the Pontiac was watching the house, had he called for backup? Unless he was very stupid, he had. How long did she have before someone else arrived, someone who could follow her when she left without leaving the house uncovered? Out. She had to get out fast. But if she went over the back fence, she'd have to leave the computer behind, and the computer was something the person who had been inside the apartment wanted.

She'd been there, already, long enough for someone else to have arrived, to be watching the back door at this very moment. It might not matter how fast she got out. What might well matter was how furtive she seemed.

She turned on the CD player and rotated the volume knob. Miles Davis blasted into the room. She opened the curtains, strode purposefully in front of the window, then made a rapid search of the apartment. An old cigar box on top of the microwave in the kitchen yielded a spare front door key. There was a laundry basket full of dirty clothes in the bedroom closet. Most of these she dumped on the floor, keeping a set of sheets and a few towels.

She flew to the phone. Depending on how long ago they had found his house, Carl's line was still secure or it was not. She couldn't risk it. She called the Yellow Cab Company and, forcing calm into her voice, requested a taxi. Then, staying out of the line of sight from the Pontiac into the living room, she detached the computer's CPU from the monitor and keyboard, wrapped it in sheets, placed it in the laundry basket, and dropped towels on top. When the cab arrived, she turned off the stereo, let herself out the front door, and locked it unhurriedly behind her.

As the cab passed the Pontiac, she turned her face away. Then, at the stop sign on the corner, she glanced back. The car had not budged and the man in it appeared to be asleep. The cab turned left, heading north as she had requested. She glanced down the alley as they passed. A silver-gray car was coming toward them—perhaps a car from one of the garages on the alley, perhaps a car whose driver was taking a short-cut, perhaps . . .

She made her voice friendly but firm. "I want you to drop me off in front of a laundry a couple of miles from here and then go around the block and come through the alley behind it. I'm dropping some stuff off there and I'll come straight through and out the back."

The driver glanced at her in the rearview mirror. "You tryin' to avoid somebody, lady?"

If he was the gallant type, confessing that she feared she was being followed would make him do what she wanted quickly and effectively. If he was worried about his own neck, she'd find herself emerging from the back door of the laundry with no cab in sight. The chances that a stranger would willingly involve himself in what might look like a domestic dispute were slim. Still, there was no logical explanation for what she was asking, except the one the driver had already guessed.

"Yeah," she said, then laughed. "The IRS thinks I know where my boyfriend banks. They want to empty his account for money he owes them and they've been to my apartment three times already. I think they were hanging around this morning and I do *not* want to talk to them again."

The IRS could strike fear into anyone, but it generally wasn't fear of physical assault. The only real problem in this explanation, she thought, would arise if the driver knew that the IRS already knows where everyone banks, because the IRS knows everyone's Social Security number. To her relief, this apparently did not occur to him.

He frowned. "Those *people*!" he said. "Just tell me where and how."

The laundry she'd used years ago was on a corner with a parking lot behind it. Doors in front and back made entering possible from Clark Street or the lot. Going north on Clark, the cab could let her off across from the laundry and then continue, go left on Foster, and come back down the alley between Clark and Ashland. In the meantime, whoever was following her—if anyone was—would have no reason to continue after the cab, wouldn't see where it went, wouldn't suspect—or not immediately—that she'd gone in the front door and out the back.

The silver-gray car was still behind them, several cars back, when the cab stopped and she hopped out. She leaned in, handing money to the driver.

"I'm talking a *big* tip the next time you drop me off," she said. "So I'll see you as soon as you come around, down the alley?"

"Look, lady," the man said, "that'll be fine. But I ain't doin' this for the money. I'm doin' this for the *fun*."

ROBERT COOPER COMPLETED a penciled note in the margin of the bid to Advance Electronics and pushed it aside. He had planned to finish a significant amount of work before this afternoon's meeting, but he couldn't concentrate, felt edgy and dissatisfied. He swiveled in his chair and looked out the window without seeing anything.

It had been a long time since anyone besides a delivery-man had been inside his house, and longer still since a woman had sat across his table. He didn't invite women to his home, went sometimes to theirs, but never the reverse. Home was where he felt secure, where he could close the door and spend his time without conversation, without interruption, without emotion.

He had been surprised, when Allison left, to find that he looked forward to going home, that he was not the workaholic she had always noted, with some pride, that he was. She had taken the Danish modern furniture, the metal-framed prints, the African carvings, the omelette pans. The house had been empty. When he replaced what was gone, he replaced it with Aunt Lillian's furniture, the furniture Allison had hated, had refused to consider putting in her home, had resented his paying the storage fee for. Now he liked going home, sinking into an easy chair, listening to music, filling the house with Vivaldi instead of dinner party guests from the university.

But last night a woman had been there, had taken long strides around his kitchen, washed dishes with sure, deft hands. "There's a dishwasher," he had said.

She looked scornful. "Did you know," she told him, "that when the first dishwasher was displayed at the Chicago World's Fair, women nearly rioted? They figured it was a plot to deprive them of the one chore they had that was reasonably peaceful and pleasant and not backbreakingly hard. Dish washing, you see, was the only respite they got. I don't know if I feel that strongly about it, and if you want to take over, feel free . . ." (He ignored this.) "But a dishwasher doesn't clean the counters or put things away so, really, how much good is it?"

She turned and looked at him, sitting in a kitchen chair with Luke on his lap, the child's dark curls against his shoulder, and he felt encompassed by that look and, at the same time, exposed, as if she could detect the band that contracted around his heart when Luke put a bath-damp hand against his cheek.

He didn't like having people in his house, so why had he felt so strangely peaceful? Chitchat didn't interest him; why did Lisa's? It seemed she had something to say about any topic in the world, and some opinion to render, but when she wasn't actually attacking him or his ideas, her chatter didn't annoy him; it soothed him, took him out of his own thoughts. Still, theirs wasn't a peaceful situation; it was, if anything, a dangerous one. Someone was looking for these strangers he had invited into his home, someone menacing. As long as he was connected to them, he could not be safe either. Whoever was looking had found them once . . .

*　*　*

LISA ASKED THE cabdriver to drop her off two blocks from Cooper's, sneering at her paranoia without being capable of suppressing it. Over the phone, Carol suggested keeping Luke for a few more hours.

"We're having a birthday party for Lauren right after naps," she said. "Her mom brought cake and prizes and so Luke knows about it. He was really hoping you'd let him stay."

"Sure," said Lisa. "I'll come for him around four?"

"Yeah. Terrific!"

It seemed strange not to have Luke with her, strange but very easy. And the unforeseen extension gave her four and a half hours to work. Not on the computer. She didn't know enough about them to attach Cooper's monitor and keyboard to Carl's CPU. She didn't even know if the machines were compatible. But the fact of Mrs. Peavy had made her realize that people, all people, exist within a context of other people. Mrs. Peavy knew Carl and, as a result, knew something about where he was. Just because he was no longer there didn't mean that no one knew where he was, only that Mrs. Peavy didn't.

She picked up the phone again and called the Alumni Office at Liberty College where she asked for and got the phone number of Beth Lawrence, the class agent. And Beth, with her blessedly organized mind, had a ready answer for Lisa's question.

"Sure, Lisa. There are lots of Liberty alums from our class in Chicago. I don't know how many of them you want to look up while you're there, but hold on and I'll get my records."

Lisa held on. It was a long shot and she knew it, but Carl had remained on a friendly basis with virtually everyone he'd ever known.

"Got it." Beth came back on the line. "Tell me if you

want work information and numbers as well as home numbers as we go."

Hanging up, Lisa surveyed her notes. Some of the names meant almost nothing to her, but there were several people she remembered and a few she had been friendly with herself. She made a list, putting the three men who'd been in Carl's dorm at the top of it.

SCOTT MURRAY LOOKED considerably more like he made his living at the Chicago Board of Trade than as a cop, which Lisa pointed out.

"Detective," replied Scott. "I'm undercover as a rich guy."

"Yeah, right," said Lisa, smiling across the table. "Has there been a sudden wave of law abiding in the Nineteenth Precinct? How'd you just happen to have time to have lunch with me?"

She had called the work number Beth had for him, discovered he was due back from court around one, and decided to talk to him in person. The desk sergeant had stopped him as he swept past her.

"Detective Murray! Lady to see you."

Scott hadn't struggled, even briefly, to place her. "Lisa Jacobi!" he exclaimed. "What the . . . ?" Nor had he been too busy to talk. "Come on, let's go grab a bite. You can tell me what the heck you're doing here."

"I didn't *have* time, doll," he said now. "I *made* time. But if a few felonies stack up in the unsolved column because I'm distracted for an hour, it's not like anybody'll notice the difference."

They ordered, and while Scott chatted easily with the waiter, Lisa sat back in the booth and scrutinized him. If he hadn't been dating her roommate junior year, she'd have been interested.

"It's great to see you, Scottie," she said, and meant it.

He indicated the menu. "You may not be into drinking at lunchtime. I'm not while I'm working . . . But they have a very nice Pinot Noir, if you still like it."

"Thanks, I do, but it makes me sleepy, so no thanks. How in heaven's name did you remember what wine I like?" asked Lisa.

"You drank it that time Sherry and I doubled with you and . . . Who was it you dated junior year?"

"Dave Kurchak." She was surprised the name came back so easily. "Good old Dave Kurchak. Who liked good wine and could afford it."

"Yeah, well, good old Dave Kurchak snapped you up, but I memorized every little detail I could, so that when I got my chance, you'd be so impressed you'd . . . you'd I don't know what, but you'd something."

Lisa gaped at him. "You never . . ."

"No. There wasn't any point. By the time you and Dave had stopped being an item, you were goofy over Carl."

Had everyone on the entire campus seen through her casual airs? She was aware that if Scott weren't looking so hangdog about her disregard for him, she would be acutely humiliated.

"Carl and I never, uh, went out at Liberty," she replied.

"Right," said Scott. "Because Carl was too dense to have the faintest idea of what a sensitive, perceptive, deep, and poetic soul like myself could see in an instant."

"I'm sorry to bring up such a painful memory," said Lisa, "but I'm looking for the Dense One at this very moment. As in really *looking.* Have you seen him? Do you know what he's doing? Do you have any idea at all where he might be?"

"Not the faintest. The last time I saw him was in September, when the Cubs played Atlanta. We went to the game, where Carl exhibited ludicrous enthusiasm for the Braves' hapless opponents. His son came too. Cute kid."

"That's right," said Lisa. "You're from Georgia. I'd forgotten."

"Wah, shuggah! Whey-ah else would ah be from?" Scott's normal voice hinted at his origins, but it was so familiar that Lisa had stopped noticing years ago. His exaggerated accent was ridiculous. Lisa giggled.

"So you're from Georgia, and you're married, and now you, too, can afford good wine. As well as"—she raised her eyebrows—"extremely nice clothes. No wonder Chicagoans complain about taxes."

Scott held up his hands. "My wife is not only clever and long-suffering, she is also very, very wealthy. It was hard to adjust, but eventually I managed. Becoming rich is like that. You get used to it. So what are you getting used to these days? And what are you doing here?"

"Oh, just hanging out for a few days. I live in Wisconsin and I wanted to see some friends . . . I'm going back soon."

"So where are you staying?"

"Here and there."

"Give me a number at least. I'd love for Gina to meet you. We could have dinner."

"I'm here for such a short time, Scott. I'm really tied up, but thanks."

"Relax," he said. "I'm not suggesting unwelcome attentions despite the depth of my devotion. I'm a happily married, solid citizen. I serve and protect. Just read the seal on one of the cars across the street. I'd like to at least check in with you before you slip away again."

She rooted in her thrift shop purse for a pen and wrote a number on a scrap of paper. "You're right. We should stay in touch."

SYLVIA TAPPED ON Cooper's door, her quick, double knock, and came in. "That delivery you told me to watch for came while you were out," she said, placing an overnight letter on his desk. "The one for Adrienne Luescher." There was a question in her voice, but Cooper ignored it. She would never openly admit to curiosity.

"Thank you, Sylvia." He indicated the bid. The meeting with Advance Electronics had necessitated only a few modifications. "Would you make these changes and get it out today?"

"A man rang up for her, for Ms. Luescher," said Sylvia, taking the papers, arranging them in sequence. "I said what you told me to say, that she wasn't in today. He asked for her home number."

"And?"

Sylvia looked offended. "And I told him we never give out home numbers, of course. As if I knew her home number. As if I knew *her*." Again the unasked, unanswered question. "He was quite insistent, for all the good it did him. I asked if he wanted to leave his name. He didn't." She sniffed. Even her sniffs sounded British. She closed the door as she left.

Cooper sat, looking blindly at a thick folder of data for the Harvest Agricultural equating study. So what's-his-name—Mickey, that was it—needed to reach Lisa. Of course he'd call here. Of course he'd use the name she'd given him for the package. Well, Lisa could call him back. Cooper picked up the phone and dialed his house. No answer.

He opened the folder and tried to focus. Why had he told Lisa about Allison? And if he was going to tell her anything, why hadn't he told her more? Like how beautiful Allison was, how crisp and lovely. How he'd fallen into a marriage with her because it seemed the sensible thing to do when college was over, when it was time to get started on being an adult. How he'd tried to please her because good men tried to please their wives and how unsuccessful he had been. How he'd never known her, never—he'd realized guiltily one day soon after they were married—even wanted to know her. Why hadn't he told Lisa any of that? Because it was none of her business, of course. But she made him want to talk. Those eyes of hers that gave everything away, that way she had of tilting her head a little while she listened. Allison had never listened. She had taken his arm in the woods, but she had never listened.

Cooper got up and grabbed his coat. Striding past Sylvia, he called back, "I'll be out for about an hour."

"But Dr. Cooper!" Sylvia was nonplussed. "There's your conference call with—"

"So reschedule it." His voice was impatient.

Sylvia sighed. It was an admiring sigh. Dr. Cooper was so sure of himself. She liked that in a man.

There was a toy store about two blocks away. Cooper had passed it often, bemused by the gaudy and often hideous objects that seemed to qualify as playthings. Now he turned in that direction. He knew exactly what he wanted. He wondered, with a pang, if he had always wanted it.

Chapter

9

I T WAS AFTER SIX. Why didn't he come home? Lisa sat on the porch swing. She was trying to tell Luke a story, but it was difficult to come up with a way to get Brown Bunny safely back to his mother and father while such a large part of her mind was screaming *Come home!*

"So the fox said, 'Ah, you look like a tasty little morsel.' And the bunny said, 'Oh, I am, sir! All the turnips I eat make me taste just like them!' Now, wasn't he clever? Because of course the fox had to stop and think about *that*. 'You mean you taste like turnips?' he asked with a shudder. 'But, of course,' said Bunny. 'Delicious, yummy turnips! Exactly like them. Lucky you.' "

"Turnips?" said Luke. "Yuck." His abhorrence for turnips was well known to Lisa, who had failed miserably in her one attempt to get a second mouthful down him.

"Well, that's just precisely what Fox was thinking too," said Lisa. "So he backed away a little and his tail was flicking and his greedy eyes were glimmering, but his mouth wasn't watering anymore. 'Bunnies don't usually taste like turnips,' he said, because he was, after all, a fox, and foxes have their clever moments. 'Oh, no,' said Bunny. 'Most bunnies just hate turnips and never, ever eat them. Imagine that! But me, I just adore turnips and never eat anything else. No carrots, no lettuce, no cabbage . . .' "

"No chocolate pie," said Luke.

" 'No chocolate pie. And to have that ordinary, boring old bunny taste, a bunny has to eat all *that* stuff.' So what do you suppose the fox did then?"

"He let that bunny go and he went to his house and he made some powidge for his supper. And the bunny went home and he never went by *there* again." Luke's voice was triumphant.

Lisa nodded. "That's absolutely, exactly, precisely what happened."

A sedate green car turned the corner and parked in front of the house. Luke, recognizing the loaner that Cooper had driven home the night before, went running, Sirius at his side. The dog, after a careful sniff to confirm the man's identity, wandered back toward the porch.

Cooper, with Luke carrying his briefcase and riding on his shoulders, came up the steps. He indicated the dog.

"I'm always grateful when he doesn't attack."

"I told you before, he reacts with hostility only to what he sees as danger. He's just a dog. He doesn't perceive overbearing arrogance as actual danger. I thought you'd never get home!"

He was surprised to hear the eagerness in her voice. "Isn't that supposed to be followed by 'dear'? And 'How was your day?' And 'Hasn't the shop finished with your car yet?' And 'My, you look tired; let me make you a drink while you put your feet up'?"

Lisa ignored him. She opened the front door and they went in, Cooper bending his knees to keep from whacking his rider on the lintel. Luke, set down, went immediately to the television and turned it on, backing away to settle in a cross-legged heap on the floor. Lisa kept walking, toward the kitchen, beckoning Cooper to follow.

"Thank God for TV," she said fervently. "One more request for a story and I was going to lose the capacity for rational thought. Did anything come from Mickey? I need some money for crayons and a toy truck. I know. I could have used grocery money from your cash drawer, but it seemed like cheating since I wasn't going to use it for groceries. We resorted to playing checkers with the pennies and nickels from my jacket pockets. And yours. Your jacket pockets no longer contain any change. You've opened your home to a petty thief. And I borrowed the chessboard from Werner—"

Cooper, dropping his coat on a kitchen chair, interrupted. "Werner?"

"Next door. Mr. Schwartz. What a sweetheart. His daughter, Mary Ruth, is coming tomorrow and he's tearing around dusting and carrying on. He's—"

"You know his daughter's first name? I've lived next door to him for nine years and I didn't even know *his* first name."

"Well, that's shameful. He's a darling. Funny and sweet. A little doddering but, heck, he'll be eighty-six in July. He and Luke had a long talk about birthdays; they're really into the whole concept."

"Allison said he was . . . difficult. She had problems with him being nosy and meddlesome, so I've always avoided him."

"Oh, screw Allison," Lisa replied, feeling, for the first time, that perhaps her host hadn't been entirely to blame for the dissolution of his marriage. "The man's a treasure."

"He's got that obnoxious, sweater-clad little schnauzer that yaps at me every time I enter my own backyard."

"Look. The dog's a fox terrier. A wirehaired fox terrier. And he has a name. Sarge. His name is Sarge. He doesn't look remotely like a schnauzer. Schnauzers aren't white and tan, for Pete's sake. And he barks because he's doing his job. *Sarge* barks at you because it's his job to bark at strangers, particularly hostile strangers, and you, who have lived next door to him for years without ever learning his name, clearly fit the bill. But I don't want to talk about Werner Schwartz or Werner Schwartz's *fox terrier.* At least not right now. I've had a horrid, awful day. I've been going nuts. And you just wouldn't come home! You've got to help me figure something out."

She had been pacing around the kitchen while she talked, running her hands through her hair so that it stood up away from her head, giving her a startled look.

Cooper was stung. How was he supposed to know the stupid dog was a fox terrier? What difference did it make? And Werner Schwartz had never shown any friendliness that he could see.

"Something came for you, aka Adrienne Luescher," Cooper said stiffly, opening his briefcase and tossing a Federal Express Overnight Letter on the table. "And Mickey called you. He didn't leave a message. I phoned to tell you, but you were tied up, I guess, with darling Werner next door."

"Mickey didn't ask for me, did he? Who talked to him?"

"He asked for Adrienne, or so says Sylvia, my secretary. She was outraged that he asked for a home number."

Remembering the disembodied voice, Lisa constructed an entire image of Sylvia. "She's probably convinced that Adrienne is a call girl you've taken up with. I wonder if he saw something. I better not call from here, just in case you're right that somebody could have figured out a link between us and tapped his phone. But I've gotta call him."

Her agitation blunted Cooper's irritation with her. "Why don't you go out and call? There's a pay phone at the drugstore down the block. I'll order pizza, since you've clearly neglected your domestic duties."

"And shame on me for it. A competent person could have thought of something to make with half a box of bran cereal and what's left of the Gouda. I didn't have time to get to the store. No, I did have time, I just didn't do it. Yeah, okay, I'll go find a phone, but when I get back, you've got to help me figure something out."

Cooper peered into the pantry. There really was virtually nothing there. Why had he ignored this part of his home? It wasn't Allison's domain any longer. It could be his. His grandmother had made casseroles and fried tomatoes and chocolate cakes in a kitchen a lot like this one. It could be filled with good smells, with a tablecloth on the table and food in the pantry. He smiled and picked up the phone.

LUKE WAS EATING PIZZA with enthusiasm. Sirius, disdainful of begging, curled at his feet, prepared for the almost inevitable happy accident. Luke had held center stage for quite some time, telling, with varying degrees of articulation, about the children and the toys and, best of all, the *kittens* at Carol's house. Now the grown-ups were talking and their conversation wasn't the least bit interesting to him. He was taking the opportunity to eat. There was sausage on the pizza. And, for some reason, Lisa was letting him have pop with his dinner. He was very happy.

Lisa was not. Mickey hadn't been at home. Whatever he had called to tell her would have to wait until he chose to come home, and she had no idea when that would be. The package from him had contained her bank card and a note:

Lisa:
    Your place looked completely normal except the back door is broken and there's a big hole in one of the kitchen walls so you can look right into the bedroom closet. Weird! No wallet anywhere, but the enclosed was where you said it would be. Justice ran around

sniffing and snuffling and whining. She could read the scene better than I could, but she's not talking. Clue me in when you can.

She described to Cooper her discoveries at Carl's apartment, her circuitous route home, and lunch with Scott. She avoided using Carl's name to keep Luke from becoming interested in their conversation.

"You knew all along you were going there today."

"I knew all along you'd tell me not to and I'd get mad and we'd say nasty things and I'd go anyway."

"If that's supposed to justify the concept of secret agendas, it's really weak. Either this whole thing is my business or it isn't. If you just intend to do exactly what you want without even telling me what that is, then you're in this alone. There's a price for collaboration. You can't have it one way when it's convenient and the other when it's not."

He was scolding her. Who did he think he was? She glared at him. Cooper turned to Luke.

"So, Buddy, do the kittens have names?"

"Sure, indeed," said Luke. "There's Pounce and Cowboy and Princess Spotty. *I* named Princess Spotty." He surveyed Cooper levelly. "Didn't you never have any animals?"

"Yes, I did. I had hundreds. I lived on a farm and I had cows and chickens and a goat."

Luke raised his chin, drumming his heels against the chair legs while he decided whether this was true. "Did them have names?"

"No."

"If I had a cow, you know what I'd name it?"

"Brisket?"

"No."

"Porterhouse?"

"No."

"Tenderloin?"

"No."

"Well, I give up. What would you name it?"

"Bob!" He giggled. "I'd name it Bob."

"Doctor Bob," said Lisa.

"Yeah," said Luke. "Doctor Bob." He returned to his pizza.

Lisa had decided to strike a bargain. Cooper wasn't the person she'd choose as a partner, but he was what she had available. And she needed him.

"Okay," she said. "Help me."

"All right," said Cooper. "You've got a CPU in a laundry basket, and I presume you want to see what's on it."

"Yeah. There were no notebooks, no floppy disks. I figured those had already gone out the window. And it seemed obvious that whoever had been in there wanted the CPU, so that made me want it. I couldn't go out the back because there was this six-foot fence and I couldn't leap it with a CPU tucked under my arm. It was just dumb luck that the door locks are the kind you have to open with a key from the inside as well as the outside, and that the only unlocked window in the place was too awkwardly situated for the guy to get through with a CPU tucked under *his* arm. Once the coast was clear, he'd be going back in for it. I was hoping your monitor and keyboard could hook up to it, but I didn't want to mess with your stuff before you got home."

"Except for pocket change."

"Right, but I didn't break *that.* So do you think you can hook it up?"

"If the monitor and the keyboard I have here are compatible, sure. But not until Luke goes to bed, because Luke and I have something to do before bedtime."

Hearing his name, Luke looked up. Cooper winked at him. "Now, I don't know if you'll like it, but maybe you could help me set up something I bought today."

"What's it be?" asked Luke, his eyes bright.

"Let's go out to the car and get it and see."

They came back loaded with boxes. "This," said Cooper, taking the tape off the largest one, "is a train set. You see if you can get that open."

Luke ripped open the carton. "They's houses and trees!"

"Yeah, there's a whole town. We can set it up almost any way we want and the train can go around the outside."

Within an hour, the dining room table had disappeared beneath a village. Lisa dragged Luke, sleepy but unwilling to depart, off to bed. When she returned, Cooper was in the study connecting a monitor and keyboard to the CPU from Carl's apartment.

"Sexism rears its ugly head," said Lisa. "I noticed who did the dishes and who played with the train set."

"Once I built a railroad, made it run, made it race against time," sang Cooper in a clear baritone. "Once I built a railroad, now it's done—"

"No," interrupted Lisa, "I can*not* spare a dime, and don't call me 'buddy' until you've helped with the dishes, at least once."

"How many dishes are there when the big, strong, income-producing member of the team orders pizza? Besides, there's men's work, babe, and there's women's work. Women, they washes dishes. Men, they got better stuff to do. Now, why don't you paint your nails or something while I engage my manly brain on this puzzling machine we call a computer. Then you can spend the rest of your adult life snooping through whatever your ex-honey put on here. Oh, excuse me, I meant 'looking for clues.' "

"Drop dead," said Lisa equably. What had happened to stuffy Dr. Cooper? Had his voice always hinted at such readiness to find amusement in the world? Had she simply missed it?

Two hours later, she emerged from the study and sank into an easy chair across from Cooper, who was sitting on the couch reading the *New York Times*. It had been difficult the last two mornings to convince Luke that a newspaper existed that really, truly, had no comics section. Cooper folded the paper and put it down. "Well?"

"There's nothing *on* it. Nothing relevant." Her voice was tired and frustrated. "There are directories for taxes and old work and personal stuff and bills. There's even a directory called 'Play,' but all it has on it is the beginnings of a *play*. Not the kind of play anybody would be after him for. And the file dates on everything are old. Carl hasn't worked in any of those files for almost two months. There's just nothing there."

"Nothing you can read," said Cooper.

"What's that supposed to mean? If it was *on* there, I could read it."

Cooper was finding himself in the pleasant situation of knowing more about a subject than his companion. "Not if it had been deleted," he said.

"If it was deleted, it's not *on* there!"

"Deleting a file doesn't mean it's gone; deleting doesn't erase. If it did, the computer would fill up with little bits of dirty rubber that you had to blow out of the CPU before they jammed the works."

Lisa was not amused. Cooper was enjoying himself. "Deleting a file just makes the space available for other data. If nothing gets written over it, the original stuff is still there. It's just not as accessible."

"And you can retrieve it?"

"Sure. With the help of a retrieval program. How much you get back depends on how much has been entered since the deletion. Of course, we don't know how much Carl kept on the computer. But there may be something."

He glanced at his watch. "We can start tonight. It's nearly eleven, but we can start."

"Can you see what you can find while I go try Mickey again?"

Cooper shrugged. "Sure. But us railroad men need our shut-eye, so I probably won't get very far."

She whistled for Sirius and let herself out. When she returned, Cooper was in the study. "Any luck?" he asked, looking up at her in the doorway. Her face was set and pale.

"Mickey was home this time," she said quietly. "But he didn't know what I was talking about. He didn't call your office."

Cooper's skin was crawling. Whoever was looking for Luke, looking for Lisa to get to Luke, was too adept at it, too thorough. "How do you suppose . . . ?"

"You must have been right. They must have seen Mickey at my house. Maybe they followed him to the Federal Express pickup and saw the address on the package he sent me. I can't figure any other way . . ."

She stopped, leaning against the doorway, thinking. "They couldn't have been sure the package wasn't really to his sister. And Great Britain's response—"

"Sylvia."

"Sylvia's response to them probably made them think that PTS is a dead end, that there really is an Adrienne Luescher, which, of course, there is, but you know what I mean. So maybe they'll stop working the PTS angle."

"And if not?"

"Well, that's the question, isn't it?"

Cooper sat, legs outstretched, looking at the toes of his shoes. His jaw muscles tightened, relaxed, tightened. He made no other movement for several minutes. Lisa sank into a chair.

"If that's what happened," said Cooper, "if they saw Mickey go to your house, if that made them wonder about his connection to you, then they probably did put some kind of tap on his phone."

"That's what I was thinking."

"Which would mean that they heard or will hear your conversation with him tonight."

"I know. I didn't say much. I said, you know, 'Hey, Mick, it's Adrienne, I heard you called today.' And he picked up on it pretty well. But I just don't know . . . If they look into it . . . Would they? If they do, there are a lot of people in town who know Adrienne. She's visited Mickey. They know she lives in Madison. And even if they don't find out where she really is, it isn't hard to find out that there *isn't* an Adrienne Luescher in Chicago."

"There really isn't any point in worrying. Let's say they figure it out, that the package was to you. Still, all they know is that someone at PTS knows you. Someone. Not me. Someone. There are eleven people on my staff. Basically, what this means is that, worst case, we have a little time."

"Maybe," said Lisa.

"We have a little time," repeated Cooper. He pointed to the screen. "I've asked the computer to tell me what files have been deleted from the hard disk but are still recoverable, to one degree or another. Here's a list. There are quite a few of them. There wasn't anything we could do a quick retrieve on, which means that none of this was just deleted today, or even very recently."

"So it wasn't whoever came in the window who deleted Carl's current files."

"If he ever had current files . . . no. Carl probably deleted these files himself. It makes sense. If he decided to store everything someplace safer than his house, then he took files off the disk some time ago. He could have locked all his files so anybody'd need a password to read them. But he didn't, so he probably just took them off."

"But if we can get at parts of them, so could anyone."

"Right. And Carl probably knew that deleting doesn't erase. So it's meaningful that he didn't bother to lock them."

Lisa raised her shoulders.

"*So,*" Cooper went on, "that means Carl knew *he* didn't know anything *they* didn't know. There was no reason to hide information from them, or at least no reason to go to much trouble about it. He had a reason to keep what he knew safe, but not to hide it from them."

"Then why did he bother to delete it?"

"Maybe because if he didn't, and somebody looked at the files, they'd know exactly how much he knew. This way, if somebody looks at it, all they know is he knows something. But not how much. If no new material had been put on the hard drive in the meantime, the deleted files would be recoverable, intact. They're not, so it seems that Carl deliberately copied irrelevant material onto the hard drive after deleting—using up the space, messing up the files. That's what he would have done if he's smart."

"He's smart," said Lisa. "Only the 'somebody' he made things hard for is me." Her voice was deliberately flat. She glanced at Cooper. "And you. Is it worth trying to get any of this back in readable form?"

"Sure, but it's going to take a while. If you work on it all day tomorrow, and I work on it after I get home, maybe we'll find something. Maybe."

He pushed a hand through his hair and gazed at her. "Did Carl's friend—the one you had lunch with—ask where you're staying? Did you tell him?"

"He asked. He was relatively persistent. I didn't exactly tell him."

"Meaning?"

"I gave him the phone number Carl and I had years ago. I've been feeling guilty about it, but . . . he's always been able to charm anyone, including me, and there's something unsettling about that. And, of course, he's a cop. I don't know. This is all just too weird."

Cooper laughed shortly. "You can say that again."

Chapter
10

L ISA SPENT THE next morning following the procedures that Cooper had explained the night before. Luke had gone delightedly off, again, to Carol's, and Lisa had stopped at a cash machine in another neighborhood. She felt much better with her own money in her pocket. But that was the only thing she felt better about.

She called up deleted file after deleted file. Many of them were garbled nonsense—meaningless series of symbols. Some contained sections of readable type, and these she read carefully until their subject matter was clear. Several, it seemed, were earlier versions of scenes from Carl's play; others were letters. The work was fruitless, and her frustration was compounded by an overpowering loneliness.

At ten-thirty, the cleaning lady arrived. Cooper had told Lisa she would be coming, and Lisa had greeted this news with a wry grin.

"I *thought* this place was just a bit too meticulously tidy. Even for a very fussy person."

"The word is *orderly.*"

"I've been in your laundry room. The word, I assure you, is *fussy.*"

When Mrs. Bukowski arrived, she bent to pat Sirius and then fixed Lisa with a stony glare. Clearly, she liked dogs better than she liked finding strange young women in her employer's home.

"Good morning," said Lisa as pleasantly as she could. "I take it you're Mrs. Bukowski?"

Mrs. Bukowski glared suspiciously at her and nodded shortly. "Dr. Cooper, he is a good man," she replied, and, with this non sequitur, disappeared into the kitchen.

Lisa was confused until she realized the woman assumed a nonexistent relationship. This was confirmed by Mrs. Bukowski's comments when Lisa entered her domain to fix a sandwich for lunch and found her industriously scrubbing the spotless sink.

"There is no food in this refrigerator," said Mrs. Bukowski, her tone accusatory. "You are making him take you out every night? Dr. Cooper, he works much too hard. He has no time for running around with nightclubs and dancing and such!"

"Good heavens, Mrs. Bukowski!" replied Lisa. "He's not my *boyfriend*!"

But Mrs. Bukowski seemed to find affront in this too. "A man as good-looking as Dr. Cooper?" Her accent made this come out "good-lookink," and Lisa suppressed a grin. "Please to tell me what is wrong with Dr. Cooper?"

"I'm sure he's . . ." Lisa groped for a phrase that would pacify the cleaning lady. She suspected that "a domineering boor" would not do the trick. "I'm sure he's a prince. He's just not my boyfriend."

Mrs. Bukowski appeared somewhat mollified, although, unwilling to allow any possible difference of opinion on the subject, she launched into a monologue while she worked. Her observations revealed a one-track mind.

"When my son got on the honor roll last year, can you imagine what Dr. Cooper did? Sent him to basketball camp.

Cost a fortune! But there's no saying no to Dr. Cooper."

"I guess not," said Lisa.

This was not laudatory enough for Mrs. Bukowski. "He leaves money, you know, so any child comes to the door selling anything—candy for school, cookies for Girl Scouts, tickets for raffles, anything—I have to go get the money and buy it." She shook her head and wrung out a dishcloth with a savage twist. "That man is going to end up in the poorhouse."

"Before or after he's canonized?"

Mrs. Bukowski ignored her, and Lisa took advantage of the momentary silence to return to the computer. A certain disregard for one's bank balance did not qualify one, in Lisa's mind, for the Walk-on-Water Club, regardless of how it impressed Mrs. Bukowski. The man might be reasonably generous with his money; Lisa had already seen that finances did not seem of particular concern to him. But did he ever do anything that actually caused him difficulty? Like attempt to look at something from someone else's point of view? She'd have to see that to believe it.

During the morning, she reached several of the other men on her list from the class agent. Pleasant as lunch with Scott had been, it had proved a complete waste of time. She could have found out he hadn't seen Carl in more than six months just by asking him over the phone. It was a lesson worth learning. Telephone conversations had revealed that either Carl's friendships were not as deep as she'd thought or that he hadn't sufficient free time to spend with people he'd been virtually inseparable from in college.

Glen Novak had, at least, more information than others. "Gosh, no, haven't seen him in over a year," he said. "But I used to see him at football every weekend, back before I blew out my rotator cuff. Him and Rick Lopas. They were always there. And I think he sees a lot of Mitchell. You remember Mitchell? He's working at some restaurant in between roles.

I think them both being actors may be why he and Carl hang out a lot."

"Anybody else you can think of, Glen? Anybody that might have seen him lately?"

"Let me think about it," said Glen. "If I think of anybody, I'll check with them, let 'em know you're here and looking. I'll let you know if I find anybody that's seen him. Where can I reach you?"

Lisa hesitated. "I'm in and out," she said.

"Well, where are you staying? I can leave a message."

"That's okay. I'd rather call you. It's just . . . easier. Thanks, Glen, thanks a lot. I gotta go."

She hung up as he started to say something else.

The number she'd been given for Rick was at Columbia College. The department secretary said Dr. Lopas was away all week at a conference. That left Mitchell. The restaurant where he worked said he'd be in on Friday. He wasn't at home.

COOPER WAS SERIOUSLY confused. His development staff had accomplished the impossible. They had written a coherent second form of the test for Northern Electric. All he had to do was review the scheduling plan. He could have done that in his sleep. He couldn't, however, do it this morning. His mind was wandering, fixing on absurd subjects, digressing from them into more absurd subjects.

At dinner the night before, Luke, intrigued by the discussion of birthdays with Werner Schwartz, had asked Cooper when his was.

"March fourteenth," Cooper replied.

Luke digested this. "My birthday's March twenty-first," he said. "Your birthday's afore mine, so you're older'n me."

"Yup," said Cooper. "I sure am."

Lisa helped herself to more pizza. "People born in March are taller than other people. And they live longer."

"Impossible," said Cooper. "Luke's not taller than you. Or were you born in March too?"

"Really, they are," said Lisa. "Except in the Southern Hemisphere, where it's, I guess, September."

"Why?"

"Because everything's backward down there."

"No, I mean why are they taller and hardier?"

Lisa shrugged. "I don't know. I don't think anybody *knows*. But they are."

The phone rang, bringing Cooper back into the present. It was Neil, whom Cooper had interrupted from data analysis earlier that morning with a request to find any studies correlating birth dates to life expectancy.

"Funny thing," Neil said. "Guess what's the best month to be born?"

"March," said Cooper.

"Yeah, how'd you know?"

"Never mind," said Cooper, annoyed at himself for wasting valuable time in an effort to catch Lisa in an error.

He wasn't like that. He prided himself on a singular lack of pettiness. What was wrong with him? Allison had never made him feel mean-spirited. Of course, there were many emotions Allison had never made him feel.

Why was he thinking about Allison? She hadn't entered his consciousness, until the other day, in over a year. Now here she was, hanging on his arm after a track meet. *Darling! You were splendid!* He had been splendid. The javelin had wings; he'd shattered the conference record. He'd felt quite fond of her, liking the admiration, liking the envy he saw in the glances of his teammates when they noticed how beautiful she was, how much she seemed to adore him.

She hadn't adored him. He wondered now if she had even liked him. But he was going places. First in his class, military service behind him but its benefits not yet exhausted, graduate school assured. She could have had anyone she wanted, one of the rich boys, one of the ones with blazing talent. But none of that mattered to Allison. She already had more money than she would ever need. She'd chosen him. She came to the track meets and the baseball games.

She'd liked track better; it was easy for her to read a book or a magazine, looking up only when his event was announced. Baseball was more of a challenge for a fan with no interest in the game. She preferred it when their team was at bat and she could ignore the game entirely until he stepped to the plate. She was like a mother who, feeling affection for only her own child, views all others with mild distaste. She'd never so much as glanced at his teammates, seeing him as an incongruous exception to the rowdy norm.

That had seemed odd to him, but he hadn't minded. He was grateful she at least watched him. She was his type—intelligent, fine-boned, delicate, so fair that the sun was a constant enemy. She was the girl who had ignored him in high school, the cool, distant one everyone had yearned for at summer camp, the one he saw in the old movies he loved. They would have a wonderful life, a series of fair, fine-boned children, a perfect house with thick rugs and antiques. He'd be dignified, respected, honored, with a wife who had a clear, sophisticated laugh and slender ankles. He would come to love her. It would be easy. It was inevitable.

How much of what had gone wrong was his fault? He knew now what he hadn't been able to accept about himself before: that he was incapable of the emotion that flowed so easily, so unstoppably, through the humanity he saw around him. He wasn't cold. He felt things. He just didn't feel love. Not romantic love, at any rate. He had loved his parents. He had most certainly loved his grandmother. But those feelings were, at best, dimly remembered. Love wasn't, after adolescence, something that happened to him. That was probably one of the things that drew him to Allison. It didn't seem to happen to her either. He hadn't mistaken for love the adoration he'd thought she felt for him. The fact that she didn't love him had made it possible for him to marry her, knowing that he couldn't hurt her in any serious way. He suspected that unrequited love would hurt.

He had accepted the way he was. But it was not in his nature to be content with what he knew was a partial life. He knew he could feel affection. He disliked the almost over-powering loneliness that came on him from time to time. There was surely the possibility of building something with someone. He'd thought about trying, with Dianne. She was beautiful, like Allison—fragile, elegant, cultured. But she had a sensitivity entirely lacking in his former wife and her respect for him was almost palpable. He picked up the phone and dialed her number. Lunch was arranged. Now maybe he could tackle the schedule.

MRS. BUKOWSKI HAD LEFT. The house seemed very empty, and Lisa was glad for the heap of solid dog lying across the doorway to Cooper's study. She crouched on the floor and looked at his paw. The fur had been shaved away on the top to allow for stitches that formed a regular, neat pattern down the side to the pad.

"Whooo!" the vet had said at the trail of blood down the hallway into her office. "I'm going to have to clean this out and stitch it. He'll have to be sedated, which means you need to leave him overnight."

"Thanks for coming in, on a Sunday and everything," Lisa had said. "It just seemed so bad."

"No, I'm glad you called. He'll be fine, but there's some tendon damage. It would have been dangerous to leave it until tomorrow."

And then something else. Nothing to do with the injured paw. What had they talked about? Somebody looking for a Bernese, that was it.

"Did that man find you?"

Lisa, distracted, hadn't paid much attention. "What man?"

"Some man who wants a Bernese. Bonnie talked to him yesterday. She'd know."

But Bonnie, of course, hadn't been there when Lisa left the office. Now she sat back, staring at her dog.

"What man, Sirius?"

Bonnie, friendly and talkative, answered the phone and remembered him well. "Some guy called last week asking about finding a dog like yours, a Bernese. For a present for his niece. He talked to Jimmy, and Jimmy said he'd heard we treated one but he didn't know anything about, like, who he belonged to. Well, you know Jimmy's always in the back. He probably never met you. Anyway, the guy came by a few days back when I was here. Saturday, I think. Yeah, Saturday. He was real nice. Crazy about this niece of his and she's got her heart set on a Bernese. He'd been looking all over, he said, 'cuz he thought a vet might be able to put him in touch with an owner and he could get from there to a breeder. You know, Bernese *are* really hard to find. I thought it was a pretty clever idea."

"Uh-huh," said Lisa softly.

"So, anyway, I told him about you and Sirius. You don't mind, do you? You're always talking about the breed . . . And having that little boy with you these days, you'd know how they were with kids. I thought you'd want to help. You know, a little girl and all." She sounded worried, suddenly unsure of whether she had done the right thing.

"Of course," said Lisa. "Was he interested in how Sirius gets along with children?"

"Oh, yeah!" said Bonnie, enthusiastic again. "He wanted to know all about it. You know, how old your little visitor is. He even wondered what his name is, but I didn't know. I don't think you ever told me."

"Hmmm," said Lisa. "Probably not." She had told no one

Luke's name, had told Luke not to. "Funny that he never got in touch with me. Did you give him my address or what?"

"Well, I wouldn't give out your *address,* for heaven's sake!" said Bonnie. "I gave him your phone number, that's all."

That's enough, thought Lisa. She improvised. "My neighbor said someone came by looking for me. I wonder if it was the same man. What did he look like?"

"Oh, gosh, he was a hunk! Really, Lisa! I wished I knew a lot about Bernese . . . anything to, you know, keep the conversation going."

"Tall, short, thin, curly hair, what?"

"Tall more than short, I guess, but nothing remarkable in any of those ways. Still, wow, you know? And he had money. He could afford some special breed, that's for sure."

"He had a diamond pinky ring? He was driving a Mercedes? What?"

"Ray Bans. You know what they cost? He was wearing Ray Bans."

Lisa guessed that in Turner Falls sporting fancy sunglasses qualified as conspicuous consumption. "Did he have a birthmark on his wrist, all over it?"

"Gee, not that I saw . . ." Bonnie hesitated. "If I'd seen that, I'd remember."

"Did he seem like he was from Texas?"

Bonnie laughed. "He was *not* wearing a cowboy hat, if that's what you mean. How else does someone seem like they're from Texas? He didn't call me 'gal.' Or jangle any spurs."

So maybe it was and maybe it wasn't the same man who'd visited Mrs. Peavy. If it wasn't, then whoever these people were, they included a disproportionate number of heartthrobs.

When she had hung up, she sat staring at the phone. The fact that a picture was missing from Carl's mantel suddenly made sense—a picture of Luke and a big, wavy-haired, tri-color dog. A Bernese.

COOPER COULD NOT pretend that lunch with Dianne had been anything short of a disaster. She would probably never speak to him again. She had been happy to see him, hadn't challenged a single observation he'd made about the world. Neither had she looked acquisitively at his dinner roll and asked him if he was planning to eat it. A perfect dining companion. He'd been bored and edgy, and his reactions, he guessed from hers, had been apparent. He sighed.

MENENDEZ WANTED THE gun back, but the man behind the desk just smiled. "You don't understand how this works," he said. "You need another gun, get another gun. Or use this one."

He opened a drawer and indicated a weapon. Serviceable. Up-to-date. Not the gun Menendez wanted. His employer watched him shake his head and closed the drawer.

"Suit yourself. Trouble is, you see, the one you want was used to commit a murder. It's got your fingerprints on it. I can't release that particular weapon because, of course, it could get into the wrong hands. Now, as long as it stays safe, with me, you're safe. And I very much want you to stay safe. Which you will be. As long as I am."

He sat back in his swivel leather chair and stretched contentedly. "Me," he went on, "I never carry a gun. I don't need to. I have a much more useful weapon." He smiled. "I use it to get people to talk to me, and people always talk to me."

This was not quite true. Women talked to him, but even women didn't always tell him everything. Menendez was just angry enough to point this out. "The old lady didn't talk," he said. "Martelli had more success getting that information."

"Martelli was lucky. Too stupid to realize that when you got a kid and you got an old lady, they gravitate more often than not, but lucky once I told you to send him in."

He tapped the side of his head. "It isn't just charm," he said. "It's charm and more brains than the rest of you put together. It isn't charm that set up this operation, put you in charge of the legit side of the business, made you the only one who knows anything at all about me. It's important to me that nobody knows who I am, nobody but you. That's the way I like it. That's why I left it to you to deal with grabbing the kid once I'd found him. A mistake, for sure, but I had no reason to think you couldn't handle it. You couldn't handle it, could you?" His voice was light, but not remotely friendly. Menendez did not reply.

The other man rose and took his suit jacket off a wooden hanger near the door to his office. It was an exceptionally good-looking jacket. It made him look quite prosperous, which, of course, he was. "I don't want to have to carry a gun," he said. "I'd have to have my jackets tailored completely differently. I don't want that. I want things to stay just as they are. Don't you?"

Menendez remained seated, looking at the toes of his oxfords. He nodded.

"Good. Well, to keep things just the way they are, we're going to have to be a little more successful in finding the kid. He's in Chicago, you know."

Menendez looked up. His eyes narrowed.

"Didn't know that? Oh, yeah. The broad McCain dumped him on is in Chicago. That means he is."

He opened the door, then shut it again and turned. "I recommend you find him. If you don't . . . well, you'll need to take out his old man, who's not really doing any damage at all where he is right now. And that would be unfortunate. It would cause me some grief. He's an old friend."

* * *

AT FIVE O'CLOCK Lisa stood up and stretched, defeated for the time being, and went to get Luke. At home again, with stew on the stove, she sifted through Cooper's collection of music.

"Vivaldi, Haydn, Haydn, Bach . . . That's what we need, Luke, a Goldberg Variation to dance to."

Finally, she found a drawer of cassettes. "Whooo! The music of a man's youth. Our Mr. Cooper wasn't always a stodge, it appears."

"What's that 'stodge'?"

"A person who likes only one kind of music, my boy."

Getting out of his car, Cooper paused to wonder who in the neighborhood was blasting Creedence Clearwater. As he came up the walk, it became obvious. Through the large front window, he could see Lisa and Luke, wild and laughing, dancing around the living room, and when the front door was opened, he could hear them slaughtering the lyrics.

"Don't go out tonight! Be sure to take your light! There's a bathroom on the right!"

He stood in the doorway and watched them. The music was so loud that they had not heard him come in. Lisa's lithe grace, her youth, her energy, made him ache. Her blue jeans were dusted with flour. Poor Carl, he thought. Imagine having her and losing her. What had he done to make her leave him, and had he gotten over it? *Could* someone get over it? Cooper was very glad she wasn't his type.

Luke, hopping sideways, arms outflung, caromed off the couch and collapsed, giggling. The song ended and Lisa bent over, her hands on her knees, panting. Feeling Cooper's gaze, she turned to him.

"For a while there, we thought we'd have to content ourselves with *The Four Seasons* when what we wanted was, you know, the Four Seasons."

"I haven't listened to any of that since . . . maybe the midseventies." He stood awkwardly, feeling out of place in his expensive suit. "Something smells good."

"It's only stew," she said. "And biscuits. I just need to add the milk and roll them out. Fifteen minutes or so?"

He went upstairs to change, found a pair of jeans. Allison had grimaced when he wore them. He dug out his favorite sweatshirt. *I thĭnk, thĕrefŏre ĭamb,* it said.

Downstairs, Lisa was brushing flour off the kitchen table into her cupped hand. "A poet-mathematician," she said. "Who'd 'a thunk? Great sweatshirt!"

"A college friend of mine made it," he replied. "Janet. Allison rolled her eyes."

"You should have married Janet," said Lisa.

The kitchen smelled wonderful and Cooper realized he was extremely hungry. He reached toward the top of the refrigerator, where Lisa had stored a large bunch of bananas.

"Hey," said Lisa. "Do you think those grow on trees?"

Cooper, peeling one slowly, regarded her in silence. I'm not walking into this one, he thought. The encyclopedia in the study yielded the information he sought. He stuck his head through the kitchen doorway. Lisa was putting a basket of biscuits on the table.

"Only an ignoramus thinks bananas grow on trees," he said. "They grow on vines."

Luke maneuvered around the table, setting down plates.

"Does he know where the silverware goes?" asked Cooper wonderingly.

Lisa grinned. "This boy is not only brave, he's clever. Show Bob where the forks go, boyo. I guess he isn't sure."

Luke counted out three forks from the drawer and placed them, precisely, on the left sides of the plates.

Cooper stood in the doorway. She called me Bob, he thought. She called me Bob.

When they had sat down, Luke patted Cooper's arm to get his attention. "Lisa thinks I'm brave," he said. "Do you think I'm brave?"

"Yes," said Cooper. "I do think you're brave. What do you think?"

Luke sighed. He had, it seemed, fooled the adults, but he hadn't fooled himself. He shook his head sadly. "I'm not brave. When Lisa said run away, I was scared. And when I *was* running away, I was scared. And when *you* was in the road, I was scared then too." It was a relief to have confessed the unfortunate truth.

Cooper gazed at the boy steadily. "Listen to me," he said. "I'm going to tell you what brave is, and I want you to remember it your whole life."

Luke nodded. He kicked his feet gently against the rung of his chair.

"When you're afraid to do something, but you know it's the right thing to do and you do it anyway . . . that's brave. It's doing what has to be done *even though* you're scared."

Luke thought about this, and a great weight slowly lifted. "I was brave!" He looked at Lisa, his eyes alight.

"Yes," said Lisa, smiling first at him and then gratefully at Cooper, "you were."

When dinner was, Cooper thought, over, he pushed back his chair. Lisa held up a hand. "As the waitress said to the Duke of Edinburgh, 'Hold on to your fork, Duke, there's pie.' "

"Pie? I've had to live a long time without pie. What kind?"

"Exist," corrected Lisa. "Without pie, you were existing, not living. Peach. Believe it or not, there were ripe peaches at the store. And Werner had a rolling pin." She cut huge pieces.

"I can't do this," said Cooper, beginning to eat. "My grandmother could, but I assumed it involved incantations. Or that it was gender related; women could, men couldn't. Like lifting a chair while your forehead's against the wall. But Allison disproved that theory."

"It's easy. You just need a person to show you how to make a crust—so you can't see a fingerprint in the dough when it's rolled out . . . Anyway, I can teach you. It's a necessary survival skill, like being able to use self-serve gasoline pumps."

"You couldn't teach me."

Luke carried his plate to the sink. "She teached *Mickey,*" he said. "You say, 'I think I can, I think I can,' and you *can.*" He disappeared into the living room.

Hearing the television come on, Lisa cringed. "But he can't read. And there's a startling absence of pictures in your copy of *Indicator Systems for Monitoring Assessment* . . . So if I make him turn it off, he'll be back in here, and I want to tell you what I found out today."

She told him about talking to Bonnie. "That's how they found us," she said. "I don't know how they knew where to start looking. Maybe Carl did or said something that pointed them north. But, anyway, that's how they zeroed in."

She carried the dishes to the sink. "All I want to do is get back on the computer. I got nowhere, got nothing, all day. But there's a lot to go through still. Days' worth at least."

"If you knew anything, a word, a series of letters that might show up in what you're looking for, you could have the computer search files for that. And if it was in there, you'd know you were onto something."

Luke had become bored with the network news. He wandered into the kitchen and stood gazing hopefully at Cooper. "We gonna play with that train?"

Cooper reached out and ruffled the boy's soft hair. "You bet," he said. "In just a minute."

"But I don't know even a word," said Lisa. "I don't know nothin'. Except that it is politically incorrect and morally repugnant for Man and Boy to play with trains while Woman washes dishes. The oppressed rise up in rebellion, you know. It's a historic truth."

"But it takes decades, sometimes centuries," replied Cooper. "I don't think you'll be here that long. It takes at least days, and whiners rarely get offered hospitality for *days . . ."*

"That sounds suspiciously like a threat," said Lisa, primly settling the dishcloth over the faucet and turning her back to the sink. She leaned against it and crossed her arms. "Don't threaten me, sir. Don't ever threaten me."

Luke pulled himself into a chair. "That's what my daddy said," he announced.

Lisa and Cooper stared at him. "What?" said Lisa. "What did your daddy say?"

"He said, 'Don't threaten me.' Me and Mayor Lin heared him when we got waked up."

"Who did he say it to? Do you know?" she asked.

"Sure I know. He said it to Gerry. You know Gerry? Gerry's daddy's friend and my friend too. Gerry's a policeman, and he's got a *gun.*"

"Wow," said Lisa. "Imagine that. Do you remember when your daddy said that to Gerry? Do you remember what night it was that you and Marilyn got waked up?"

"Course I do," said Luke. "It was just afore we came by your house. Daddy and Gerry was making noise and it waked us up and then I went to bed again and then Daddy waked me up again and we got in the car and we drived a long time and we came by your house."

The dishes sat, ignored, next to the sink while Lisa bolted for the study. She surfaced, twenty minutes later, and murmured over the dull clacking of the train, "There's no Jerry with a *J* anywhere. But there are six files that contain Gerry with a *G*. Six files!"

"A place to start," replied Cooper. "Why don't I deal with bedtime and you go on with it." He grinned, the smile lighting his eyes. "Go on. Then we'll both be doing what we want."

"Great," said Lisa, retreating to the study but turning to glance back at him as she went through the doorway. He grinned again. Settling into the chair, she wondered why she hadn't really noticed before how nice-looking he was.

An hour later, Cooper came in and stood behind her chair, looking over her shoulder at a list of addresses on the screen. " 'Needham and Charles. Walker Insur . . .' Those two are at the same address. All of these are in the Loop, but what are they?"

Lisa pointed to the telephone book next to her. "I looked them up. They're insurance agencies. Or brokers. See, they're grouped by location. If I remember downtown correctly, the names in each group that aren't at the exact same address are located within a block or so of each other. Do you know any of these addresses? Like, what else is there?"

Cooper pointed to the first address on the screen. "That's a huge building. It's got a number of businesses—lawyers and accounting firms and a little bit of everything. I don't know either of the two addresses in this next group, but you're right, they're around the corner from each other. This stuff is in a file that contains the name Gerry?"

"Yeah. I've looked at most of the Gerry files. They're all largely written over with garbage. Some of them have what I guess are names and addresses, but not downtown. One of them didn't make any sense at all, but I wrote down the English words or parts of words." She handed Cooper a legal pad.

"Seifert . . . irgin Isla . . . Mino . . . ke Forest." The rest of the notes were similar scraps of names, partial phrases.

"Let's think about this. Who could Gerry be? Luke seems to know him pretty well. Do you?"

"The only Gerry I know of that has any connection with Carl is a guy we went to school with. He was Carl's roommate junior year and I thought he was a creep. His last name was . . . damn! What was his last name? Martelli. He dated freshman sorority girls. Lots of them. And played football. He was . . . seamy, but Carl didn't see it. Gerry was . . . funny, charming, a good guy, but only so long as it was easy to be one. Not the kind of person who'd made some actual commitment to being a good guy."

She reached for the phone book. "Maybe it's the same Gerry, though it's hard to imagine him pledging to serve and protect. He wasn't around Chicago while Carl and I were together, but that wasn't for long." She ran her finger down a page. "There's one here."

There was a phone on the desk. Lisa pulled it toward her, put a foot on the edge of the chair seat, and dialed. In a few seconds, she spoke. "Hi. I'm calling on behalf of the Alumni Office at Liberty College. Could you tell me if this is the correct number for the Gerry Martelli who graduated six years ago?"

She listened intently and Cooper saw her brow furrow. "I'm sorry to have bothered you. Thank you. I'm . . . so sorry." She hung up, but her hand remained clenched on the receiver. "It's the same Gerry. That was his mother. He's dead. They found him, Wednesday afternoon, shot to death in the woods, not far from here. He'd been killed that morning."

Cooper lowered himself into a chair. He felt weak. The same fear that had tightened his chest in the Wisconsin woods was creeping through his bones. Lisa stared over his shoulder at the wall, her eyes filling and overflowing.

"That's the day I was at Carl's," she said. "I was there while Gerry was . . . It's even worse than I thought. Dying didn't make Gerry a wonderful guy, but he shouldn't be dead. And if he is, is Carl?" She turned her gaze to meet Cooper's. "I thought I would know if Carl was dead. I thought I would just know. Something would feel different, and I would know."

Damn, thought Cooper. She's in love with him. An unfamiliar nausea clutched at his stomach, interrupted the terror. For the first time in his adult life he was jealous. He'd forgotten what an ugly feeling it was. He kept his voice relaxed.

"Don't think that way. It doesn't help anything. We'll give ourselves a few days. If we don't know a lot more by then than we know now, we'll go to the police."

"But—"

Cooper didn't let her continue. "But nothing. We don't have any choice. You said yourself that if the police are involved in this, it's hardly the whole force. Maybe Gerry was, himself. Maybe his partner. But not the whole force. I was around in the sixties and even I know *that.*"

"I'm not an idiot. Don't patronize me." Lisa's dismay had intensified the sense of vulnerability she'd been struggling against. She felt raw. "It doesn't have to be the whole force. The one thing Carl said not to do was to go to the police. Damn it, Cooper! He had a reason, and I don't intend to run right out and do the one thing he told me not to do."

This was impossible. He was older and more experienced. He knew more about the world than she did. As soon as he behaved consistently with those facts, she accused him of patronizing her.

"Fine," he said shortly. "Gerry was a cop. Gerry's dead. When a cop gets shot, the first people *I'd* suspect are other cops."

Lisa looked away. Did all men do this, or was it just men who had been the boss too long? She took a breath. She couldn't afford the animosity; he was her only ally. Calm down, she told herself. Think!

"I didn't say it was a cop who killed Gerry. I just said we don't know how they're involved, how many are involved . . . all right, *if* they're involved. But it seems that Gerry threatened Carl, and the question is why. Maybe he'd told

Carl something, or done something—showed off in some way—that made Carl tumble to some department corruption Gerry was in on. That would explain a lot. The police have resources, resources they can use to find people."

Cooper's eyes narrowed. "And plain, black shoes," he said.

Chapter

11

SYLVIA HEALY GAZED around the lobby of the huge office building at the address Cooper had given her. Her assignment was a simple one. She walked purposefully to the directory and noted the office number of Walker Insurance on the fourteenth floor. Then she looked slowly and carefully around her. What might connect this building and another three blocks away and another seven blocks away? A man in light blue was removing a panel from the lobby ceiling. Sylvia, wandering past his ladder, looked up at the writing on the back of his coverall. "Maintenance" was all it said. The security guard was looking in her direction. She walked over.

"I'm so sorry to bother you," she said, laying one perfectly manicured hand on the top of the tall desk behind which the guard was perched. "Could you by any chance tell me who takes care of the office cleaning in this building?"

The guard looked at her quizzically. "There's a cleaning staff for the building," he said. "None of them are here right now. They work at night. But the supervisor's around. Do you want . . . ?"

Sylvia raised an eyebrow. "Oh, no, please don't bother

anyone. I'm looking into . . . job opportunities for recent immigrants, and I want to talk with some people who have experience with hiring, shall we say, unskilled labor? No, not unskilled. Perhaps, non-English-speaking. But the cleaning staff here works only in this one building. Is that correct?"

"Far as I know," said the guard. "It's a big building. Keeps everybody pretty busy. Like I said, you could talk to Mr. Miller. Rob Miller. If he's available."

"No, never mind. I really need to find a, well, a bigger operation. But thanks awfully." She graced the guard with a slight curve of her lips, walked sedately out of the building, and headed toward the next address on her list.

COOPER, FOR HIS PART, was poring over microfiche. The newspaper office had, as Sylvia had assured him it would, indexes referenced by names as well as subjects. There were two names he was looking for and they were not hard to find.

The first, Seifert, had occurred in an article dated January 6. Another article, from February 2, contained the second— Minot. After reading those articles, he had no trouble deciding what else to look for. Articles about robberies, a series of robberies, in the wealthy northern suburbs.

LISA MOVED SIRIUS'S paw off her knee and pulled her eyes away from the monitor. "I'm sorry," she said, dropping a hand to the silky head. "I know it's too boring. With Luke off at Carol's and no rabbits to chase, life's a drag. Hang in there another half hour and we'll go out and get your antibiotic. That'll be a walk at least."

She yawned. It had been a long night. They had worked until three, combing the disjointed files, pulling any names, dates, addresses, whole or partial, they could find. They had made lists, compared them. They'd found nothing that meant anything. But maybe by the end of the day it would mean something. If not . . . She didn't want to think about that.

Something had been different last night. Cooper had taken over the computer, but Cooper took over everything, so that wasn't it. He'd issued orders—take this down, make a note of this, look this up in the phone book. That was hardly new.

Sirius nudged his head under her wrist, lifting it off the keyboard. She scratched him slowly behind one ear. "I didn't mind," she said. "That was it. I didn't mind. We were getting through the stuff. It made sense to just do it his way." She had sat, pencil poised, watching him hit keys, scan the monitor. And she'd noticed the little vertical lines at the corners of his mouth and the way his eyes darkened when he thought hard.

She'd become annoyed only once. "You can tell someone what to do or you can tell them how to do it," she'd said. "Not both. Only a boor does both."

His voice was cold. "I'm sorry you feel that way."

She had started to giggle. She knew it was rude but couldn't stop. The laughter grew until she was gasping. Cooper had gazed at her, at first offended and than—comprehension striking him—amused.

"I mean, I'm sorry," he said. And he'd laughed too. She had never heard him laugh before. He had a nice laugh.

COOPER SAT IN THE back of a cab, staring at the notes he had taken. He tried to concentrate. Sleep deprivation, he thought. The whole country is wandering around in a state of sleep deprivation all the time. This is just an extreme example. They had worked too late, straining to make some sense out of what was most often nonsense. It had been confusing and frustrating, but Lisa had been right with him, having no trouble with the logic he tried to impose on the scraps of information, catching him when he missed a connection. He wasn't used to working with people who could keep up. Her hair smelled of lilacs.

THE MORNING CREPT by as Lisa searched for deleted files that contained any of the names or addresses they'd found last night. It was slow and aggravating and tedious, and, as she'd realized the other night, too indirect. If she could find Carl, she wouldn't have to try to find bits and scraps of his thought processes. Find Carl! But at that effort, she'd had not the slightest success. She went over, again, each bit of information she'd gathered from everyone—well, nearly everyone—she knew who also knew him. Rick Lopas. She could find Rick. Was there anyone else?

She put herself back on campus, walked through the library, glanced in at the student union, surveyed a crowd in the stadium, pushed a tray along the food service counter in the dining room. She put Carl in each place and looked to see who was with him. She still needed to find Mitchell and Rick. Was there anyone else? When the doorbell rang, she started violently in her chair.

There was a woman on the porch, a small-boned, lovely woman in a beautifully cut linen suit. Lisa opened the door and spoke through the screen.

"Yes?"

The stranger raised one perfectly shaped eyebrow. "Is Bob here? I called his office and they said he was at home, so I thought . . ."

"No, he's not here. Could I tell him something for you?"

"Well, I'll just come in and leave a note." She turned the handle on the screen door and opened it, but Lisa did not move. "Excuse me, dear," the woman said, a hint of exasperation in her voice. "I'm his wife. I'm allowed in his house."

Lisa stepped aside, silencing Sirius's incipient growl with a small movement of her hand. "I wasn't aware that he had a wife . . ." She let her voice trail off, as if in vague confusion. "Oh, you must mean his *ex*-wife."

"Exactly," said the woman, looking around and wrinkling her exquisite nose. "I'm glad he's getting some help around here. I'm Allison. Allison Grahame. And you're?"

"Not his wife," said Lisa. She smiled sweetly. Allison sat down gracefully on the edge of an overstuffed chair, managing to give an impression of both elegance and fragility. She looks, thought Lisa, like she's dressed to star in the movie of her life.

"Of course," said Allison. "Well, I need to talk with him about a summer job for one of my husband's students. I'll leave a note, but perhaps you could tell him I stopped by?" She took a small notepad and a pen out of her purse, wrote on a piece of paper, and tore it out neatly. She held it out to Lisa. "Would you see he gets this?"

Lisa smiled. "Of course." She did not get up from the rocking chair she had sat down in. Allison's eyes narrowed with annoyance. She rose and took the step needed to hand the paper to Lisa, then sniffed delicately.

"It's none of my business, of course, but are you making pot roast?"

"Uh-huh," replied Lisa, stubbornly refusing to follow her father's orders to always say yes or no instead of their more guttural substitutes. "Are you hungry?"

"No, no," laughed Allison. "I didn't mean . . . Well, you see, I'm sure you're a wonderful help to Bob, but, well, I don't know how to say this graciously . . . It's just that perhaps you ought to know he positively *hates* pot roast . . ."

"Really," said Lisa, standing and moving meaningfully toward the front door. "How interesting. I guess he'll have to make a sandwich."

Allison was momentarily silent. She gazed at Lisa appraisingly. Lisa gazed back. Sirius, sensing a degree of emotional turbulence in his god, waited for some sign that he should encourage the interloper's departure. It was not forthcoming.

"Did Bob get a dog?" asked Allison.

"No," said Lisa. "He positively *hates* dogs."

SYLVIA TAPPED ON the door to Cooper's office. "I'm back."

"Come on in and shut the door."

Sylvia was a snob; there was no getting around it. She was sometimes a bit pushier than was gracious. She was far from introspective. She was not, however, stupid. As a matter of fact, it was really Sylvia who figured it out.

COOPER LOCATED LISA at the corner of State and Madison—just where he'd told her to meet him—but not without some difficulty. He had been admiring a young woman whose skirt swirled fetchingly around pretty knees, grateful that he lived in such a windy city, when she turned, and he realized he had found her. The extra inches added by the heels on her Italian shoes made her almost his height.

"Carol said Luke was welcome to stay until whenever I could get back," she said, "but what are we *doing*? Why am I dressed up? There had better be a good reason; if there's one thing I can't stand, it's a meaningless sacrifice."

"Blame Sylvia," said Cooper. "She came back to the office and started putting two and two together and, well, it's an idea. But somebody's got to check it out, and I thought you and I could do it."

"Check what out?"

They were walking west on Madison. Cooper took her elbow to pull her closer as a woman pushing a stroller negotiated passage on the sidewalk. His grip on her arm took her by surprise. It was firm, stopping just short of uncomfortable. Her hip bumped against him and she felt suddenly shy.

He spoke quickly. "Each of the Loop addresses we have is,

Sylvia confirmed, a large office building. What is the one thing, besides elevators, that all large office buildings have?"

"Come on," said Lisa, her unfamiliar self-consciousness making her irritable. "I hate guessing games. Oh, all right. Animal, vegetable, or mineral? Please don't say mineral."

"Animal."

"Men in suits. Women in suits, with slightly different ties. Secretaries. Republicans." She stopped, wheeling toward him. "Security guards. They all have security guards!"

She was so close that Cooper felt rather than saw her slight trembling. "And security guards," he said softly, "are often ex-cops or moonlighting cops. And they wear plain, black shoes."

They divided the list and arranged a meeting place, Cooper agreeing to Lisa's suggestion of a restaurant on Adams. "Don't get into conversations," said Cooper. "Just check their uniforms, badges, whatever will tell you what company they work for. One of them might have been inside your house, seen you. You look different, but not completely different." He took a pair of glasses from his pocket. "Woolworth's. Clear glass. It works for Clark Kent."

With the glasses on and her hair brushed behind her ears, Lisa looked like an assistant D.A. "Someone expecting you would know you were you. But it would take a minute," he said. "You look . . . severe. A bit dour."

"I *beg* your pardon?" said Lisa, surveying him coldly. She turned neatly on her heel and walked briskly away.

By the third address on her list, she knew they were onto something. What, exactly, she didn't know. But something. All three guards, solid, steady-looking men in dark blue uniforms, wore the same badge and a small inscription above the pocket. "Total Security," it said. None had given her more than a glance.

She was waiting at a table at Keefer's when Cooper came in. He sat down and raised his eyebrows. She nodded.

"Total Security," she said.

"Yes," he replied, glancing at the menu. "Now let's sit here for a few minutes and think."

A waiter approached, the waiter whose station Lisa had requested when she'd been guided to a table. He'd been a theater major and her physics lab partner sophomore year. They'd had coffee in the student union, cramming for the midterm. More important, he'd lived in Carl's dorm. He looked at Cooper inquisitively.

"Do you have a cold beer in a long-necked bottle?" asked Cooper.

"Yes, sir."

"Does it cost less than a hundred dollars?"

"Yes, sir."

"Then that's what I'll have."

The waiter turned to Lisa. "Miss?"

She looked at him through the glasses. "I was so lost in admiration of your manly forearms," she said breathily, "that I haven't given a thought to my other appetites."

Cooper was appalled. Frowning savagely, he saw her push the glasses up on her head and grin. "Hey, Mitchell," she said.

"Lisa!" The waiter lost his startled look. "How ya been?"

They exchanged a few minutes of chatter. "I see you're still pursuing theater," said Lisa, with a gesture toward his order pad.

"You bet," said Mitchell. "With some small success. I had the lead in a Pinter up at North Light. Carl came. Ask him how great I was. I assume you're still in touch, you were such pals at school."

Right, thought Lisa. Pals. But she smiled. "I will, as soon as I see him. I wanted to look him up, but he seems to be away. You got any idea where he is?"

"I dinna ken, lassie," said Mitchell. "I no ha seen Carl, or

146

the wee bairn." He sounded as if he'd just tramped over a moor.

"You're in *Macbeth,* is that it?"

"Don't I wish, though the Bard requires less of a brogue than voice-over work. I'm doing a commercial for short-bread."

"I remember your flawless cockney," said Lisa. "I just didn't realize your range. But back to Carl. I've really got to find him. Who'd know where he might be?"

"Did you try Joe?" asked Mitchell. "A few weeks ago, he and Carl were in here a couple of times, huddled at a table for hours. Remember Joe? We all thought he'd be in the Senate before he was thirty. He's an insurance broker. Right around the corner. Oh, well. I thought I'd be on Broadway before I was thirty."

"And you will be," said Lisa. She already knew that Joe Thatcher had gone into insurance. But Joe hadn't been in Carl's dorm, hadn't been one of his closest friends; she'd put him lower on the list.

"Beware when you find McCain," said Mitchell. "He'll stop at nothing to recruit you for the team."

"What team?"

"Our *raison d'être,* my love. Theatre League softball. You remember. Didn't you play on the team for a few games back when you and Carl . . ." He hesitated, unsure of the relation-ship between his customers.

"When Carl and I were together." Lisa was calm. "Yes, I did. It was fun. But I'm not recruitable these days. I'm living in Wisconsin."

"Trust me. Carl will try. We had to take the penalty for not fielding enough women in almost half of our games last year. You were fierce, I remember. And if I remember, he surely will. He's managing the team and gets more than a little fanatical. He'll have you in the starting lineup before you know it."

"Kind of a long commute. And I'm not exactly in theater, Mitchell."

"So you'll be a ringer. It's allowed, for the gentler sex. Or, at least, it's inevitable. Moving you down here might pose more of a problem, but Carl will try. Forewarned is forearmed." He glanced at the man with Lisa and decided his tip was safer if he returned to business. He poised the pencil over his pad and looked back at Lisa. "Did you want something to eat?"

"Does a walrus have teeth?" asked Cooper.

When Mitchell left, Cooper brought Lisa up to date on what the newspaper files had revealed. "For some reason, Carl seems to have been interested in people who were recent victims of robberies. And he was interested in insurance."

"And Joe's in insurance. And Carl was huddled in here with him not long ago. Maybe they were comparing notes on how much they'd contributed to the Alumni Fund, but maybe . . . I'd better get hold of Joe. If he's free for a drink after work, can you get Luke?"

"Sure," said Cooper. "I can even fix dinner. Would you prefer Cheerios or Wheaties?"

"There's pot roast on low in the oven," said Lisa. "I understand you positively hate it, but Luke loves it."

"Hate pot roast? I don't hate pot roast. I used to hate Allison's pot roast, but she made it with capers and . . ." He shuddered. "No, if anything could ruin your appetite, it would be for me to describe what Allison put in pot roast. But why did you think . . . ?"

Lisa described Allison's visit. "I resisted the urge to offer to unscrew the cap on a bottle of wine. It wasn't easy."

Cooper smiled at the vision. "Well, I'll call her. Someday."

"I have to admit," said Lisa, "that the two of you don't make a lot of sense. She doesn't seem like someone you'd marry, like, well, like your type."

Cooper just grimaced. He was reluctant to admit the truth: that Allison—beautiful, delicate, poised Allison—was exactly his type, in a hundred different ways.

"So tell me about her." Lisa was frankly curious.

Mitchell set down their order. "Good luck finding Carl," he said. "I'm sure he's around. Lorna told me he was going to take care of her dog while she's in L.A., and she's not back yet. If you need anything, holler."

Lisa watched him walk away. "He's taking care of a dog? I don't *think* so. Certainly not Lorna's dog. Mitchell's a great actor, a terrific shortstop, and, it appears, a decent waiter. But I've found the limit to his talents. There's no way he got *that* right."

"What's the problem? Dogs or Lorna?"

"Not dogs so much as Lorna," she replied. "Lorna's the only person in the world Carl doesn't like. It goes deeper than that. He can't stand her. She quit a show he was in, midrehearsal, to take an Equity part. He used to mimic her. 'They made me an offer I couldn't refuse.' He's never forgiven her, and he never will. Lorna may have told Mitchell that she was going to *ask* Carl to take care of her dog, but I wish I'd been there if she did, indeed, actually ask him." She grinned and shook her head. "But we were talking about Allison. Or I wanted you to."

Cooper ignored the tall empty glass and took a long drink from the bottle. "Allison's not all bad. She does a lot of work in the arts, she volunteers at museums, that kind of thing. She's bright. She does what she thinks is right. She's just . . . concerned about things, a lot of things, that I don't understand being concerned about. And she's *not* concerned about a lot of other things."

"And those . . . differences weren't obvious."

"No, I think they probably were quite obvious," said Cooper. "I wasn't paying attention."

He looked across the table. Lisa was finishing a flaky raspberry pastry, which she had been eating with neat efficiency. She lifted her coffee cup and looked at him over the rim. Yes? her eyes said. Go on. He went on.

"People tell you who they are if you listen to them. It wasn't her fault that I didn't." He paused, memory bringing a wry smile. "We went out to dinner for her twentieth birthday. It cost me two weeks' salary from my student job as an assistant to the buildings and grounds crew. We shared a bottle of Cabernet Sauvignon, and she told me she would rather drink from her cupped hand held under a faucet than from a glass that wasn't crystal. Obviously I heard her; I can quote her today. But I wasn't listening."

"Twenty-year-olds rarely listen."

"She was twenty. I'd been in the army, so the government would help pay for school. I was twenty-four. That's creeping up on the ripe old age you've attained. You, I think, listen."

"Sometimes." Lisa's voice was soft. *Mea culpa.* "Tell me about the brilliant Sylvia. You sent her off to check out these addresses, and she came up with the security guard connection?"

"Yup. Not an uncommon burst of genius for Sylvia. She's quite bright."

The pressure of Cooper's grip on her elbow slid into Lisa's memory. She found herself feeling uncharitable about Sylvia's brilliance. "And she does anything you ask because you're the boss. You tell her to run downtown, she runs downtown. Or did you tell her why?"

"Of course I didn't tell her why. I told her I wanted to find out what could conceivably connect those buildings. And, yeah, she does what I ask her to do because I'm the boss. Or because of my undeniable charm. It *could* be that."

Lisa snorted. "Sylvia's got a crush on you?"

"What?" Cooper was shocked.

"Well, it wouldn't be the first time a secretary got a crush on her boss. I don't know about undeniable charm, but you're not completely repulsive."

"Wait a minute, I've got to put that down in my little Book of Memories," said Cooper. He took a small leather-bound book and a pen from his jacket pocket, opened it, and paused, pen poised. "April seventh, Lisa used the words . . . Could you just repeat that, so I can get it exactly right? Was it 'not repulsive'?"

"Not *completely* repulsive. You're avoiding the question."

"There was no question."

"You're avoiding the implication."

"I'm not avoiding anything. I have had no experience with a crush, actively or passively, since the one I had when I was nine and Betsy Blackaby transferred to my school." He sighed and raised his eyes heavenward. "I still dream of Betsy. She wore saddle shoes and double-cuffed her socks. She had perfect little wrists and knees that never bore a scab. She was my ideal nine-year-old. She would undoubtedly be my ideal forty-two-year-old if I could find her . . ."

"I know Betsy Blackaby," said Lisa, "though she goes by 'Lizzie' these days. She's got a goiter and most of her hair has fallen out. She drools. Thyroid deficiency, I think. She still double-cuffs her socks, but she wears them with house slippers. She watches soap operas and eats large boxes of store-bought cookies. She is fascinated by the fact that they are all exactly the same size and hasn't figured out yet how that's possible. Forget her. It's best for both of you."

"Not a chance. I'll never forget Betsy. And she wouldn't go near a large box of anything."

"Oh, *that* Betsy Blackaby," said Lisa. "Sorry. I got confused. I know that one too. She goes by 'Lissa' now, and her favorite restaurants are the ones where lunch costs twenty-seven dollars and consists of a small mound of an exotic food product centered on a very large plate. She's perfect for you. She's just like Allison."

"That," said Cooper, "was uncalled for. You're just in a snit because I know there is a woman in the world more perfect than you, and you can't stand it."

Lisa was unperturbed. "Well, you may have lost Betsy, but I'm sure Sylvia bats her baby blues in your direction."

"Sylvia," said Cooper firmly, "is a rock, a jewel, and a reward from heaven for something good I once did. Undoubtedly something that risked my life. It is not one of her sterling qualities, however, to be able to discern any significant difference between me and a toad."

He drained the last of his beer and gazed at Lisa. He was comfortable with her. She didn't fuss, didn't dart sly glances at him. She moved confidently and easily. And when she wanted to know something, she asked.

"We've spent a good deal of the day detailing the loves of my life," he said. "How about you? Tell me about Carl. If it's not too personal a question, why did you dump him?"

Lisa paused, her coffee cup halfway to her mouth as she stared at him. She put the cup down. "I didn't dump Carl except in the most technical way of looking at it. I left Carl to keep him from dumping me."

"Well, then, why would he have?"

"We weren't right for each other." She made a face. "I know that sounds like the charm-school explanation for every breakup, but it happens to be true." Cooper's question was an easy one. She had, many years ago, given it a great deal of thought.

"I didn't matter enough to him. There was nothing about me that spoke to anything essential in him. Everything important to him existed outside *us*. He wanted somebody a lot different from me. He told me that, in a hundred ways. He could have had any of those women he pined for, the willowy ones, the sophisticated, chic ones; he just didn't know it."

She looked across the room and signaled Mitchell for more coffee. When it had come, she looked into her cup.

"He never chose me; he just let me choose him. As soon as somebody closer to what he wanted also chose him, he'd be gone. As kindly as he could go, of course; he's not a cad. There was, you see, nothing to stop him. Losing me wasn't much of a threat. And I preferred for him to find the right person after I left rather than before."

"And did he?"

"I think so. I think his wife was probably the right person for him. I don't think he would have married someone who wasn't. They probably had a good marriage. He's a nice guy. Everybody likes him; they can't help it."

I could, thought Cooper.

"I'm going to go call Joe," said Lisa.

He watched her move through the tables to the back of the room. He wondered if Betsy Blackaby took neat little steps or if she moved fluidly, like Lisa.

Chapter

12

THE MAN THEY called the boss, and who was aptly named, gestured toward a leather chair, and Menendez sat down.

"It's the same girl," said Menendez.

"How much does she know?"

Menendez shrugged. "Something. She's gotta know something. Or what's she doing? But it all depends on how much McCain told her. We don't know how much he knows."

"He knows shit," the other man replied. "And we're going to keep it that way. But he may have told her what he was up to. So let's assume she knows everything he knows. That's still not much. He doesn't know about me."

"So I should . . . what?"

"Same agenda. Find the kid. That might be a piece of cake now. If not . . . if he's not with her, well, we'll go at it from another angle. Pick up McCain and work the more direct approach."

"You want me to pull somebody else in to help on the tail?"

The other man was quite attractive when he smiled, and he smiled now. He picked up a paperweight and turned it casually in his fingers. "If you think a broad who doesn't know you're there can shake you."

"EXCUSE ME, MISS," said a stocky, athletic-looking young man with eyes such an odd shade of blue-green that women, after spotting him at the grocery store, were often inspired to do their shopping on a nightly basis. "I'm looking for a robustly smashing woman I used to know, undoubtedly wearing blue jeans and a sweatshirt and quaffing a brew, but you—you doe-eyed, feminine lovely—are sitting where I expected to find her. Do you know what's become of Lisa?"

Lisa fluttered her lashes, languidly crossed her legs, and leaned back in the chair to gaze up at Joe Thatcher. "Perhaps I could entertain you while you wait for her."

Joe straddled the other chair and lowered himself into it. "Boy howdy! You look great! How ya been, cutie? And whatcha doing in proper shoes?"

"Fine, mostly," said Lisa. "And these are not proper shoes." She stuck one foot out from under the table and looked at it appraisingly. "Decorous, yes. Gorgeous, yes. Proper, no. There can't be anything proper about a shoe suitable only for dainty, mincing progress along a pavement. But to get rudely right to the point, I need to find Carl and I can't. Do you have any idea where he is?"

"Not a one," replied Joe, catching a waiter's eye and pointing at Lisa's glass and the empty place in front of himself. "He didn't show up for football on Sunday, which is mainly where I see him. He moved, you know."

"Yeah, and I've been there. No sign. I ran into Mitchell and he said he'd seen the two of you huddled at Keefer's. So I was hoping you might have a clue."

"Not I. Or why would they call me Clueless Joe?"

Lisa rotated her margarita glass and sipped. It was a good margarita. "Did you guys talk about what he's working on these days?"

"Of course. He's working on a play. But this time he's writing it. I told him to forget it, go for the big time. If you're going to knock yourself out, write a screenplay, for God's sake."

"Mitchell said you were filling out forms . . ."

Joe waved one hand dismissively. "Yeah. Like I don't see enough of those during working hours. You want to know about *that*?"

Lisa nodded. "Really. I do."

Joe sighed, then grinned and cocked a finger at her. "Okay. But if you make me spend this whole, potentially delightful meeting talking insurance, you're buying the drinks."

Lisa smiled. She was enjoying the flirtatious turn this encounter was taking. Joe was decidedly nice-looking and he'd gained the air of authority that so often accompanied success. It was pleasant to have him look at her the way he was looking at her.

"Not the whole time. You can also tell me all about how you got to the point in your career where you can afford a Rolex watch and how many beautiful women you number among your conquests and anything else I wouldn't have found out by reading the alumni magazine. But first . . ."

"Yeah, yeah. First the most fascinating subject, which, of course, *would* just happen to involve Carl." His tone was not mocking. It was, in fact, slightly sympathetic.

Joe smiled at her, friendliness sparking his voice and making his eyes even more eerily beautiful. "Some people he knows are out of the country and want to change insurers. He was helping them with the details, feeding me the application stuff, getting the schedules together, all that."

Joe glanced up at the waiter, approaching with his drink.

"Then he just dropped the whole thing."

"Dropped it? How do you mean?"

Joe raised his glass. "To Jimmy Buffet." He sipped and swallowed. "Did you know that Jimmy Buffet made *millions* last year? Doing what, I wonder . . . Yeah, dropped it. The application's just sitting in my files. I got a bunch of estimates together and gave them to Carl, and he was going to fax them to these people in Europe and get back to me with a decision. But I haven't heard from him in the two weeks since I gave him the information."

"So the application's just, as you said, sitting there."

"Yeah. Maybe they didn't like the quotes."

Why, Lisa wondered in frustration, would Carl have done such a thing? Why in the middle of what he had perceived, correctly as it turned out, as danger to Luke, would he spend hours helping some rich people apply for insurance? It had to be related. But how?

Joe looked at her quizzically. "So, other than needing to find Carl, you're okay? Where are you living these days?"

"Yeah," Lisa lied, smiling. "Wisconsin. In the woods. Like Laura Ingalls Wilder—a little house in the big woods."

"I thought that was the prairie."

"She wrote more than one book, doofus. What did you read when you were a kid? *What Every Boy Should Know about Liability Law*?" She studied Joe, feeling more of her tension dissipate. He was nice and funny and very smart. If she just told him everything she knew, everything she needed to know, would he be able to help?

"Wisconsin, eh? So whatcha doing here? Looking for Carl, I know, but why?"

She gestured vaguely, still undecided about involving him. "I left some stuff with him a few years ago. I hope he still has it."

"Well, I may run into him. Or hear from him. Where are you staying? I'll let you know if I do." He held up a hand as a waiter passed. "One more? Or how about dinner?"

"No, thanks. I've got to get going."

Joe shook his head and the waiter went on his way. "Leave me a number."

"Great," she said, trying to overcome what she knew were paranoic hesitations. "I'm at the Palmer House. But I don't know for how long. I'll call you."

Outside the restaurant, Joe hugged her. The smooth wool of his suit jacket felt good. The embrace felt good. It lasted long enough to communicate affection, and that felt good too.

She turned right and headed toward State Street, aware of the safety in crowds. So many anonymous people. She was quite sure none of the security guards had looked at her twice. Still . . .

She hurried into Marshall Field's and got into the first elevator she saw, noting the other occupants. Choosing a floor at random, she got off. Two women and a man got off with her. She took an escalator back down to the first floor and stopped at an exit onto Wabash, looking around. None of the people from the elevator was anywhere in sight.

She hurried up the steps of the el station, remembering that two separate lines circled the Loop. If she got on the wrong one, she'd end up in Oak Park, miles from Cooper's house. A train was standing at the platform, people boarding hurriedly. It was the right line—Ravenswood. An A train. She stepped through the door and to one side to make room for the people crowding on behind her. There were no seats, but here, right inside the door, there were railings to lean against. She leaned as people pushed past, and then sighed disgustedly. Right line, wrong train. At rush hour every train didn't stop at every station. She'd have an extra six blocks to walk from an A stop, and her feet, unaccustomed to heels, were killing her. How long could it be before a B train came? She stepped off as the door slid closed.

A woman holding a little girl's hand glowered at a man who jostled her roughly in a quick but futile attempt to get from the aisle to the door before it shut.

The girl tugged on her mother's skirt. Her face crinkled in delight and her eyes were gleeful. "Did you hear what that man said?"

"Yes," said her mother shortly. "I'm sure we *all* did."

The train moved slowly away.

"YOU WAITED DINNER for me?" said Lisa, sitting down at the kitchen table and looking up at Cooper. "Now I know how working mothers feel. Guilty. I've barely seen Luke all day. Thanks for getting him fed and into bed. And thanks for this." She gestured. "You even set the table."

"Well, I got Luke to show me where the forks go."

She glanced down at Sirius, who had placed his head in her lap. "Ooops, sorry, fella," she said. "You need your dinner too, don't you?"

"I managed to figure out which grocery item was intended for the dog's consumption," said Cooper. "He's eaten."

"You fed him?"

"When I came home, I detected a slight movement of his tail," replied Cooper. "I thought I should reward the sentiment."

They had sat in the living room while Lisa told him about what Joe had to say, and he'd listened intently but without giving voice to a brainstorm. He sat down now across from her and unfolded a napkin.

"Shall I ring up Allison?" he asked. "I could ask if she wants to come over and see how normal people eat pot roast. No? But this is our first meal with just the two of us. Will we have anything to talk about?"

"Gee, I don't know. We just found out that every Loop building on our list employs the same security guard agency and has at least one insurance company or broker in it. We just found out that Carl spent hours with Joe, who's in insurance, setting up some big-time policy. Clearly we've got all *that* figured out. So let's talk about the Cubs. You're a businessman; maybe you can tell me why a team that makes so much money can't afford any pitchers. Or was there something you preferred to discuss?"

"What do security guards and insurance companies have in common?"

"Crime. Prevention of and coverage for." She ate silently for a few minutes, thinking, and didn't taste her dinner.

"Coop?" Her voice was hesitant. "If I had inherited a priceless silver tea service from my grandmother, who'd know about it, besides all the ladies I had over for watercress sandwiches?"

"Your insurance company." He put down his fork and leaned forward. His eyes were thoughtful. "And assuming that your use of *priceless* was not precisely accurate, your insurance company would know just about exactly what it was worth."

"Wouldn't they also know if I kept it, say, on the kitchen counter instead of in a safe? And if I could do that with relative safety because I had a burglar alarm? And what kind of burglar alarm? Would they know all that?"

"I think they would know the model number of the burglar alarm."

"But the insurance company isn't going to send thugs out to pinch Grandma's tea service."

"No."

"And they're not going to display my insurance application and the special rider I have for the tea service down in the lobby of their building . . . so how is somebody else going to find out?" She waited. Was the idea taking shape in her mind as logical as it seemed? She didn't have to wait long.

"Total Security."

She nodded, and he went on. "They have keys. At least the security guards we use at our building have keys. I think it's up to the building management, maybe even to individual tenants, if guards have office keys. But I'll bet they often do. A security guard could go through any hard-copy files he wanted."

"So Total Security could find out who had what, how much it was worth, and how they protected it. But . . ."

"But what?"

"How do they know when no one's home? There hasn't been a rash of home invasions with residents tied up in their closets. No one was at home in that series of robberies you read about."

Cooper thought. "Travel agencies would know. Are there travel agencies in the same buildings as the insurance brokers and companies?" He looked at his watch. "Let's leave the dishes and apply our waning energies to looking at the stuff on the computer again, the files that didn't make sense."

Three hours later, Lisa was sitting on her heels, gazing at the notes she had spread out, when Cooper came back from the kitchen and handed her a bowl of popcorn.

"When I was about thirteen," she said, "my friends and I spent one slumber party describing the men we would marry. Everybody had details. They knew how tall these men would be, what they did for a living, what color eyes they had. I knew only one thing—he made popcorn. So the question is, will you marry me?"

Cooper leaned against the doorway. "Not likely," he said. "Your standards are too low."

"The hell they are," she said. She turned back to the papers on the floor. "There's got to be something here, some kind of pattern."

"Okay. We printed all the Gerry files, and we're not finding anything complete enough to make sense. I found one odd list of names before you got home." He sat down at the computer and tapped keys. The file he'd been reading earlier came back on the screen. "This stuff looks like names, but it doesn't make a lot of sense. Most of the first names are missing."

He paused, irritated by the illogic facing him on the screen. "There's a dog in here. At least I think it's a dog, unless some poor sucker's actually named Pekinese. Why would he list a dog?" His eyes narrowed. "Here's somebody's entire name. Somebody named Shiba Inu lives in Winnetka. It doesn't say if that's Mr., Mrs., or Ms. Inu."

Lisa jumped up from the floor and looked over his shoulder at the monitor. Cooper had deleted the meaningless symbols to compress what was left. What was left was addresses, some just fragments, others more complete. Several had names with them.

"Bouvier, Vizsla, Pekinese, Tervuren, Papillon, Wheaten, Shiba Inu," she read. "They're *all* dogs, Cooper. All of the names are dogs. That isn't a person named Shiba Inu living in Winnetka; it's a Shiba Inu *dog.*"

"That's it," said Cooper. "We already figured Martelli was crooked. Now we know the details. He was taking payoffs from dogs, not your ordinary city dogs, wealthy North Shore dogs. Maybe he was springing them from the pound."

"Yeah, well, it doesn't make any sense to *us,* but it makes some kind of sense."

"Or Carl was working on an 'I Yip for Yummies' commercial."

"No; this is going to help us. It's got to."

"Downtown addresses—office buildings in the Loop. North Shore addresses. Robberies at a number of those. Dogs. Well, I'll print this file and we can add it to the other stuff we've got, but it sure doesn't make any sense."

Lisa yawned. "I can't think. I'll work with this some

more tomorrow, but it could be clear as a bell and I wouldn't see it tonight. I want to go out and call Mickey in the morning, see if anything's happening up there. Other than that, I'll just keep blundering through this stuff."

Cooper turned off the monitor and swung around. "Do you miss him?"

"Mickey?"

"No, Barry Bonds. I've never had a friend that was a woman. It's never even seemed possible. But you and Mickey are actual friends, right?"

"Yeah, we are. He's not the best friend I ever had, but he's definitely a pal. He's one of those irrepressible people, cheerful, ready for anything. He's funny and he's nice and we help each other. I help him cut firewood; he helps me when somebody's got to hold the pipe in place and somebody else has to turn the wrench. Or when I want to go someplace and can't take Sirius. He'd hate a kennel, so I just wouldn't go if I couldn't leave him with Mick. Of course, I do the same for him, watch Justice when he can't take her with him. Living where I live would be a lot harder without—why are you staring at me?"

"What if you didn't have Mickey, didn't have a friend you could leave your dog with? What if you were going to the south of France, or Hawaii, or . . . it doesn't matter where, just someplace you weren't driving to? What if you were going on a long vacation, and there was no Mickey in your life?"

"The south of France? Is this supposed to be a difficult question? Sirius would get used to life in a kennel."

"And say I worked at that kennel—"

"In which case you should sue your career counselor."

Cooper ignored her. "Say I worked at the kennel. What do I know *for a fact* when your dog shows up there?"

It was coming together now for her too. "That I'm going out of town."

Cooper sat back, folding his arms and gazing at her. "And that there's no one else at your house, or why did you bring your dog to the kennel?"

"And you'd know," Lisa said slowly, "or you could find out in about a second, how long I was going to be gone." She sat, staring at Cooper, not seeing him, seeing a list of dogs on a computer monitor. "It's perfect. What are the odds that every robbery victim used the same two or three travel agencies? Even the same dozen? But there are very few kennels that people are going to feel comfortable leaving their pets in for extended periods of time. They may board them at the vet's for a weekend, but for a cruise, for a long trip? No way."

IT WASN'T HARD the next morning to get enough facts from information to cross-reference the list of addresses and the names from Carl's computer files. There wasn't a perfect match, but by ten o'clock she had enough to go on—seven names that had listed phone numbers. Next to each name was a breed of dog.

She picked up the phone again, took a deep breath, and dialed. Lying made her jumpy. "Hello, this is Wendy Morrison; is this Mrs. Fontaine?"

The voice at the other end was brisk and wary. "Yes."

"Oh, good. Well, Mrs. Fontaine, I was talking to a woman at a garden-club meeting the other night, a tall, attractive woman with brown hair, a friend of yours but I'm afraid I've forgotten her name—"

"Leslie Harris?" The voice indicated relief that the call seemed not to be sales-related.

"Yes, that's it! And she said that she thinks you sometimes board your Shiba Inu when you go out of town, and we're new to the area—just moved here from Atlanta—and need to board our Shih Tzu and I wondered if you could tell me what kennel you use and if you're satisfied."

"Why, of course." Mrs. Fontaine lost her reserve, verged on friendliness. "We use The Retreat. It's marvelous. Nice, roomy runs and personal attention. You'll be very pleased. It's right on Laurel Drive."

"I can't thank you enough," said Lisa sincerely.

Over the next half hour, the lies began to come more easily. "Yes, of course! I knew her name was Marge, but I couldn't remember if it was Cotter or Carter. So embarrassing! Anyway, she said that she thinks . . ."

Despite dealing with an answering machine, to which she responded by hanging up, her results were as close to conclusive as she could have hoped. "The Retreat" had been traced over on the tablet by the phone five times. There were five check marks next to the name.

There was one more call to make. A Harold Minot residence. It was another answering machine. It was lucky that this person wasn't at home, she thought, since she would have given her deception away by failing to pronounce the name *Min-OH,* as did the pleasant, recorded voice. She would have liked one more confirmation, but it didn't matter. She had enough.

Chapter
13

THEY WERE THERE, where Lisa had hoped to find them. About a dozen men in sweatpants and long-sleeved jerseys, playing touch football on the east edge of Welles Park. Plus ça change, plus c'est la même chose, she thought. People can get married, have children, change jobs, buy houses; they find some way to keep on doing the things they really love. For this group, at least one of those things was football.

She recognized Rick Lopas immediately—tall, bulky, still curly-haired, and younger than he looked. He went deep, hooked to his right, and glanced back for the pass, which sailed over his head. Lisa sat down on a bench and watched. The park was pleasant, with dogs scampering after tennis balls and joggers making the circuit. Across the field, a playground was full of children. It would have been nice to bring Luke instead of imposing on Cooper to watch him, not that Cooper had seemed to mind. But she took Luke no-where with her anymore. She couldn't shake the feeling that things were closing in, that neither of them was safe, and that Luke was less safe when they were together. The number of people who knew she was in Chicago had grown and she had come to believe that it would have been better for no one to know that.

If her inquiries had led her to anything, it might have been worth the increased vulnerability. But they had led her nowhere. She knew more, knew a series of facts she mulled over again and again. Still, that's all they were. A series of facts. Not a picture, not even the sketchiest pattern. Rick was unlikely to fill in any gaps, and yet she needed to try.

The game broke up, its participants leaving on bikes or in cars. Rick walked toward Lincoln Avenue, and as he neared her, Lisa waved.

"Hey, toots!" he called out cheerfully, recognizing her. She wondered if he ever used a woman's name. She'd never heard him address any female as anything but "toots." His lighthearted kindliness took any offense out of what would be, in a cruder man, a questionable idiosyncrasy.

They sat on the bench and talked. "So I'm looking for Carl," she said. "And I remembered that you and he used to do this. Clearly you, at any rate, still do."

"So does he, except lately," said Rick. "He didn't show up last week either. I knew you were looking for him. Glen left a message with my wife a few days back and she told me. I would have called you, but Glen didn't leave your number. Anyway, I don't know where he is; haven't seen him for about a week and a half. But," he said, pushing cleats off his feet and dropping gym shoes onto the grass, "I expect to see him again soon."

"When?"

He shrugged. "Don't know for sure. But he borrowed a shitload of AV stuff and said he'd get it back to me soon. Which he'd better do, seeing it isn't all mine, and I've got to get it back to the department."

"What did he want AV stuff for?" asked Lisa.

"Exactly what I asked him. He said it was a long story. But I'm going to turn down Carl? The man got me *through* Major English Poets."

"So you don't know where he is? I need to find him, like, right *now.*"

"Yeah?" Rick looked at her closely. "What's up?"

"Talk about long stories . . ." She smiled. "It doesn't matter. I just need to find him."

"Sorry, toots. I don't even know his phone number. I tried calling the number I had for him, and it was disconnected. But he lives up near Wrigley Field."

"Yeah," said Lisa noncommittally. "Say, did you hear about Gerry?"

Rick didn't answer. He leaned down and tied his shoes. When he straightened up, his eyes were hard.

"I heard about Gerry. I wasn't surprised."

Lisa felt, for an instant, where her skin stopped and air began. "Why not?"

He hitched sideways on the bench and leaned forward, his arms on his knees. "Look, we don't know each other all that well, so I probably shouldn't say anything. But that man . . . He was a cop, you know. Worked out of the same precinct as Scott Murray. Well, I'd bet money he wasn't straight."

"Why?"

"Why wasn't he straight? That's a little deep for me. Or why do I think he wasn't? That's easy. He had too much money."

"There *are* cops who have independent incomes, you know," said Lisa. She really had no interest in defending Gerry. She had disliked him forcefully herself. But she did want to know where Rick's suspicions came from. "Family money?"

"That's what he told people," said Rick. "So that's what everyone thought. But his parents came to graduation.

168

Those people were not wealthy, believe me."

"Okay, then, a second job."

"Right. A second job. He had one, doing something. You knew Gerry. How hard do *you* think he worked? All right, maybe. But it wasn't just the car he drove or the vacations he took. It was *him*. There was always something about him, something not quite right. Look, I wouldn't have had anything to do with the guy, but he was really tight with Carl, and Carl's okay. So I saw Gerry now and then—at these goofy football games we play on Sundays, or when Carl had poker at his place. The result was, I saw him more than I wanted to. Let me say this about that. Nothing I saw dispelled the idea that the man was out for whatever he could get."

Strange, thought Lisa, pedaling away from the park on the ancient bike she'd borrowed from Werner Schwartz's garage. His reaction to Gerry was more than indignation; it was bitterness. Stranger still was Carl's need for audiovisual equipment. He'd never had any interest that she knew of in cameras of any kind except for being in front of them. She certainly hadn't seen any AV equipment at his apartment.

CARL MCCAIN WAS dreaming. He was walking on the beach and someone was coming toward him, running, waving, calling out. The sound of the waves obscured the voice. He didn't know whether to hurry forward, see who it was, or turn and run. The figure got closer. It was waving more frantically. It was a man, muscular, dark-haired. It came closer. It was Gerry, with a look of stark terror, tears running down his face. And then Carl realized that the noise wasn't waves. It was a train, and it had materialized behind Gerry, overtaking him. The sand Carl was walking on was between tracks, and now he began to stumble over the ties. Gerry glanced back over his shoulder. The train was looming. He couldn't outrun it. *Get off the tracks!* Carl was trying to scream, but his voice was tiny, weak. The train bore down and Carl realized the figure it was bearing down on wasn't Gerry at all. It was too small to be Gerry, too young, too . . . It was Luke. Carl began running, struggling for speed, desperately trying to make a sound. *Get off the tracks!* He would never get to him in time. Louder, he had to shout louder. Louder! *Get off the tracks!*

The hoarse sound of his shout woke him. He lay on the foam mattress, heart pounding, gasping. He sat up, still shivering with fear, adrenaline surging. Through the small window, high above the street, he could see children playing. No one pursued them. Their fathers hadn't held them up like bait, hadn't stupidly, criminally victimized them in some crazed notion that things could be made to work out.

Carl gulped air, trying to calm the nausea that had overcome him. It wasn't the first time he'd had the dream, or versions of it. Ever since Wednesday afternoon, when he'd gone out for a walk, stir-crazy and bored, and come back with the paper. Ever since he'd seen the short article on page three, headlined "Off-Duty Cop Found Shot to Death," and read the copy, he'd been having the dream.

Until then, he'd clung to the belief that, given time, he could convince Gerry that he could cause some pretty major trouble, at least for Gerry himself. Turning state's evidence would start to look to his friend like a good idea. Even if the Lake Forest house didn't lure Gerry's associates into providing the proof Carl needed, Gerry's basic intelligence would prevail. It had to.

Now there wasn't even that slight possibility. He wasn't going to get any help from Gerry. Gerry hadn't even been able to save himself.

What Carl knew was on computer disks in a safe-deposit box and on paper in a sealed envelope in his lawyer's office. What he needed was what the borrowed video cameras and tape recorders and his own eyes and ears would reveal if his plan worked. But it hadn't worked yet. He was into his eighth day holed up in this glorious Lake Forest house, holed up with the silver and the art and the coin collections. Or so it looked on paper. The application for household insurance listed everything, identified the security system, detailed the methods taken to protect so many priceless possessions. There were pages of riders, which Carl now knew were called schedules, specifically covering the most valuable items. The owners of the house, Mr. and Mrs. Franklin Pierce, were enjoying a long vacation in Europe. The fact that their most valuable possessions were locked safely away in bank vaults until their return, some three months from now, was not revealed on any of the paperwork.

He'd have to go out soon, go out and find something to eat. Then he'd try Lisa again. He'd been calling for four days. Where could they be? On the first day, he'd talked briefly to the answering machine. "Lisa, it's me! Pick it up, if you're there." She hadn't picked up. He hadn't been too concerned; he knew she took Luke out for long walks; they went to town. But she hadn't been home the next day, or the next, or the next.

If no one answered today, he'd have to drive up there tomorrow. He couldn't stand the worry much longer. He'd been concerned, of course, ever since he'd left his son in Turner Falls. But concern intensified to severe anxiety when he noticed the missing picture.

He was standing in his living room, mentally checking his preparations for this stay in Lake Forest, when he glanced at the mantel. Something was wrong, but what? It took him a full minute to realize that the picture of Luke and Sirius was gone. The remaining pictures had been adjusted to take up the space. How long ago had the picture been removed? He had no idea.

The fact that it was gone meant several things. Most obviously, it meant that Carl had been located. It did not, at least yet, mean that Luke had been located. If that were the case, Carl would have heard about it. Luke, after all, was merely a means to get to him. But what if he'd been found since Carl left home, during his lonely sojourn in Lake Forest? Carl couldn't have heard about that. No one, absolutely no one, knew where he was. And if Luke was safe, where was he? Where was Lisa?

She must have taken Luke somewhere, on some kind of trip. That's all it was, some kind of trip. But someone had called the number he'd left with her. A woman had called looking for him. Maybe Joanna, maybe . . . oh, any number of women. Maybe Lisa.

He couldn't take more than another night anyway. Another night of starting at every tiny noise, of listening to the polished wooden floors creak with the footsteps of nonexistent invaders. The whole plan had been a long shot, but it had been the only plan he could come up with. His experience in front of a camera had helped enormously in trying to work behind one. Behind several. He'd set them up, obscured by shrubbery, outdoors. They turned on automatically when the motion-detector lights turned on. But so far, they'd recorded nothing more interesting than the neighbor's cat, though they'd recorded it repeatedly.

If no one came tonight, he was packing it in. He'd have to just pick out a police station and walk in, cross his fingers, hope they could fill in the missing pieces, hope they could get the evidence he lacked, hope, most of all, the officer he spoke to wasn't involved and wasn't reporting to anyone who was.

He went out the back door, walked three blocks to his car, drove toward the business section of the town, and parked in front of a small grocery store. A dark blue Pontiac cruised past and stopped a half block away.

* * *

"You color the trees and I color the deers." Luke handed Lisa a green crayon and a black one. He patted his chosen page in the coloring book and selected a tawny brown from the new box of crayons. Cooper had purchased the largest size, which was, to Lisa's mind, completely unnecessary. "Some of them is green and some of them is black."

"Some of what is black?"

Luke looked at her patiently. "Some of the trees."

"I never saw a black tree except at night. I can *make* them black, if that's what you want. I just never saw one that color. Well, maybe the trunks, if they're wet. They might look black."

"Some trees *is* black. All over." He pointed to the leaves, branches, and trunks. "Black, black, black. My grandma said so."

"Your grandma said there are trees with black leaves?"

"Uh-huh." He bent over the page, casually secure in his knowledge.

"What, exactly, did your grandma say?"

"She said about going to the black forest. So the trees there is *black*." He colored diligently for a few minutes. "She's going to bring me a present when she comes back. And me and my dad, we'll go to her house and play pool just like we used to do. Except someplace else 'cause they's moving. My grandma and my grandpa."

So that's where she was, Germany. Carl had been more vague. Did it matter? She couldn't help find her son from Germany. Or could she? Might she possibly know something Carl's closest friends didn't know, have some idea Lisa hadn't thought of? She would try to help. Lisa, having met her once, was sure of that.

She had come to opening night for a show Carl was in. An attractive, efficient woman, pleasant and cheerful, married to a man who wasn't Carl's father. There had been something odd about her. What was it? The memory was gone. Whatever it was, it had nothing to do with a lack of friendliness. Even if Lisa said nothing about Luke, nothing to frighten her, she would try to help. She was the type. And maybe she'd point in a direction Lisa hadn't thought to go. But how could one find a person in Germany? If she was even *in* Germany.

Lisa colored carefully. Luke had high standards. Neighbors. That was it. Neighbors might know. Carl had grown up in . . . where was it? She had known once. He had grown up there, which meant that neighbors might be longtime friends.

"They haven't moved yet?" she asked.

"They *gonna* move. Too cold by Chicago."

"Where does your grandma live now?"

"I said already, where the trees are black. She's coming home someday and she's bringing me a present."

"But where's her house? The one she'll come home *to* before she moves away?"

Luke shrugged. "Not so far."

Luke was right; it wasn't far. Lisa had never been there, but it couldn't be far. It was close enough to drive into town with some neighbors for the opening of a minor play in a minor theater in which one's son had a minor role. The neighbor lady had been quite striking, amiable, straightforward, and clearly crazy about Carl. The next month, a Christmas card had come from her. Lisa remembered pronouncing the name mentally and having no idea who the sender was until Carl said her name out loud. What had that name been?

More important, what was his mother's name? She was married to someone with a president's name. Lisa remembered that. An old-time president. Not very famous, relative to Washington, Madison, Jefferson, et al. Mrs. Benjamin Harrison?

"What's your grandpa's name?"

"I got two."

"The one who's married to the grandma you've been telling me about."

"Grandpa Frank."

Franklin Pierce. Mrs. Franklin Pierce.

"I'll be back in a minute to finish the trees," she said, heading for the kitchen phone. "In just a minute."

Information for the northern suburbs revealed that there was one listing for a Franklin Pierce. In Lake Forest. "Here's your number," said the operator, and the line switched to a prerecorded voice before she could ask the address. She called Name and Address, gave the number, and got an address. Tomorrow, first thing, she would go up there and talk to the neighbors.

Luke was carefully coloring a doe's eyes a vapid baby blue. "Can we go to the playground?" he asked.

"No," said Lisa. "It's almost dinnertime."

"Bob's not here. We gotta wait for him. We could go to the playground 'til he comes home."

"He's not coming home for dinner. He's got a meeting tonight with somebody he's doing work with. It's just us, boyo."

COOPER CHEWED THOUGHTFULLY on a mouthful of broiled salmon and looked across the table at his potential client. The fish was good, the salad was acceptable, and the chef had done a masterful job with what, in a lesser restaurant, would have been merely boiled new potatoes. The wine was exceptional. He wondered if Lisa would like it here. He wished he were eating at home. Well, he'd be home soon. This meeting appeared to be more of an excuse for Larry Steiner to avoid eating alone than an actual exploration of the proposal PTS had submitted to his company.

"So explain this 'point biserial' statistic again," said

Steiner. "I didn't understand that one." He didn't really care about point biserials, and Cooper knew it. He was, however, making a good show of having an inquiring mind. Which was fine with Cooper, who enjoyed talking about statistics. How many people ever asked?

"It's a way of measuring a test item's validity. If, in general, people who do well on a test as a whole do poorly on a particular item, that item has a low point biserial. You don't have to know *why* those able examinees do poorly on that item; the fact that they do poorly on it means that it's, well, counterproductive. What do you learn from it? Nada. Or worse than nada. Because you may think you're learning something, but it probably isn't what you think you're learning. Maybe your keyed answer's just wrong, but if you check that and still think you keyed it correctly, well, a heck of a lot of bright people are disagreeing with you. So get rid of it."

"So when my kid takes a standardized test in school, that test's been through all this kind of analysis?" Steiner reached for the wine and refilled his glass.

And this whole conversation isn't really about what PTS can do for your company, is it? thought Cooper. You dragged me out on a Sunday night to talk about why your kid's test scores are lower than you think they ought to be. "You bet, Chet," he said. You bet, Chet? Was the wine getting to him? "You know, the tests we're proposing to develop for you aren't going to be much like nationally standardized tests, right?"

"Oh, sure. Sure."

Steiner's questions had so far seemed to reveal an entrenched distrust of testing. Whether that indicated he was the wrong person for Pacific Machineries to have sent out for this meeting or the right one, Cooper was still trying to decide.

Steiner sighed. "You got kids?"

Cooper shook his head. If the man wanted to ask him about standardized tests, the kind Steiner's kid was probably having trouble with, why didn't he just ask him? That would be a more fruitful exploration than the conversation they were supposed to be, but had not yet been, having.

"No, no kids," he said. He'd answered the question many times before quite casually. Ever been to the Hebrides? No, can't say as I have. Now he found himself wanting to add "yet."

"Yet," he said.

Steiner leaned back, hooked a thumb over his belt, and smiled. "Ah. Married?"

"Nope." This time he added nothing. His personal life was not a topic he had any desire to open to scrutiny. Or even light conversation. He looked around the restaurant, searching for a phone. Steiner had waved away the dessert menu, which meant this meeting was almost over. They'd leave; he'd drop Steiner at the Palmer House; the rest of the night was his. There was a design of some sort to the puzzle he and Lisa were working on. Maybe they'd put one piece in place tonight. He pushed back his chair.

"I've got to make a quick call, Larry," he said. "I'll be right back."

The phone at his house was busy. Well, it didn't matter. He'd be home in half an hour. He went back to the table and beckoned to the waiter.

"So, Dr. Cooper," said Steiner, leaning forward. "Let's get down to brass tacks. How about we talk things over at the bar on the ninety-fifth floor over at the Hancock? There's just a few details to hammer out, and we can close this deal."

Cooper looked at him in blank dismay. Irritation made him rude. "Do you mean the Signature Lounge? It's on the ninety-*sixth* floor."

Steiner seemed not to have heard. "I told Susan I was going to the ninety-fifth this trip if it killed me."

It might, thought Cooper. It just might.

LUKE WAS ASLEEP and the dishes were washed. Lisa had tried the Pierce number before taking Luke up to bed, in case he was wrong and they were back. The answering service was bland, efficient, and obdurate. "No, I can't give you any information whatsoever. I will be more than happy to take a message."

She stared across the kitchen at the refrigerator door waiting for pieces to fall, arrange themselves, make sense. Those insurance forms that Carl had been filling out with Joe Thatcher, filling out while he had been frantically trying to stop the danger to Luke, to himself . . . were they for his mother and stepfather? If so, why hadn't he told Joe that? Or had Joe just forgotten? The forms would have the applicant's name and address. It was worth checking—if Joe remembered any such details.

She went in search of the notes from her conversation with Beth, the class agent. Back in the kitchen, she tried Joe's home number. The answering machine picked up, producing Joe's familiar friendly drawl.

"Hey! Don't go away! Leave a message, and I'll get back to you."

She hung up without waiting for the beep. He wouldn't remember the name and address from a form he'd last looked at weeks ago. And what if he did? What if it *was* insurance for the Franklin Pierces of Lake Forest who were traveling in Europe? What did that have to do with anything? And then, suddenly, she knew.

She felt sick. Insurance brokers—at least one per relevant address downtown. Security guards—the same company working each of those buildings. Robberies in houses where the owners were away and the dogs were having canine cocktails at The Retreat. Carl's desperate rush to situate a thick insurance application folder in a file drawer at an insurance office. An insurance office in a building guarded by Total Security. She didn't need to put it together; it put itself together. And, as it did, she remembered.

Mrs. Harold Minot, robbery victim, was Carl's mother's neighbor.

She dialed the Minot residence. This time, an actual human being answered instead of a recording.

"Mrs. Minot?"

"Yes?" The voice was casual, friendly.

"Hi. I met you once years ago. My name's Lisa Jacobi and I'm a friend of Carl's, Mrs. Pierce's son."

"Oh, yes!"

"I'm calling because . . . well, this is an odd question, I know, but did you have a robbery lately?"

"Why, yes. Did Carl tell you?"

"No. Does he know?"

"Oh, yes. He stopped by to sympathize, the dear. We chatted for a long time."

"Did Carl ask a lot of questions?"

Mrs. Minot hesitated.

Lisa took a deep breath. "Mrs. Minot. I know it seems like I'm the one who's asking a lot of questions, but if you could just humor me. I'm taking care of Carl's son, Luke, and there's a reason that I need to know. It's important. Really, it is."

"All right. The answer is no, not a lot. He didn't, well, he didn't pry or anything. I remember he asked me about the Tressori."

"The what?"

"Oh, we had a wonderful little reproduction of a Tressori. You know, the Italian sculptor? It was a very nice copy, made from the same stone as the original. Most people thought it was genuine and, I admit, we kind of displayed it as if it was. But it wasn't, of course. A real Tressori doesn't belong anyplace but in a museum. Ours was just worth maybe a few hundred dollars. We listed it on the police report that way, naturally. I mean, it was just insured the same way as the TV—not ridered or anything like the original artwork. But losing it was upsetting because we can't get another. At least not one nearly that fine."

"So you told Carl it was a copy?"

"I assume so. I don't remember."

It didn't matter whether Carl knew or not. What mattered was that he was interested. What mattered was that he was somehow involved in a series of robberies on the North Shore. Just one more question.

"Do you have a dog that was boarding someplace during the robbery and did you tell Carl that?"

"I think I told him. Bitsy was staying at a lovely place, thank goodness. The Retreat."

The Retreat. Lisa breathed a hurried thanks and hung up. She was a fool, an idiot. She was horrified by how stupid she'd been. Mitchell had handed her a crucial bit of knowledge and she'd ignored it. Worse than ignored it, dismissed it. Carl *had* offered to take care of Lorna's dog. Information gave her the number she sought.

"Hi, sorry to call so late, but this is Mrs. Franklin Pierce and we just got back to town—had to cut our trip short—and I've forgotten what the earliest time is that we can come get our dog."

"We open at seven-thirty for pickups." The young man was bored but polite.

"Great. But look, could I bother you to check something for me?" She flecked her voice with mild insinuation. "I would be so grateful and . . . by the way, what's your name, so I can be sure to leave a little something for you?"

The young man would, he assured her, be glad to help. No trouble at all. And his name was Howard.

"Would you just look up our file. Pierce is the name." She spelled it and kept talking, afraid Howard would ask what her dog's name was. "Just look it up and make sure everything is fine. My husband won't be able to get to sleep until he knows. You'd think he could wait one more night, but he's like a mother hen." Needing to be sure he had actually located a file, the Pierce file, she added, "And tell me what the darling ate for dinner. I can't thank you enough, Howard."

She waited. Either Howie had trouble alphabetizing or he wanted her to think this was an extremely time-consuming task, or . . . or there was no dog belonging to the Pierces at the kennel.

"Professor is fine, Mrs. Pierce." Howard was soothing. "He had four cups of Science Diet, just like your husband requested. And a cookie."

"Oh, thank you," said Lisa. "You're just a dear. Good night."

The dog registered as belonging to the Pierces did not, in fact, belong to them. Lisa had recalled the odd thing about Carl's mother. She was terrified of dogs.

Lisa had found Carl. She knew that with certainty. What she didn't know was if she'd found him in time.

Chapter
14

WERNER SCHWARTZ'S DAUGHTER, Mary Ruth, opened the door to Lisa's frantic knock and agreed, with friendly enthusiasm, to lend both her car and her baby-sitting skills.

"Dad and I can play cribbage just as well next door as here." She exhaled a cloud of smoke. "The car's a mess, honey. I hit every fast-food place between Albuquerque and Chicago, and most of the White Hen Pantries. And Jeff—he's my oldest—he's fooled with the engine and the muffler, so you may get invited to drag . . ."

Lisa didn't care. "I don't know when Cooper'll be back. He may beat me home. I don't know how long I'll be."

"Well, we'll stay 'til somebody gets there. If Dad nods off, I'll send him home. I never go to bed before two, so don't you worry."

Mary Ruth was right. The car looked like a pit crew had camped in the backseat on the way to and from its last raceway engagement. No, Lisa decided, pit crews probably drank something besides sixteen-ounce bottles of Coke. It was a Cub Scout troop that had camped in the car. She drove conservatively, aware that she invited suspicion and that, driving without a license, she couldn't afford it.

The northern suburbs were easy to reach from the Edens Expressway, and the street map from Cooper's desk showed Whittier curving gently through Lake Forest. Lisa noted the closest exit and headed for it, stifling the urge to exploit the big engine. Cars whizzed past her.

Inside the boundaries of Lake Forest, tranquillity hung in the air, thick enough to smell. Sections of the winding road were as dark as the lanes through the woods near the cabin, but it was impossible to believe that rabbits died among these trees or, indeed, that any battles ever raged there. She drove slowly, pulling over from time to time to check her progress on the map. She passed huge homes, sedate and confident, and smaller ones, jauntier but still composed. It was late, close to midnight, and no children played outside to disrupt the serenity with shouts or jeers. Disagreements, if such things occurred behind the thick doors and leaded glass, retained their privacy.

She turned left onto Whittier. According to the map, there wasn't far to go. She felt the tight clutching inside that comes from a knowledge that you're completely unprepared for the inevitable, as in a dream where not only is the final Comparative Government exam unexpectedly occurring at this very moment, but the political science building, where you're supposed to take it, isn't located where it always has been.

The road curved gently. A massive brick house rose on the left behind a deep front yard. The porch light glowed, revealing brass numbers above the door. Next to it but decently distant, a more graceful Victorian frame house sat slumbering behind a wide veranda. It, too, was set back from the street. On the right, a stark, modern house blazed white in the darkness.

The next house, around another bend, was 946. Lisa drove another hundred yards, pulled to the side, and parked.

Oak and maple grew close to the road and formed wide, wooded barriers between the house and its neighbor on either side. In the yard itself, magnolias survived Illinois's frigid winters by their proximity to the lake. Their buds had begun but it would be weeks before they exploded into masses of delicate pink.

Lisa moved quickly and silently through the thicker trees. It was very dark. One light, in what was probably a bathroom, gleamed dully but failed to illumine the yard.

She took a deep breath, crossed the grass to the house in a few quick steps, and pressed against the stucco. Here, next to the walls, the grass had been dug away to be replaced by annual beds and the earth was soft under her feet. The foundation of the house rose three feet before the wooden frame began, making the first floor high. The windowsills were on a level with her chin.

A light came on, to her right. Lisa, keeping her back a scant inch from the house to prevent the stucco from catching on the fibers of her sweater, moved sideways toward it.

The curtains were closed. The heavy fabric hung, impenetrable and gapless. There was a murmur of voices from inside the room but the words were undetectable.

Something pushed against Lisa's leg and she gasped and crouched, stifling a yell of surprise. A very large, somewhat fat cat pressed its head against her hand and mewed softly. Ask, and it shall be given you, thought Lisa. She picked up the cat and stood. Seek, and ye shall find.

Lisa let out a furious meow, loud and harsh in the darkness. As the curtains parted, she tossed the cat gently into the yard. It landed and glared back at her. A flashlight beam pierced the blackness outside and picked up the feline's indignant stalk toward the trees.

The inside of the room had been revealed for a brief instant. Not long enough to count the people, only to see that there were several, that one of them had his hands tied behind his back, and that the bound figure was Carl.

Lisa moved back to the corner of the house and sprang to the shelter of the trees. She needed help—fearless, preferably burly, help. But though running to a nearby house and calling the police would undoubtedly provide it, the idea of law officers banging on the door of 946 Whittier left her with hideous visions of Carl as a hostage.

She broke through the trees onto a wide, dark lawn. The police had to come, had to keep Carl from being dragged out of the house and thrown into a car, to depart to heaven knew where. But they had to leave the people at 946 believing that, while a quick departure was desirable, the police were not coming for them. They had to leave Carl behind.

She raced up the road to where she'd left the car. She gunned the engine, drove fifty yards, and slammed on the brakes. The car squealed in protest and skidded sideways. She jabbed at the radio, searching for the right station, and when she'd found it, cranked the volume and rolled down her window. Wheeling into a three-point turn, she gunned the engine again, releasing the clutch enough to lurch forward briefly. She slammed on the brakes. The car rocked forward, slamming her against the steering wheel.

Lights came on in bedroom windows. Come on, thought Lisa, come on!

Mexican music pulsed into the night. Lisa laughed loudly and hysterically. "¡Te voy a matar, cabrón! ¡Hijo de tu chingada!" The vulgar phrases fit her mood.

She stepped on the gas and laid rubber down the road, squealed to another stop. Come on! her mind was screaming. You know you can't venture into the darkness to check me out; I might do anything. I'll probably pull out a knife and cut off your nose! There are at least two of me, maybe more. I am not the neighborhood kids, am I now, am I! Come on!

She cruised around the bend in the road toward 946 and started up the driveway. Fifty feet from the house, she stopped again and aimed a Coke bottle at a tree. It made a satisfying, tinkling crash as it shattered. She laughed hysterically again, barreled backward to the road, and pulled over. She yanked open the glove compartment. There were maps for every state from New Mexico to Illinois and several books of matches. She got out without turning off the engine, allowing the radio to continue to blare, and ran toward the house, through the trees next to the driveway, stopping only long enough to sweep up an armful of damp leaves.

Circling around toward the yard on the opposite side of the house from the room where Carl had been, she knelt on the dark lawn, ripping the maps apart and crumpling the paper. The car radio howled from the road. The papers caught on the second match, crackling into fire. She tossed on a small handful of leaves, more paper, more leaves.

They're on their way, she thought. They're on their way or I'm wrong about this entire community. She ran back to the car and turned off the engine and the radio, straining to hear. A car was coming, maybe two, coming fast. She turned the engine on again, leaving the radio off, and drove just into the long curve of the neighbor's driveway. She got out and walked to the road, waving at the police cars as they approached and stopped next to her.

A policeman rolled down his window. "You the lady that called?"

"No, but thank goodness someone did!" Lisa gestured furiously. "They were driving a big, dark car. Maybe dark blue. I think it was a Pontiac. God only knows where they are now!"

"Didn't see anything suspicious coming this way," the policeman's partner muttered, twisting around to pull a nightstick out of the backseat.

Lisa let out a small shriek and pointed at 946. "Is that smoke? Oh my God; it's smoke! Nobody's living in that house; there's no reason for smoke unless . . ."

The policemen looked confused. The smoke was completely invisible against the sky's blackness. This wealthy young woman had either incredible eyesight or a bad case of hysteria.

"Can't you smell it?" shrieked Lisa.

A faint whiff of a disturbing smell reached the policemen. "By God, she's right!"

The police car backed into a hasty turn and careened into the driveway of 946. Lisa faded quickly into the trees, willing her thought waves into the stucco house. They're coming to check things out. Leave while you can!

She moved through the thicket. Emerging from cover near the back of the house, she ran quickly toward the door. Either the men had left it unlocked during a hurried departure, or they were still inside.

She yanked the door open, closed it behind her, and waited for her eyes to adjust to the more complete darkness inside. There was a thumping sound ahead of her in the caverns of the empty house, and she felt her way slowly toward the noise.

She was through one doorway, then another, and in the same room with the sound. She struck a match.

Carl sat against the wall, wrists and ankles tied. His mouth was taped. His eyes were open and Lisa, kneeling beside him, saw fury give way to startled confusion.

"Shhh," she whispered. "Be very quiet. We're getting out of here." She waved the match out as its creeping flame burned her fingers, and lit another. Holding it in her left hand, she used her right to rip the tape off Carl's mouth.

"Sorry."

"Lisa! What—"

"Shhh." Digging her pocketknife out of her jeans pocket, she cut through the cords around Carl's wrists, then his ankles.

"Come on," she murmured, taking one of his hands in hers. "Back door."

Outside, she could see the rotating light from the police car on the far side of the house and hear one of the policemen talking into his radio. She pulled Carl across the lawn to the trees.

Thirty feet in, she stopped at Carl's insistent tug. He clutched her, one cold hand holding her head against him. His jawbone dug painfully into her temple. His grip was strong and firm. She put her arms around him, wanting time to stop.

"Luke?" he whispered.

"He's fine; he's fine."

"How . . . ?"

"I'll tell you everything when we're away from here."

They reached the car and started slowly down the road. A police car approached from the opposite direction. Lisa blinked her lights and stopped, leaning out the window.

"My husband and I wondered if you found the car . . ."

"No, ma'am. There's sure no sign of anybody now."

The news was depressing but not surprising. Lisa waved and smiled gratefully as the policeman pulled away, shaking his head bemusedly at the eccentricities of the rich lady who drove a beater. He turned into the driveway where his co-workers were stamping out the remains of a small but smoky fire.

IT WAS EASIER to talk to Carl than it used to be. Maybe, thought Lisa, because she was so relieved to have found him. She told him about the attack on the cabin, about Cooper, about Joe, about calling the kennel.

He leaned back into the seat and put one long-fingered hand on the back of her neck, rubbing gently. "And here I thought you were one of those girls too gorgeous to have a brain."

The immediate danger past, fear and dread had departed, leaving him exaggeratedly casual, flip. Lisa knew it wouldn't last. "It's just more pleasant for you," she said, "to think that I'm brilliant than that you're intensely stupid and any fool, gorgeous or not, could stumble onto what you were up to."

"There you go," said Carl. She glanced over at him. She could see him now in the highway light. He smiled, his wide, heart-stopping smile. He looked sleepy.

"They're just more careful than you could have guessed, darling boy," said Lisa. "Which is one reason nobody's caught them. They must have been watching the house for a while. They probably watch every house, for at least a day, before they break in."

She hesitated and went on. "We're amateurs, Carl. It doesn't matter if we're smart or stupid . . . or, at least, it doesn't matter enough. We have to tell somebody, somebody with the resources and the experience and . . . We have to tell the police. Even if there are more cops in this thing besides Gerry. Cooper says, and I know he's right, that—"

"I don't really care what Cooper says." Carl's voice was strained. "It's not the idea of a conspiracy that's stopping me. I'm not a fool, Lisa. But if I have to turn in the statue, I've got nothing. What stopped them from wasting me back there? Not their tender hearts."

He told her about Luke's discovery of the statue and his own foolish curiosity. "When I found out who insured all the victims and where their offices were, it started to come together. I only noticed that the buildings all used Total Security because I'd seen Gerry in his uniform so often. It's a big operation, Leese. This isn't a couple of moonlighting cops gone bad; it's a lot too well organized for that. And, right now, the whole thing could tumble if they can't retrieve that statue."

His voice had lost any trace of lightness. "That's what they're after, Leese. They told me they had Luke, and not having been able to reach you, I was pretty close to believing them. So they probably would have gotten it. And once they'd gotten it—maybe, at this point, even if they hadn't gotten it—the next you would have heard of me would have been a news report in a few weeks about unidentified remains found in a forest preserve. Or, more likely, you would never have heard anything."

He was right. Lisa knew it. She tried out the vision it called up and rejected it. Some ideas were better left unexplored. A driver, annoyed at the legal speed she maintained, pulled around and cut back into the lane. "What do you mean, even if they hadn't gotten it?"

"It's gone on too long. I think the statue kept me alive at the beginning. I don't think it will anymore. Reading that they'd murdered Gerry . . . that made it pretty clear that they're fixated on ending this thing."

"But you can't prove anything, even with the statue. You don't *know* anything. If the cops had the statue, why would anyone bother with you?"

"They don't know how much I know. They don't know how much Gerry told me. For all they know, I'm looking for the last name or the ultimate proof or . . . Why would they risk it? They don't risk much of anything. That's why I needed the videotape. See, they disarm the alarm systems. They cut the phone lines to the police station, or . . . Well, I don't know what all they do, but the alarm systems never work."

Lisa slowed to let a merging driver into her lane. "So how were you going to survive? If they hadn't known you were there, which they did, how were you going to ever get a chance to get out of there with whatever videotape evidence you had? Once they got in, they'd find you. They *did* find you."

"Yeah. They did find me. But only because they knew I was there. They changed everything. They came in the front.

They *never* come in the front. I didn't have an alarm rigged there; I didn't even have a camera set up out there. I never even heard them."

He sighed. "It wasn't really so stupid, Leese. All I was counting on was logic. They'd come in, I figured, in their normal way, through the back or a window. Probably the back since the windows are high. They'd see that there wasn't anything there, because there *isn't* anything there. Why would anyone go searching for coin collections in a house that doesn't even have furniture? My mother's putting the place on the market after they get back from Europe. She's already moved everything to Arizona. So who'd stick around? Who'd go looking in the attic for me, snuggled up with a book, a flashlight, and a cellular phone? They'd have to figure their information was wrong, that's all. The insurance papers listed the wrong address, or somebody fucked up, or . . . It doesn't matter what they thought about why the house was empty. They'd see it was empty and they'd leave. And I'd have them on tape, breaking in. I'd have their conversation too, while they discussed it."

"No, it wasn't stupid. All that was stupid was trying to do it on your own. Why didn't you at least tell Joe? He could have helped, couldn't he? I mean, he wouldn't much care for the idea that the security firm that guards his building is rifling his files."

"Right," said Carl. "I tell Joe exactly what I'm up to. I tell him to just act normal, just put the application where he'd always put a new, pending policy. Don't act strange, I tell him. Don't look funny at the uniformed guy in the lobby. And, for heaven's sake, don't protect any of your hundreds of trusting clients by locking up the paper copies of their policies with locks the guards don't have keys for. Oh, and by the way, Joe, don't say anything to anybody. This? To Joe? He's a great guy, but he's got a major flaw—he knows better how to do everything. In an entire semester with him as my partner in chem lab, I never so much as lit the Bunsen burner. He would never have let me just do what I had to do. He would have had a better way. Only he doesn't have Luke, so I don't want any part of his better way, whatever it might be."

Yes, thought Lisa. That was Joe, all right. Maybe that's why she had liked him more the other evening than she'd remembered—she was getting used to men who always knew better how to do everything.

"I would have loved to tell him," he went on, "or Scott or Rick or Mitch or Glen. Someone."

"Well now you have to," she said. "Because they'll find you again. Or they'll find Luke again. Maybe soon. You can't do this by yourself. We can't by ourselves. It just comes back to that."

Carl didn't answer. Tomorrow, thought Lisa. He couldn't think tonight and neither, really, could she.

Chapter 15

COOPER AWOKE SLOWLY, struggling toward consciousness. He lay still, aware that he was angry, wondering why. The night before came back to him—his frantic waiting and then the sound of footsteps on the porch.

Oh, she'd explained her sudden departure. She'd made sense out of why, when he came home ready to work, he found Werner and his daughter huddled over the kitchen table moving pegs on a board. Yes, she'd told him what had happened. But it was clear he was out of it now, an interloper in his own home.

Let them figure it out, make their decisions, do what they had to do. It was their business. Except for Luke. Luke was his business too, whether they wanted him to be or not. He could wash his hands of Lisa. It would be a relief. The way she'd hovered around Carl made him shudder. He didn't know her after all.

Carl looked exactly like he'd pictured him. Dark brown hair that fell forward when he bent over. Thin skin over good bones. Tall, bony, and very young. Like Lisa. Not that Lisa was bony. Slender but not bony. She was . . . He sat on the edge of the bed and shook his head angrily, seeing the tenderness in her eyes when she looked at Carl.

He got up and went into the bathroom to shave. He had planned to spend the day trying to take thirty thousand off the bid for Larry Steiner's company. That plan was gone. The price was a bargain at the bid amount, and if Steiner couldn't see it, let him take his business elsewhere. If Steiner hadn't had to have those last drinks, hadn't had to talk and talk so endlessly about his aggravations with the labor unions, Cooper would have been home in time to go with Lisa. Damn Steiner. He should *add* thirty thousand to the bid.

His angry face stared back at him from the mirror. He knew Lisa was up; he'd heard her moving quietly downstairs. She probably hadn't slept well on the couch. Tough. If she wanted to give up her bed to Carl, let her.

He didn't want to see her, but he couldn't leave the house without going downstairs. So he'd go down. It was, after all, his home. Lisa and her boyfriend could gaze soulfully at each other all day and make whatever plans they wanted. He had a company to run. He'd got his car back at last—fuel gauge working and everything functioning properly. He could drive to work again. Shortly now, he'd get his house back, his privacy back, his life back. The sooner the better.

Lisa, sitting at the kitchen table and cradling a cup of coffee, looked up eagerly when he came in. "I didn't know you were up," she said. "No 'That'll Be the Day' reverberating off the bathroom walls. I've been waiting for you. I was going to come get you if you didn't haul your rear end down here pretty soon."

His anger fled. This person was again, however temporarily, Lisa. He poured coffee for himself and sat down across from her. The office could wait. Having abandoned any thoughts of revising the Steiner bid, all he really had to do was sign it.

"Didn't want to wake the company," he said, glad for an easy excuse. His earlier determination to relinquish any involvement in the problem that faced them all had muted along with his indignation. Now the question that he had wanted to ask Lisa when he got home the night before came back to him.

"Tell me about Gerry."

Her face lost its animation. "I told you about him."

"Tell me again what he was like. Tell me what you remember about him. What did you like—not much, I know—or particularly dislike? Just talk."

Lisa leaned back in the chair and looked past him at a fingerprint Luke had left on the wall. She began in a sing-song voice, like an obedient child asked to recite, but as she talked, her voice slowed and deepened with interest.

"Gerry was a handsome, shallow, conceited, sneaky man. He was one of those people who . . ." She searched for the right words, the words that would make the Gerry she had known somehow visible to someone who had never met him. "One of those people who exist on the fringes of what's allowable, crossing over to prohibited behavior only when there's no chance of getting caught. He cheated on tests, but never by writing facts on the cuff of his shirt. He cheated by getting somebody to give him copies beforehand."

She turned her eyes to Cooper. There was bitterness in them. "Yeah, I disliked lots of things about him but I guess what I hated most was the way he'd string girls along. Every attractive female on campus got the eye from Gerry, the 'Whoa! Lookin' *good*!' comment, the deep, meaningful gaze. He couldn't have cared less that there were hearts beating inside those bodies, as long as the bodies were alluring."

She stopped and thought. "Okay. Here's an example. On Tuesday or so, he'd start tucking in coffee in the union or some other fast, easy, fifteen-minute 'date' with the girls who were his second and third choices for Saturday night. So if things didn't work out with his first choice, he had backup. At the last minute, he'd call some girl who thought he really had a thing for her. He'd act like he'd been planning all along they'd spend the evening together. My own roommate sophomore year fell hard for him. She'd turn down dates, thinking he'd call at the last minute. And he'd call at the last minute just often enough to keep her going."

"He covered his ass."

"Well, that's one way to put it. He sure did. And he'd use *any*body. Any class he was having trouble with, you could bet he'd be dating a girl who was acing the course. As soon as Laura got him through anthropology, she stopped hearing from him."

"What did you ever do with him? How'd you know him?"

"I played poker with him because Carl would invite him. He was terrible at poker." She frowned, remembering. "He made the mistake of never getting caught bluffing. So you knew he had it. He's raising on you when you look like you've got a flush? He's got the boat. Not maybe. Absolutely. So you fold. It cost him, but he couldn't help it. He was almost incapable of taking what he saw as a real risk."

Cooper's voice was quiet. "So why did he crawl so far out on a limb with these guys? Was he stupid enough not to know what he was doing?"

"You know, there were times when he seemed stupid and, I guess, he could be. But it wasn't a lack of brainpower. He was stupid in the ways that pathologically self-centered people are. Or when it suited his purposes."

"So, since he wasn't a complete dolt, he had something on them. He had something that he thought would protect him. But it didn't. What was it, and why didn't it work?"

"Because they found whatever it was."

"Or because they didn't know he had it. Maybe he didn't realize that his time had run out. Maybe he had a high card down and didn't know it was time to show it."

Lisa was sitting up straight now, leaning forward. The

bleakness was completely gone from her voice. "It wasn't the statue itself—that wouldn't protect him unless it had their fingerprints all over it, and it wouldn't have. So what was it, and where'd he put it, this high card?"

Carl came in and stood behind Lisa, yawning. It took her a moment to notice him, but when she did, her heart gave its habitual lurch. Cooper saw the almost imperceptible heightening of color in her face and, with sullen determination, pushed his resentment aside. He kept his voice even, casual.

"The statue, Carl. How was it packaged?"

Carl put his hands on Lisa's shoulders and kissed the top of her head. "It was in a box, with some padding stuff. I didn't notice anything else."

"Did you put it back in the same box, keep the same padding?"

"Of course. Why wouldn't I?"

"*Could* there be anything else in there? A paper, maybe a tape . . . ? Anything?"

Carl pulled out a chair and sat, one elbow on his knee. He closed his eyes and rubbed his forehead.

He's playing *The Thinker,* thought Cooper, impatient.

Carl's voice, when it came, was low and critical. "I missed it. Of course. Gerry told me to give the man the *statue.* He made a point of it. Not the package, he said, the *statue.* I thought it had to do with fingerprints, or heaven knew what, that he was going to try to deny being the one who'd actually taken it, plead some kind of innocent ignorance, say he hadn't realized what was in the box. And the box or the wrapping would have nailed him. *There's something in the box.*"

"Yes," said Cooper. "There's something in the box."

LISA STAYED AT the house with Luke while Cooper and Carl went to the bank. "Call me!" she ordered as the door closed behind them.

The crumpled newspapers that supplemented the cotton wool in cushioning the angel Gabriel, when uncrumpled, had clearly been intended to protect Gerry as well. Each piece contained a news story about a North Shore robbery. There were some from the big downtown papers, others from suburban weeklies. In the margins, in Gerry's cramped scrawl, were a series of notes.

Peters drove—Buick Regal (ZR 6141), charged gas at Mobil sta. nr. Willow/Edens. Flynn pocketed silver lighter. In at 1:40, out at 1:58. P. cut himself on glass bkcs getting coin coll.

Each story was so accompanied.

"Lisa was right about him," said Cooper. "The man wasn't stupid. Some evidence room somewhere has the glass with Peters's blood on it. Now they can match it. And if that causes problems, there are credit card records to place him nearby on the right date. Flynn may still have that lighter. There's this kind of stuff on every single break-in. Why don't you call Lisa and tell her it's all here? I'll find a way to copy this."

Cooper spoke quietly with the bank manager outside the safe-deposit vault and arranged for the use of a copier.

"We'll leave the original stuff here," he said when Carl had rejoined him. "All we have to do now is decide whom we take it to and I, for one, would rather take copies."

Carl nodded. He felt weak, dizzy. Relief had hit him hard.

"I've got to swing by the office," said Cooper. "There's a bid I need to sign, but I'll drop you at the house and meet you and Lisa there soon after." He peered at Carl. The younger man looked sick. "Just a few hours now, kid. You can do it. It's almost over."

ACROSS THE STREET from PTS, in front of the bookstore, a man in a car drank coffee and grunted monosyllabic replies to his companion.

"We just gonna sit here waiting for the guy that drove up in the Lincoln to leave?"

"Yup."

"Aren't the chances that he's gonna be here all day?"

"Yup."

"We got any good reason to think that's the same Lincoln?"

"Nope."

"You gotta smoke those things?"

"Yup."

"Damn. Makes the windshield look like a can of peaches exploded in here."

This comment didn't merit response, even monosyllabic. The driver gazed out the side window. The door to the office building they'd been watching for the last seven days opened, and the Lincoln's owner appeared. When he'd slammed the door and pulled away from the curb, the other car made a looping U-turn and followed.

"THE COMMISSION ON Organized Crime," said Lisa. "How about them? Those guys are really, really good. If they don't think this is their bailiwick, they'll point us to the right place."

"Yeah, maybe," said Carl. "Maybe that's the way to go."

"Just decide, Carl," said Lisa, irritation evident. "They found Luke once. I think I know how, but it's staggering that they were able to do it. Somehow, they knew to look in Wisconsin. How'd they *know* that? Of course, it doesn't really matter how anymore, but if they could do it once . . . You've got to move on this."

Carl stared at her. "Do you think I don't realize that? Do you think there's anything in the world more important to me than protecting him?"

"No! I just mean let's *go.*"

It was strange to her, sitting and talking with this somber man. Carl had always been cheerful, easygoing, good-natured. She'd assumed he worried; everybody worried. But she'd never seen its effects on him. It made him slow. It made him paranoid. She wished that Cooper had stayed inside after he'd come home, that he hadn't thrown such a strangely dark look in their direction and gone out into the backyard to, of all things, spread wood ash on the peonies. Cooper would have got this *done.*

Carl put his hands flat on the table and stared at them. "I don't know where I stop and he begins," he said. "What if what we have, what we know, isn't enough? We've got a statue. We've got Gerry's notes with some names on them. Evidence from a dead man. And, yeah, it's more than just his word. But we don't know who's running this thing. We don't know how far it goes, how deep. We know Total Security is crooked—or a lot of its employees are, but we don't know which ones. Somebody at The Retreat either works for them or sells them information, but we don't know who. We've got nothing on Gerry's murder, so the most serious crime anybody can pin on these guys is the break-in at your place. If you can ID anybody. With your testimony, that's attempted kidnapping as well. With my testimony, we've got the men I saw last night on whatever crime it is to break in, grab somebody, tie them up, and threaten them. The rest of it's just plain old theft. Breaking and entering and theft. What's going to stop the top dogs from getting rid of us? We know too much to risk leaving us alive. We don't know *enough* to protect ourselves."

Lisa had listened in complete silence, every nerve protesting at the suggestion that the search, the agony of ignorance, must continue.

"No! We don't need to know everything! The cops know how to do this, Carl. We *don't.* They can unravel it. We have much more to give them than a mere thread. The people Gerry named . . . they'll talk. The cops will give them lots of reasons to talk. They know. The cops will put things together. We *can't.*"

Carl moved over to the window and looked out. Cooper was leaning on a shovel, talking to Luke. Luke said something and reached up. Cooper took off his sunglasses and handed them to the boy, smiling. Carl sighed.

"They won't tell the cops who's at the top, Lisa. They won't tell them because they don't know."

"What are you talking about?"

"They were talking last night while they were looking for me. I could hear every word. They didn't know that. They knew I was there, but they didn't know about the mikes. They had no way of knowing I could hear them. When they found me, then they knew, of course, but not while they were talking. The top person talks to one guy, and the men in the house, probably some of the same men in Gerry's notes . . . they don't even know for sure which one of the people in the meetings, which one of the men that go out on the jobs, that one guy is. They think it's Mendez, or a name that sounds like that, because he gives the orders to them. The one who's calling the shots has something on Mendez, something big. They don't know what, but they know it's big. The boss—that's what they call him, the boss, like some really bad movie—he's not directly involved in the actual break-ins. He does do some of the tricky stuff, I gather, though. 'The boss knows how to track this guy,' they said, 'this guy' meaning me, I presume. 'He found his kid and the old lady. Now he's found him.' Until you showed up, I thought 'found his kid and the old lady' meant Luke and you." He shuddered, remembering.

He opened the refrigerator and took out a beer, looking questioningly at Lisa. She shook her head. He twisted the bottle open, took a swallow, and went on.

"Gerry sure didn't know who he was. He told me that, and he wasn't lying. It scared him."

"So he's the one who went to the vet's office. And he visited Mrs. Peavy. That means that Bonnie and Mrs. Peavy have seen him."

"Yeah, but say they could describe him really well. So any sketch artist could come up with a useful likeness. Doubtful, but let's say they could." Carl had been leaning against the sink. He crossed the kitchen now and straddled a chair across from Lisa. "What I heard is all that connects those visits to what's been going on. Once they found me last night, they took the tape. So the only way the police can get this guy is for this Mendez guy to give him up, or for what's-her-name and Mrs. Peavy to describe him so well they can locate him. And *that,* then, would mean they'd have to live long enough to tell some courtroom who they saw. And I'd have to live to tell some courtroom what I heard. You think he'll risk that?"

"Which means, if what you heard is right, if this guy really has something on Mendez, that you're not safe, that Bonnie and Mrs. Peavy aren't safe, that Luke isn't safe until we know who this man is or, at least, what that *thing* is."

Luke came in from the backyard wearing Cooper's sunglasses. He looked like an alien. He tipped his head backward to keep them from slipping off his nose and looked back and forth from his father to Lisa.

"Bob's just *working.* They's nothing to *do.*"

Lisa took the glasses off and put them on the table. They were expensive, far too expensive to serve even briefly as a child's toy. Cooper had a lot to learn about four-year-olds.

"Your daddy and I need to talk for a while, honey," she said softly. "You could color, or play with the train, or watch TV if you want. But you have to do it by yourself."

Luke sighed. There was a finality in her tone that discouraged negotiation. He trudged out of the room.

Lisa gazed at the glasses. Ray Bans. Something flickered in her mind. She picked up the glasses and sat, turning them in her hands. A patternless jumble shifted and the design emerged.

"The mind behind all this . . . the person who runs the whole thing . . ." She looked up and her eyes were bleak. "Carl, I know who it is."

Chapter
16

L UKE WAS PLAYING with the train. He would miss the train. He wondered if Bob would let him come back and play with it after his dad took him home. Maybe Mayor Lin could come to Bob's house too. Bob would like her. Luke would show him where she liked to be scratched on her stomach and how, if you did it just right, she'd curl up in a ball and grab your arm with her paws. Then you could just scoop her right up. It was like a trick. Bob would be good at it. And maybe he'd finish the story he'd been telling the other day about the brother and sister named Macaroni and Cheese. It was an exciting story because Macaroni was always very bad and Cheese was always very good and they had so many adventures. That was probably because they lived all by themselves and didn't have any parents. Somebody with parents, or even one parent, couldn't have adventures like that. But parents were better than adventures.

He twisted around to look into the kitchen. His dad and Lisa were still talking. His dad put his hand under Lisa's chin and tipped her head up so she was looking right at him. Maybe Lisa would be his dad's new girlfriend. That would be nice. His dad's other girlfriend never sat on the floor and didn't understand how the little bent piece off the end of the vacuum cleaner hose could be a gun. She wasn't very smart at all, and although that made him feel sorry for her, when she was around, they always went to restaurants, which was really boring.

LISA HAD REPEATED, as close to verbatim as she could, her conversation with Bonnie. Now she repeated the critical fact. "One of the reasons she couldn't describe the man was that he was wearing Ray Bans."

Carl felt his face go slack. "Are you saying he wasn't on that road by accident? The car wasn't really out of gas? You've been staying all this time . . ." He swallowed, trying to think while terror crawled up his spine.

THE TRAIN WASN'T as much fun to play with alone. The only disaster Luke could think of was having the bridge fall down. Bob knew a lot about trains—what was in all the cars and what Russell the Engineer said. But Bob was out in the backyard. He'd come home from work and changed his clothes, and Luke had hoped that meant he'd play with him. But he'd gone straight out to the yard. Maybe he'd come in soon and do something fun.

LISA STARED AT CARL. "Cooper? Heavens, Carl, not Cooper!" She was sincerely shocked by his stupidity, then realized with a twinge of guilt that the reaction wasn't fair. Even she, who knew him far better, couldn't have articulated why such a conclusion was unthinkable.

"I would trust Cooper with my life," she said. "That's not who I'm talking about. Listen. You said yourself that the men last night knew you were there. How? Sure, maybe they watched the house, saw you coming or going. But you went in and out, what, maybe once a day?"

"Not much, that's for sure."

"Okay. So that means they watched the house *a lot*. Or they were very lucky. I don't think it was either one. The only thing that really makes sense is that someone knows you—knows you and figured out your plan. Any other way, there's too blasted much coincidence—too much in this whole thing, and there can't be. There's someone who pulls it together."

She was not talking about a someone. She was talking about a very specific person, and Carl knew it. He could see in her eyes that she didn't want to tell him, wanted him to figure it out too, make it real.

"You didn't recognize any voices last night because the one who knows you wasn't there. Mrs. Peavy and Bonnie aren't the only ones who have seen him, Carl. You have too. Mrs. Peavy said he talked like Fred. Fred was from Texas. Think! Who do you know, who do we both know, who talks like that *and* who would be much harder to describe when he was wearing sunglasses? Whose involvement just makes *sense*?"

Carl's confusion fell away as the logic of what she was saying hit him. He swore quietly.

SIRIUS PUT HIS chin on Luke's lap and deposited a tennis ball. He stood back and looked up at the boy, his tail waving.

"Okay," said Luke. "Just a minute."

He got down off the chair and glanced into the kitchen. His dad was looking in a phone book. He'd better not go in and bother him. But Lisa always let him throw the ball for Sirius. He wouldn't go down the street to the playground or do any of the things he needed to have someone do with him. He'd just take the ball and go out by the sidewalk. Maybe Werner would be out there watching for the mailman. Maybe Werner would talk to him.

He opened the front door quietly and gazed out through the screen. Across the street, a little girl was playing in her front yard. Maybe she'd want to come over and see the train. He'd just go to the curb and ask her. He dropped the tennis ball and bumped the screen door open. Sirius, picking up the ball, tried to push out with him.

"Wait a minute." He pushed the door shut. "I just going to talk to that girl. You stay here case she's scared of you."

The dog watched Luke descend the steps. He whined faintly, pushing his nose against the screen. Luke reached the curb and stopped. The girl's mother had come out and got in a car and now the little girl was getting in with her. They were driving away. Luke turned, disappointed, and started back. Sirius's tail began to move slowly.

A car with two men in it had pulled away from the curb down the block and now it stopped in front of the house. One man jumped out. He was only about twenty feet from the boy. Sirius's eyes sharpened and he growled softly. The man overtook Luke, slid one hand over his mouth and the other under his arms. He lifted the boy into the air and turned for the car.

Sirius roared in outrage and slammed his body against the door. The screen bulged and the dog slammed into it again, ripping it from the wood. Scrambling over the frame, he launched himself from the porch, reaching the curb as the man threw Luke inside the car.

The dog sank his teeth into the man's buttocks and the man screamed, flailing. Sirius pulled backward and his enemy fell on top of him. The car door slammed shut. Sirius squirmed out from under the twisting body and, snarling, dove for the man's throat.

Inside the car, Luke was yelling, thrashing, trying to twist away from strong hands. He felt his arm jerked toward the steering wheel and held fast. He tried to pull away, scrambling toward the passenger door, but something bound his wrist.

The man inside the car with him was cursing. Reaching

under the seat and pulling out a gun, he kicked the driver's door open and ran around the front of the car.

In the kitchen, Lisa and Carl had heard the clamor. They were now halfway down the front steps, their eyes wild, Lisa a half step in the lead. A bullet tore out a piece of the bottom step.

"Hold it!" The man moved his weapon back and forth, from Lisa to the twisting mass of dog and human on the ground.

Lisa had stopped faster than Carl and he thudded into her. Now she could feel his hands on her waist, moving her to the side. He was going past her. She threw out an arm to block him, hearing running footsteps coming through the side yard.

"Wait!" she said quietly. "We'll get him out of there."

When Cooper, if that was Cooper, came in view, there would be three targets and perhaps enough confusion to allow a dash for the car.

Carl hesitated. The thrashing pair on the ground was the only motion on the street. No shades flew up; no cyclists careened around the corner.

"Jesus! Get him off me! Kill him!" the man on the ground was shrieking. His voice was high with terror.

The man with the gun moved forward, trying to get close enough to send a bullet into the dog's brain instead of his partner's. Sirius let go of a fruitless hold on the man's jacket collar and plunged for his face. One eyetooth opened a furrow on the man's cheek. The man with the gun realized what he had to do. He drew back a foot to catch the dog in the ribs, lift him off his writhing victim, get a clean shot.

Cooper emerged from the side yard. His heart had lurched at the sound of the dog's furious barking, and he hadn't known if the scream, *Luke!*, had come from him or from indoors. He'd bolted for the front of the house, still holding the garden spade, but as he ran, he found himself settling into the even stride he'd used twenty years before. He jogged the spade handle backward, gripping it closer to the blade, getting the balance of the weight right in his hand, raising his arm without thinking about it. Now, as he came around the corner, the sight in front of him filled him with a fury so visceral that thought of any kind was impossible.

His mind went blank. He knew only that this throw was odd. The weight in his hand was too heavy, and it was strange to aim as one hurled. He'd never cast at a target before. His arm went back, his body turned to the right, and his arm came forward as he twisted and flung the object he held. He took the familiar, hopping steps on his left foot that allowed him to keep his balance and watched the spade crash into the shoulder of the man with the gun, shattering the bone, sending the gun skidding along the sidewalk. The man fell, cracking his head on the pavement, and lay very still.

Next door, Mary Ruth flew down the steps behind Sarge, who was barking furiously. Her father, gripping the handrail, was close behind her. Sarge sailed to the bigger dog's side and made eager, rushing motions at the prostrate foe.

Lisa moved forward, slid her hand under her dog's neck, and pulled him away from his victim. The man was jabbering, twitching. He sat up, his leather jacket shredded, his face white except where blood flowed from the gash on his cheek. He skittered backward, pressing against the car, shrinking from the excited fox terrier.

Carl was inside the car, smiling at Luke, helping him scramble into a sitting position. Luke's face appeared, wide-eyed, trying to see over his father's shoulder. Carl twisted around, his face strained but his voice deliberately casual.

"Cooper, can you find something to cut plastic with? Luke's wearing a giant wristband, and he doesn't much like it."

Cooper was running his hands, none too gently, over the man pressed up against the car. There was no gun.

"What'll cut it?" he asked, speaking close to the man's ear.

There was no reply. The man shivered, staring at the dog.

Cooper looked up. Werner Schwartz stood a few feet away, holding the gun he'd picked up off the sidewalk.

"Werner," said Cooper, the unfamiliar name coming easily, "I'll take that if you could go get the pruning shears off my back porch."

The old man nodded grimly. "Mary Ruth went to call the police," he said and departed, appearing a moment later with a pair of shears.

"A plastic restraining cuff," he said, looking curiously at the smooth strip that held Luke's arm tightly against the steering wheel. "I've seen 'em on TV. See, he could've slipped out of regular cuffs."

"Get that *off* me," said Luke.

"You bet," said Carl. He slid one blade carefully through the plastic loop and pressed the handles together. Luke rubbed his freed wrist and looked up at Werner Schwartz.

"You saw it on *TV*?" he asked.

"Why don't you two go in and call Mary Ruth? Make sure she got through to the cops," said Cooper. He wanted the boy away.

Carl nodded and carried his son up the steps. Luke was pushing himself away from his father so that he could look directly into his face. "Did you see, Dad?" His voice was shrill; his eyes were very bright. "Sirius bit that man in the butt!"

"Yeah!" Carl's voice floated back. "He sure did."

Sirius was keeping an eye on the man by the car while trying, simultaneously, to lick Lisa's face.

"Good dog," she murmured, smoothing the bloodied fur under his chin. "Good, good dog."

A siren cut off as a blue-and-white police car pulled into the curb and screeched to a halt. It was over. Why, wondered Cooper, struggling to remain standing, was he so tired?

He looked over at Lisa, talking quietly to an officer while his partner knelt by the unconscious man on the ground. Another police car pulled up. Lisa gestured toward Cooper, turning to gaze in his direction. He smiled at her, perplexed by the faintly startled look that came into her eyes. She and the policeman walked toward him, and by the time they reached his side, the look was gone.

THE POLICE DETECTIVE was someone to be contended with, Lisa could tell. She would not want to go up against him. It wasn't that he was particularly bulky; he wasn't. His pale brown suit jacket hung rather dejectedly from his shoulders and gaped unattractively when he sat. The man who wore it, however, loved his job. There were lines of weariness around his eyes, but the eyes themselves were intelligent and interested.

A woman from the D.A.'s office sat next to him at the conference room table, facing Lisa and Carl. Cooper was out there somewhere, on the other side of the solid door, showing Luke what a police station was like. Carl had given the background, and then Lisa had filled in what she could of the details surrounding the attack on the cabin, the fight with Luke's kidnappers, and the intervening days.

"What we need to know," Lisa said, "is whether you found the gun that killed Gerry Martelli."

The detective did not, as she had expected, say that such information was not available to the public, that such details could not be divulged since they were involved in an ongoing investigation. He said no.

Lisa turned to Carl. "So that's probably what this guy has on Menendez."

The name was not Mendez. Several hours of questioning

Chaco and Phelps had disclosed that it was Menendez. And Menendez was, at this moment, occupying a cell in the precinct's holding area. Menendez was not talking. Except to say that the firm he owned, Total Security, was completely legitimate, Menendez was not talking at all. His lawyer was wearing a suit that did not gape unattractively, and Menendez was not talking.

Carl opened the yearbook he'd retrieved from his apartment. He leafed through to the section for seniors. His finger ran down a page and stopped at a good likeness of a friend.

"When Mrs. Peavy gets here," he said, "show her this."

Even to an elderly lady who had to peer carefully through the reading lenses of her bifocals in order to see clearly, the smiling face in the photograph was immediately recognizable.

"Why, yes!" she said, smiling and patting Carl's arm. "There's your cousin, right there. That is most certainly him. He looks different in the picture for some reason, but that's him. It's not just that he's a little older now, though of course he would be; it's something else . . ." She shook her head. "I don't suppose it matters, but I wonder what it is."

Lisa put a hand on Mrs. Peavy's shoulder. "It's a black-and-white photograph," she said. "So you can't see the blue-green color of his eyes."

She turned to Carl. "The only thing Joe ever cared more about than his class standing was Barry Switzer and the Sooners. I wonder if he'll say 'Boy howdy!' when they pick him up."

He didn't, of course. He didn't say anything except to make a firm request for counsel in his casual voice with its almost imperceptible drawl. Counsel was less helpful to him than he would have wished. The search warrant obtained on the basis of Carl's and Mrs. Peavy's information had turned up the murder weapon in a safe in Joe's office.

————

Chapter 17

A RABBIT EMERGED into the clearing in front of Lisa's cabin. The big dog on the porch stirred and sat up, his eyes glittering and his body stiff with interest. Slow as the movement was, it did not escape the rabbit's notice, and the wary animal retreated hastily. The dog sighed and lay back down, moving his chin to the top of Lisa's foot.

Lisa put down her book. It was a glorious Tuesday, sunny and clear but mild for mid-June. She was aware of the beauty around her; it just didn't matter.

At first, when the statements had been made and signed and the charges had been filed, and she had been free to go home, each breath seemed a gift; each daybreak filled her with euphoria. Everything bad was over, and the very air seemed charged with possibilities.

Carl and Luke drove her to the cabin and stayed for two weeks. Luke had suffered from nightmares, but surprisingly few of them, and they had gradually faded. They talked with him, she and Carl, every day about what had happened and how it couldn't happen anymore. One memory had, if anything, sharpened as the days passed, but Luke did not seem to be upset by it. He looked from time to time at Sirius with a wondering smile and repeated his earlier observation. "He bit him right in the butt!"

She sat across the breakfast table from Carl, morning after morning. The sky had never seemed so blue.

And then, so gradually that she couldn't put a time to its beginning, the euphoria dimmed. She began to feel bored and restless.

"I need to get back to work," Carl said one morning, and she felt a surge of guilt when she recognized that her reaction contained more relief than regret. "This has been . . . great. You've been great, Leese. But I've got to get my life back."

He reached across the table and put his hand over hers. "Do you want to come with us? Should we try again?"

Lisa smiled at him. "We weren't trying anything before, Carl. We just fell into being together because I wanted you so badly and you didn't mind."

"You minded, though. And that's why you left."

"Yes. I minded a lot. I still mind a lot, but it's different. I mind now for her, that girl I was, the one who loved you so much. You know how you can feel sorry sometimes for the person you were once? It doesn't seem like self-pity, because you're not really that person anymore?"

Carl uncovered her hand and sat back, his eyes serious. "I know what you're saying. But you were wrong about me. I did love you, Lisa. I still do."

"I know." Suddenly she wanted very much not to hurt his feelings, to keep him from knowing just how much her own had changed.

"I love you too." She smiled at him. "But we're balanced now, with something that's more like affection than the kind of feeling people make a life with together."

He left the next day, driving away down the winding lane with Luke waving from the window, and Lisa was suddenly lonely. It was almost as hard to accept the end of her passion as it had been to live with it. Standing against him and feeling the sharp bones of his shoulder blades beneath her hands had not stopped her heart, and she had felt oddly wistful.

Another two months passed. June had come and was going by, and there was something very wrong. She missed Luke, but it was more than that. She felt distracted and dull, and her friends irritated her.

"Maybe you should go see that Cooper person in Chicago," Mickey said, one afternoon when she sighed and dropped her end of the branch they'd just cut off a dead apple tree. "You talk about him all the time; do you ever talk *to* him?"

"I do not talk about him all the time!" Lisa was astonished.

"Oh, you do too. I know about his ex-wife and his neighbors and his job . . . Criminy, Lisa, I know the man sings in the shower. I know *what* he sings in the shower."

"You do not."

"Otis Redding, Buddy Holly, Paul Simon, the Beach Boys, Mel Tillis . . ."

"Hardly any Mel Tillis. And that was just to annoy me."

"Yeah, well, now he's singing to Rhonda . . ." He dropped his own end of the branch and assumed a guitar-strumming pose. "Help me, Rhonda! Help me get her outta my heart!" He bent over his phantom instrument and began the *dah, dah, dah* part of the refrain, while Lisa looked at him in disgust.

"You are insane." She picked up the branch and dragged it toward the woods. Mickey's voice followed her.

"Don't be an ass," she called back over her shoulder. But she was unnerved. Mickey's teasing had brought a swell of confused emotion.

Suddenly she was in the front yard of Cooper's house again. She was turning to point him out to the policeman and, seeing him, standing quietly, relaxed and competent and self-contained, she'd realized something. She'd realized that her time with him was over and that she didn't want it to be. It had confused her, and she'd put it away to think about later, but it hadn't been easy to think about. She dropped the branch again, confusion fading and startled dismay taking its place. So that was what her problem was.

Since then, four days before, things had simply gotten worse. A constant hollow aching had taken up residence just behind her sternum. For a while she'd probed the discomfort, seeking a sense of its depth and veracity. Now she knew. It was extensive and it was real, and that meant something had to be done. She felt edgy and raw. Sleepless nights and the itch of unfinished business were taking their toll.

At least, she told herself, gazing dispassionately at a hummingbird that she knew should be making her feel something more than mild admiration, it's better to know that you love somebody, once again, who just doesn't love you back, than it is to go on blaming all the wrong things for the fact that life isn't any fun anymore. Yes, something had to be done. But what?

Then again, maybe there was a reason why she was irritable and agitated instead of depressed. She wasn't, she realized, at all depressed. That didn't make sense unless . . . unless something in her believed that the way she felt wasn't so one-sided. The thought had no sooner occurred to her than she realized it was true. She did believe it or, at least, believe it possible. When she'd left, she'd hugged him goodbye, and he had not released her until she'd pulled away. Then, putting his hands on her shoulders, he had looked closely at her. What had been in his eyes? She'd gotten into Carl's car and been driven away.

But what had been in his eyes?

She looked down at Sirius. "I could call his office," she said. " 'Sylvia? Could you leave a message? Tell Dr. Cooper I need to know how he feels about me. And let me know as soon as possible, would you?' Or we could go to Chicago and find out for ourselves. What do you think?"

Sirius whined and wagged his tail at her inquisitive tone.

"Okay," she said. "As long as you agree. We'll go in the morning. Get there about when he gets off work."

SYLVIA WAS WORRIED. The door to Dr. Cooper's office was closed again. It was always closed these days. For a while, a few months back, he had changed. She knew the word *blossomed* wasn't used to describe men. Certainly not men as impressive and competent as Dr. Cooper. But it was the only word she could think of to describe what had seemed to be happening to him. And then it had all stopped. He'd gone back to silence, back to his brisk, businesslike approach to life. No, not back, beyond back. He had always been pleasant before, even before the—she stumbled over the word again—*blossoming*. Now he wasn't even pleasant. Not rude, really. Not harsh and sarcastic and domineering, like some bosses. But definitely curt. The smile that had lit up the office for a while was gone. She remembered, though, and so did Clarisse and Marsha in Editorial and Neil in Research.

Everyone was nervous these days. Dr. Cooper hadn't lost his competence. He still had, as Marsha said, a firm hand on the tiller. They weren't going to sink into the void that could swallow a small business when its guiding force lost sight of the original, inspirational vision . . . at least not immediately. The accountant was calm, but the accountant didn't work there every day. The people who worked there no longer enjoyed it.

Sylvia had worried when he went through his divorce several years back. That was nothing compared to this. He'd been distracted, but not, it seemed, particularly burdened. Not grim, like this.

Mondays were sometimes all right. Sylvia found herself looking forward to Mondays. She didn't know what he did, from time to time, over the weekend that lightened his step as the week began, made him occasionally inquire how she was doing, whether her nephew had passed the bar exam, or if she'd changed her hairstyle. And Thursday mornings, she'd noticed just recently, were pleasant.

The phone rang and she recognized Carl's voice. "Yes, he's in," she said. "Let me put you through."

It was odd that Dr. Cooper had become friendly with that lanky young man. They were so different—the one so cheerful and casual, the other so stormy and reserved. The younger man came by once in a while and called from time to time. Lately, the calls came while Sylvia was doing the preliminary work on the books. Which she did on Wednesday afternoons, meaning that Carl called on Wednesdays. The same day that Cooper might announce he was leaving early. The day that came right before Thursday. She wondered vaguely if there was a connection between Carl and her boss's sunnier moods.

Cooper turned away from his computer screen and picked up the phone.

"Got you batting cleanup this afternoon," Carl informed him. "It's an early game, so we can have some infield practice beforehand. Can you be there by four-thirty?"

"Sure," said Cooper. "This place runs itself. I just give myself a paycheck as a matter of habit."

Carl laughed. "Well, try. We've got a chance today, and I don't want to blow it. Not much of a chance, I'll admit. Tanya's got a callback this afternoon and will probably miss at least the first few innings, maybe the whole game. Which means not only are we missing the 'Hey! Get your head in the game or *don't play*!' reminders, but we gotta put Cheryl in at first, and that's risky at best."

He paused. Should he mention Lisa? Cooper was touchy on the subject. His eyes went flat when her name was mentioned. It wasn't lack of interest; it was too deliberate for that. What was going on there? Two of the women on the team had shown a decided interest in the new third baseman. Cooper hadn't even noticed, and when Carl teased him about it, he seemed pleased but ultimately indifferent. Carl made up his mind to try again.

"Yeah, it would help if we had a little more depth in the feminine portion of the team. As I've said before, we need Lisa."

You can say that again, thought Cooper. A thought of her hovered. It shimmered, then held. A tremor passed downward from his breastbone, and he winced. He did not reply.

Carl noted the silence but refused to take the hint. "Yeah, we need Lisa, all right. Too bad I couldn't convince her to move down here."

Cooper felt a coldness at the bone. "You tried?"

"Yeah, I tried. She gave me the old heave-ho." He chuckled. "Ah, it wouldn't have worked anyway. She was right. I thought maybe we could pick things up again. But something's changed with her. She just plain doesn't adore me anymore. Hard to believe, isn't it?"

It was hard to imagine Lisa adoring anyone. "Doesn't put too much of a strain on *my* imagination," Cooper replied. "What's hard to believe is that she ever did, and I've just got your word for that."

"Nice," said Carl, amusement evident in his voice. "Real nice. Maybe you won't be batting cleanup today."

Cooper made an appropriately indecent remark and hung up. He sat gazing at the phone. If Carl was out of the picture, out of the picture at Lisa's request, then maybe . . . No, it was impossible. Lisa was content the way she was, alone. The kind of person whose only deep needs were for solitude and independence. She was, indeed, the kind of person he had thought for so long he was.

About himself, he'd been wrong. It had taken him several weeks after Lisa left to realize he wasn't the person he thought he was, but when he'd realized it, he hadn't fought the insight. He'd sought to use it. It had led him to get hold of box seats for the Cubs, had made him make the first call to Carl to suggest an outing for Carl and Luke and himself to Wrigley Field, had resulted, eventually, in occasional and extremely welcome Saturday afternoons with Luke. And it had quickly resulted in a starting position on Carl's softball team.

"You played college ball?" Carl had asked, glancing at a team picture on the wall in the study, his eyes speculative. Cooper was helping him set up a personal budget on the computer. "Played any since?"

"Not much," Cooper had replied. "Don't have the range I had once."

"So, no left field . . ." Carl was thoughtful. "But it would be a shame to waste your arm on the right side." He remembered, with clarity, the spade cutting through the air, dropping the man with the gun. "We can have one man on the roster who's not directly connected with theater. You interested in being him? Wednesdays at five-ten or six-twenty. You don't need too much range at third. Our third baseman got cast in an Equity show. Means he's not available for any late games, and he's never been dependable for early ones. Besides, slow-pitch softball is a hitter's game. If you can come through at the plate . . ."

It sounded immensely appealing to Cooper. Far better than the lonely jogging he'd taken up. Better than the gym workouts. Of course, he couldn't just substitute one weekly hour on a diamond for more regular exercise. Still . . .

A softball didn't go as far as a baseball. Especially the sixteen-inch softball that was Chicago's answer to limited park space. It was like hitting an angel food cake, though line drives made the thing feel like a cannonball. Still, gym workouts had brought back the muscle tone that had started to slide, and he'd quickly become the team's long-ball hitter.

It gave him joy. He found that as Wednesday afternoons

approached, his depression lifted. He even stopped dwelling on Lisa, stopped hearing her voice, or heard it with something akin to fond memory instead of cold unhappiness. He hadn't been able to hold on to that, but any respite was better than none.

The degree to which he missed her astonished him. When the old, pink roses bloomed, all he had thought was that their beauty was wasted without Lisa to show them to. The garden had chosen this year to outdo itself, this year, when he didn't care.

The idea that moments with her had slid by without his taking the opportunity to memorize them filled him with regret. That she didn't feel the same way was simply an unfortunate fact; there was, after all, nothing he could do about it. But that he'd wasted chances to find out what she'd wanted to be when she was little, what her favorite flower was, what kind of movies she liked, depressed him. Now he'd never know. All that time together. How prodigal he had been.

A few more hours before practice and the game. He'd finish reviewing Cheryl's copy—it was good; she was coming along nicely—and go home to change.

LISA DROVE EAST on Irving Park. Sylvia didn't know where Cooper was, just that he'd left early. She volunteered that this was not unusual for a Wednesday. When pressed, she remembered that Carl had called and that such a call was not unusual for a Wednesday.

Lisa had sat in the car next to the pay phone outside the White Hen Pantry, thinking. Carl and Cooper had become friends? It seemed an unlikely alliance. Well, maybe not. Carl tended to like people. Cooper, less blithely accepting, had doted on Carl's son. Maybe it made sense. So what was with Wednesdays?

Now, driving around aimlessly, waiting for Cooper to get

home, was making her jumpier than she was already, so when she passed Greenview Avenue, she turned at the next corner and wound around to park in front of Mrs. Peavy's apartment. She was greeted with enthusiasm.

"Why, what a surprise!" said Mrs. Peavy. "Of course your lovely dog can come in! Luke has told me all about him." She ushered Lisa to the living room and settled herself in an upholstered rocking chair. "Did you come to see Carl and Luke?"

"Not actually, but of course I'd like to see them. Carl wrote that they'd moved back to this building."

"I didn't give the poor boy much choice," replied Mrs. Peavy. "When I read about the indictments and really understood what had been going on—Carl, that slyboots, had never told me—I called him up and left a message every day until he called back. 'That child should have somebody that loves him right close by,' I said. The idea that my baby was . . . And to think you never even gave a hint! I wasn't too happy with Carl, or with you, my dear. But all is forgiven, so you just sit right there while I find something for us to nibble on."

Something to nibble on turned out to be an enormous plate of white-frosted ginger cookies and mugs of steaming coffee. "Now, you just tell me how you've been. You look a little peaked, dear."

Lisa was tempted to do exactly that, just for the luxury of having someone to talk to about it. Mickey had not been the person, his tender attachments being, typically, so fleeting. Then again, Mrs. Peavy was inordinately fond of Carl. Could she understand? "I've been fine," she lied. "And you?"

"Lonely!" said Mrs. Peavy. "For Marilyn, of all things! I finally decided a few days ago that I'll just get myself my own cat now that she's gone back to Luke. But other than that, I've been just fine. It's so nice to have Carl and Luke in the building again, though they're across the courtyard now, and that's not quite as handy. Still, except for Wednesdays, they're always home by five-thirty, and it's just so nice to know they're there."

She regarded Lisa shrewdly. "If you're anxious to see them, you could run over to the diamond."

The diamond? Of course. Wednesday was Theatre League softball. That's where Carl was and, perhaps, Cooper. Why Cooper would have started going to Carl's games, she could only guess. Maybe he kept an eye on Luke. Maybe he just liked going. At any rate, it was possible he was there.

"Good idea," she said. "I'll do that. But I want to see you again before I go home."

"Anytime," said Mrs. Peavy. "Anytime at all. I was planning to make doughnuts tomorrow . . ."

"Then it will be tomorrow," said Lisa, grinning.

Remembering where the league had played in the old days, she headed up Clark, turned on Montrose and again on Marine, and parked in the first available space. There were three games going on. Neither Carl nor Cooper was on the closest field. Then she saw Carl, a hundred yards away, running in from center to snag a pop fly. Even at that distance, there was no doubt in her mind about who the fielder was. She scanned the sidelines for Cooper.

A child that might well be Luke was standing behind the backstop. No one bearing any resemblance to Cooper was near him. Now that she was here, her nervous dread of doing what she had to do had reached an alarming level. She tried to reassure herself. When I see him, she thought, I'll know what to do—something or nothing. I'll *know*. But she was just as glad Cooper wasn't there. She could go over and watch the game and talk to Luke, assuming the child was, indeed, Luke. She could go out for a beer with the team, chat with Carl, find out how Cooper was doing these days. Yes. This was good.

She started along the periphery of the park, keeping

Sirius close enough not to interfere with a play. Carl's team was still in the field. She recognized Mitchell at shortstop, as much by the fact that he never wore socks as by his stance, poised and casually ready. She hoped he'd get a play while she was watching; he was as fluid, as quick, as a cat. The batter cracked a sharp grounder down the third-base line and the third baseman moved sharply to his right to field it cleanly, pivoted, held the runner at second, and made the throw to first, catching the runner by a good five feet. The first baseman ignored the woman edging well off second, looping an underhand throw to the pitcher instead, and the runner (who should, Lisa thought, have been less tentative) scurried into third. Too bad. The third baseman had been ready for the throw, ready to make the tag. Robbed of the opportunity, he now left the base, yelling "Nice catch" instead of what Lisa would have been tempted to yell.

She stopped. Her knees, suddenly weak, had recognized the voice before her conscious mind did. She stared at the field. Cooper, in a jersey with the arms cut off and light-weight sweatpants, was playing third. Mitchell made some comment, inaudible to Lisa, that made him respond with a shrug and a friendly grin.

The batter took two balls and a strike before popping up to the pitcher. Cooper trotted toward the bench. The game was going well. He'd doubled his first time up and was look-ing forward to another trip to the plate. There was a dog standing behind the backstop with Luke. A big, shaggy, blackish dog. It looked like Sirius. Cooper stopped short. It was Sirius.

An arm curved around his back, gripped his shoulder lightly. "Never pictured you in the hot corner," said the voice he'd been hearing for months. "I've been practicing double-cuffing my socks."

The umpire rubbed his neck and sighed. Actors! What were they rehearsing now? *Romeo and Juliet*? The third baseman had made a nice play, but why the fair-haired newcomer was making such a big deal out of it was beyond him. And why the man had stopped dead in his tracks and was responding with such theatrical enthusiasm seemed hardly reasonable, given the fact that there were five more innings before the game was over. They were behaving, the two of them, as if it had already been decided. Or—he looked again—as if *some*thing had.